ghost

fligh t

A MOSS REID MYSTERY

Prologue

"Sunt lacrimae rerum."
"There are tears at the heart of things."
— Virgil, Book I of the *Aeneid*

"What did he used to call it?" Mrs McGann is about to show me out to his ... "Oh yeah, his *den*," she says.

Terry McGann's den. I half expect a glorified potting shed. Instead, it's one of those fancy "garden offices". Double-glazed, plastered, fully insulated. Its centrepoint is a large wooden desk flanked by two tall bookshelves.

I run a hand over the rough surface of the desk, trying to get a feel for this Terry McGann guy. Open the desk drawers. The usual biros and staplers clobber. Nothing jumps out from the shelves either. I could spend all day on those shelves, stuffed this way and that with books, books and more books.

That's the difference between real-life PI work and the movies. It's messy. Mundane. Half the time you're stuck in your car or stuck into webpages. Interviewing people, typing up reports or – as in this morning – poking about in a dead man's shed.

Why am I telling you all this? To give you some idea of where I'm coming from. I'm not quite sure what I'm looking for and can't think of anything better to do. So do what you're paid to do: plod away in the dark at fifty an hour plus expenses, checking the desks and dens of three missing men to find, well, who knows?

Rummage around in another drawer, move on to the next item to catch your eye.

Like that oil painting over the desk. Renaissance is it? Pre-Raphaelite? Don't ask me – I'm a private investigator not an art collector.

Is it a clue? If so, a clue about what? His *art*? Art as in his art collection? Or art as in his artful skill in amassing it? Is the painting simply a reflection of a dead man's wise investment choices – or a dirty old man's proclivity for Victorian nudes?

Put on the reading glasses. Mrs McGann seems puzzled or annoyed. Impatient anyhow. As if to say, "Not you too with the nudes?" Or, "What d'you hope to find in that old shite?"

On closer inspection it's not an expensive original but a print. At its centre a young man is sprawled out on a sort of couch of golden brown feathers, on a large flat boulder. He could be asleep, in a coma, dead. Sprawled out on his rocky bed, surrounded by calm waters of a murky green-brown sea and – oh yeah – by the three naked women. His body is cradled in the arms of one of them. All that naked flesh, yet it's not unlike a biblical scene. A Pièta, a Golgotha, the place of the skull.

Around each forearm he has leather straps. These are attached to the pair of huge wings with their giant feathers. So: not quite the fallen angel, more the lost birdman.

There's hardly a stitch on him. Not a scratch on him either. An autopsy wouldn't find a pinprick, though maybe something might turn up in the toxicology report.

As if.

What do we have so far? A birdman with broken wings. An adult male Caucasian, possibly Arab. Or at least deeply tanned. The nymphs with their pale skin, by contrast, have never been near a sunbed. He's young. Far younger than Mrs McGann's husband would have been when he disappeared. And in modern parlance he's "fit". Not a *pumping-iron rugger bugger with biceps fit to burst* kind of fit. More the *lean soccer type from Serie A.*

In the distance the sun is setting. Or is it rising?

Like I said, I'm no art critic. Can't even decide whether it's dawn or dusk in the picture, let alone whether the …

Hold on.

4

There's small print near the bottom, a caption in the white margin: *The Lament for Icarus.*

Despite Mrs McGann's impatience, all this nosing around takes less than a minute. Less than a euro's worth of my time, and Patricia McGann isn't even paying for it.

Another blind alley, perhaps, but life's like that. Plenty of dead ends. You wouldn't make much of a living if every case solved itself in five minutes.

OK. What else do we have? And what possible connection could it have with the disappearance of three businessmen in a light aircraft off the west coast of Ireland?

Or with one of these men being spotted again five years later by his sister-in-law, after she bumps into him in the south of France?

Then she too disappears?

Nothing makes any sense. I have the nagging feeling that I'm missing something. Something so obvious that …

My eye has strayed to something else: a garish yellow paperback on a bookshelf. Something about professional cycling, with what looks like Domestos in the title. No, not Domestos. *Domestique.*

I wave the book at her. "Mind if I borrow this?"

"Go ahead," Mrs McGann says. "Sure I've no use for it."

What use have I for it either? What can you possibly learn from a dead man's books? Why this particular book – the one about cycling with the day-glo cover? What has any of this to do with my case, even remotely? I don't know, and, at this particular moment I really don't care. I just need a good bedtime read.

On to my next probing question.

"Was your husband into cycling?"

"Terry? Hardly. The opposite really."

Give the painting one last look. Icarus. Some people would call that ironic. Icarus the mythological smartarse who should have heeded his father's warnings: *Don't lose the head, don't fly too high or too low, listen to the experts, play it safe.*

Everyone remembers the disaster waiting to happen, the hubris, the crash part. But most people forget the other part, just before the downfall. That, for a brief while, Icarus did actually manage to fly.

Yet something doesn't add up. There's something totally wrong with that picture, and I can't for the life of me …

Frank Ferriter. You'll also hear about Frank briefly, because he too is part of the story. On its margins, yet there at the very start as it were. When it started to become a real, tentative, breaking story.

I happen to know Frank. And Frank just happened to be on the newsdesk that night.

Up to then it had been a slow news day. Maybe even slower than usual until the first reports trickled through. The excited stringer told Frank that she still had "just the bare facts". Slow down, he told her. Start at the beginning, with everything you have.

Fact: it was a missing plane. "An executive jet" she called it.

Fact: it was a Beechcraft Duchess (with propellers, not jets; a subeditor would later correct that little faux pas).

Fact: it was perfect flying weather. A crisp November day, blue skies, hardly any air traffic.

Fact: the three passengers were leading businessmen from Dublin – John ("Johnny") Kettle, Kevin Reilly and Terry McGann. At least the stringer got their names right.

Fact: McGann was the pilot. The stringer said she was "still trying to ascertain whether he owned or leased the thing". Everyone still had quite a lot of ascertaining to do.

And fact: their plane had disappeared. That afternoon. Somewhere out in the Atlantic.

"Seems it was three suits on a jaunt," she added, with the salty cynicism of a well seasoned hack. "Well for some, eh, Frank?"

Their plan had been to take off around midday from the Weston aerodrome eight miles west of Dublin, head across the island to Connemara Airport, land and drive into Galway for a late lunch or a quick pint. Afterwards they would take off again, hop down the coast to the Cliffs of Moher, skip up to the Aran Islands, turn east again to Galway Bay, and be back in Dublin in time for tea.

That was the plan. But after taking off from Galway they were last seen flying over the Dun Aengus Fort on Inis Mór. Heading due west in a straight line, next stop Newfoundland and the New World.

Or not quite due west. Shortly before the Beech Duchess went off the radar it began to drift slightly northwest. After that, no radio message, no Mayday call, nothing. Not even a postcard from Greenland saying *All's well, ran into a few lads after work, may be home late.*

It was a complete mystery.

Frank Ferriter's newsroom and all the other newsrooms went into overdrive in the following four hours or so, trying to muster any other facts to hand.

For a start, how Terry McGann was an experienced pilot. Since obtaining his licence he'd clocked up hundreds of hours of flight time. And, it turned out, he did own the aircraft rather than leasing it. The weather people confirmed that conditions at the time were near perfect, or "CAVOK" in pilot-speak (Ceiling And Visibility OK). No clouds below five thousand feet, visibility ten kilometres, no bad weather now or in the pipeline.

See? Perfectly CAVOK.

And isn't that the thing when mysterious air disasters hit the headlines? All that technical mumbo jumbo about engines and aircraft types, cumulus this, cumulonimbus that, all those aviation acronyms that mean nothing to us mere mortals. Sheer CAVOK.

It can take hours for the corpse of a wildebeest on African grasslands to attract a decent swarm of hyenas, flies and vultures. An air disaster, on the other hand, takes minutes. In this case the descending vultures were aviation experts, leading authorities in international relations or international terrorism. All male, all subscribers to *Jane's Defence* and *Jane's This and That,* all planespotters since childhood, all versed in pilot-speak and techie talk.

And, of course, all great for bandying around the flying odds. How you'd need to get on an airplane every day for six thousand years before anything bad will happen to you. "That's the statistical probability," they'd say. "Six thousand years. You'd have to clock up one heck of lot of air miles."

So, for the three businessmen in the Beech Duchess, it seems their six thousand years were up.

Or so it seemed at the time.

After two or three days on the front pages the trio from Dublin – soon dubbed the "Galway Three" – became yesterday's news. The story, like the airplane, simply faded away. Like most people at the time, I thought no more of it. It was like a strange dream that had never happened.

The case of the Galway Three would always be about absences. Odds and probabilities, happenstance and coincidence. And an absence as empty as the skies they'd flown into. Possibly a crash at sea, but literally unfathomable, with no wreckage, no floating bodies for a postmortem or an inquest by the Air Accident Investigation Unit. They were swallowed up by sea or sky. Now where have I heard that before?

Two months later, two wives and one ex wife – "the three grieving widows", one tabloid called them – held a joint memorial service in Dublin. After that the story faded from the headlines, yet lingered on in the deep recesses of folk memory. Unresolved mysteries tend to do that, like the Loch Ness monster and the *Mary Celeste,* or where Lord Lucan rode off to on Shergar the night he killed the nanny. That's how the story of the Galway Three ended up. As a perennial item in RTÉ's *Reeling In The Years* show – a blip on the screen, a fleeting moment to be resurrected, then just as quickly forgotten before the first commercial break.

Almost completely forgotten until, more than half a decade later, one or two bodies began to turn up again.

One

Áine rang the doorbell. The curtains twitched. Definitely a twitch.

Bet Patricia McGann is standing behind them, dithering, wondering *What's that Áine la-di-dah Kettle doing on my doorstep this afternoon with that gob on her?*

Áine had, admittedly, turned up out of the blue. It would be perfectly understandable if Patricia McGann were to dither for a bit before opening the ...

"Oh. Áine. How *are* you?"

"Trisha! Long *time* no.

"Must be five years now."

Áine had been here once before, with Olivia Reilly. The time the three of them met to make arrangements for that stupid bloody memorial service.

It was one of those ecumenical things, worse than a folk mass, with memories and eulogies instead of the *Kumbaya My Lords*. A wake without a corpse, like a military service for a solider missing in action.

The Catholic curate was a right eejit, winging it with vague nonsense and fluff about "fragile threads of hope".

At least the Anglican canon cut to the chase, talking as if they were indeed dead. And at least the canon knew all three husbands – "hadn't we been to college together?" If you were to sum up his homily for, say, Twitter, you'd have to include the words "tragic loss", "three great mates", "inseparable" and "though while our paths would later cross less frequently ... " Even so, his homily was a tad long. The Anglican canon wasn't the Twitter type.

Since then she and Trisha had hardly seen or spoken to each other – apart from a few phone calls early on of course. Sure what did they have in common? Nothing except their missing husbands. Or ex husband in Olivia Reilly's case.

Five years now.

"Five already? Doesn't time fly."

Fly?

Patricia McGann sounded chirpy this afternoon. Hers wasn't a small house. Not as big as Áine's of course, and it still had that awful old pebbledash. At first Patricia only let her in as far as the hallway. Probably dithering about which room to entertain her in.

Entertain. Like a performing seal.

Probably thinking the best room was too formal, the kitchen too familiar.

Patricia's hallway had enough room for a unicycle, but hardly enough for two unicycles. Áine could see through to the conservatory. A right tip with piles of exercise books; must have caught Patricia in the middle of marking. Today's kids with all their laptops and tablets, yet homework still came in dog-eared exercise books.

So not the conservatory then.

In the end Patricia parked her in the kitchen with coffee and biscuits and a cafetière that hadn't had a proper wash in ages. Áine thought Terry and Trisha would have had one of those shiny new Lattissima machines, not a dirty old cafetière. Maybe they did have a fancy yoke back then. Wouldn't they have been loaded at the time?

"Yes, all these years and still no news," Patricia said.

Patricia was always doing that. Repeating herself, stating the bleeding obvious, was that a teacher thing? It also made it hard to figure what Trisha was thinking. Did she think Áine was angling for another bloody memorial service? To mark what? The fifth or sixth anniversary? And more nonsense in All Saints with the priest and vicar, the three widows without a coffin or a headstone to rub between them? If poor Trisha was thinking all that she should get a grip.

She should have moved on long ago. Everyone else had.

"Can I get you something to eat?"

"Ah no," Áine said. "I'm only after having lunch."

So they sipped coffee and small-talked around the fine weather and Áine's nearly grown-up brats and this and that, and stared out the window through the rain at Terry's den at the end of the garden. That flaming shed.

Áine's Johnny didn't do sheds, not in a den sense. They did have one for the strimmer and broken lawnmower and the rakes and whatsits. But not a "home office den" kind of shed. Johnny didn't even do the mowing. The gardener did all that.

Yes, our husbands really were chalk and cheese.

Enough about sheds. Time to get down to business, even if it came across as a bit, well, blunt.

"Did you ever think my Johnny was having an affair?"

Trisha nearly spilled her coffee. "What? Whatever gave you … I mean … I can't see … "

Trisha was dithering again. Probably about to say she couldn't see Áine's husband as *that type*. What type was that? The same type as Trisha's Terry? The type to carry on with a floozy from Waterford, and the wife always the last to know?

"I … I don't know," Trisha went on. "I hardly knew your Johnny."

"Sometimes I don't think I did either."

They drank away in silence. Two women with nothing in common apart from a shared emptiness, a lump of their lives gone missing at the same time in the same stretch of ocean. Somewhere that used to be vague names on the sea area forecast. *Rockall, Malin, Hebrides.* That's all they shared really: virtual widowhood, a financial mess, a shared absence, shared coffees and strange dreams of deep oceans.

Before, long before everything had happened, Áine loved to nod off to the shipping forecast. All that *Southwest gale eight to storm ten veering west* stuff, a babbling lullaby with you tucked up in your bed while huge waves crashed against the hull of a small fishing-boat far out to sea. Or crashing and smashing up a plane wreck.

Rain, then squally showers. Poor, becoming moderate.

Trisha broke her out of her reverie: "It's a right mess, isn't it?"

"Course it's a bloody mess. Flying off like that, leaving us stuck in a legal bloody quagmire."

"Don't get me started," Trisha said.

"Don't get *me* started." Which Áine did anyway. She started with Johnny's will and the problems with his pension, or rather her non-widow's non-pension from the bloody bank. And the life insurance. As for the children – as in her kids because Trisha and Terry didn't have any – where do you start? With Orla's business folly? On top of Orla's disastrous marriage? Or Simon's bloody college fees? Orla's negative equity, Orla's mortgage arrears timebomb, and Orla's …

"Can I get you another?" Trisha asked.

Áine shook her head.

"A drink then?"

Because it was already well past six.

By the time they'd demolished one bottle of Sauv Blanc and attacked another – unfortunately that was the only wine Trisha had in the house – the two virtual widows had tackled all the troubles of the world. Lawyers. Bank managers. What it's like when you're not technically a widow. Johnny's disastrous investments – "you'd think a banker would know better". Oh, and his *Busty Babes* porn collection that Simon came across on the family's PC.

Trisha was plain Trish now. Trish too had a good rant about bank managers, Terry's life insurance – "then I found he didn't have any because he figured he was going to live for ever" – Terry's expensive gadgets and gizmos, his gambling debts, the huge loan he'd taken out for his stupid bloody jet. Which, Terry was constantly reminding her, wasn't a jet because jets don't have propellers.

Anyway, he'd say, *you need big-boy toys to reassure the clients and impress the investors. Entrepreneurs have to splash the cash to get more cash.*

That's what he was always saying. Him and all the other bloody chancers.

Áine poured herself another glass. She'd have to ring a taxi.

"Trish, do you ever feel guilty?"

"About what? It's like you said. *They* weren't the ones left to clean up the mess. *We* weren't the ones swanning off in the middle of the bloomin' Atlantic Ocean. *We* weren't the ones having a bloody affair."

Trish stopped herself, with one of those oh-shit-too-much-information looks on her.

"So you *do* think my Johnny was having one," Áine said.

"Don't be daft. I meant … " Trisha obviously meant her Terry. Him and the tart from Waterford.

"Exactly," Áine said. "We're not the guilty ones."

"Can we drop it?"

"Yeah, sure." She took another sip of wine. "But you know my sister Niamh?"

"Of course," Trish said. "Where is she this weather?"

"In France."

Of course Trish knew Niamh. Everyone did. Niamh was a great mixer despite her "condition". Mixing not only with Áine's friends and Trisha McGann and Olivia Reilly but also with all three of their bloody husbands.

That was the problem with Dublin. Everyone knew everybody else. Like you were in a huge extended family where your dad is a politician, your mam's a saint, the eccentric uncles are a disgraced bishop and a crooked but moderately successful entrepreneur, the aunts a lapsed nun and a performance artist, your gran an ex-terrorist, and various offspring include a poet, a guard, three fascist solicitors, a mendicant and two or three perpetual students. Who are all, in turn, friends or relations of someone else's extended family.

"Áine! You're not saying your own sister, that he and

she were … "

"Now who's daft? Lookit. My Johnny could have been shagging every young one in the bank for all I care. But he wasn't. Even if he were I wouldn't care any more. I dunno about you but I drew a line years ago. He's gone, past tense and good riddance. I just wish I had his body. No, don't laugh, I mean for the pension and the life insurance. Anyway, he wasn't exactly God's gift was he? Who'd have him?"

"Busty Babes?"

They both giggled. Panic over.

Now it was Trish's turn to cut to the chase. "Look. This is all lovely but you didn't come here to shoot the breeze about legal hassles and all that living-in-limbo stuff."

"Something's up," Áine said. "Niamh rang from France this morning."

"And?"

"She's bumped into Johnny. She's *seen* him. My dead husband. He's very much alive again."

Two

Niamh put her handbag down, turned on a tap, splashed cold water on her cheeks and looked at the face in the mirror. The face was vaguely familiar. It was hers.

Then she thought about the other face. The one she'd just seen out there, at the table on the terrace.

The restaurant was still busy with the lunchtime rush, yet the ladies' loos were empty. And clean. Despite the reputation of French toilets for being festering old sewer pits from Napoleonic times, these ones were modern, spotless.

"I *know* him," she told her reflection. She was absolutely almost a hundred per cent sure of it. But who the feck was he?

Admittedly – Niamh reminded herself for the gazillionth time – she wasn't great with faces. Faces or putting names to them.

This wasn't some vague, minor affliction that crept up on you when you hit forty, as in how she'd finally given in last March and bought her first reading glasses. No, in Niamh's case she'd always had this problem, this condition. Had it as long as she could remember. It was all she knew.

Imagine the opposite. The shock of waking up one morning and suddenly having that problem – after, say, slipping and banging your head on the side of the bath. At least she'd had years to grow used to it, to her condition. To seeing the world as a sea of unfamiliar faces. For every passer-by to be – as far as she was concerned – a complete stranger.

Face blindness, they called it. But it's not as if you can't see or make out the various parts of a face – like there's a blank spot where a nose or mouth should be. Of course not. Not that kind of blindness. The problem is how to see them as a whole, the jigsaw pieces of a face you might know.

It was no laughing matter. There you are, minding your business in a cafe in town, when this nice old lady sidles up and says hello. You exchange pleasantries, yet there's this throbbing strangeness — *Who the hell IS she?* So you try to end the conversation as quickly as possible. The trouble is, this old biddy seems to know you. You probably know her too. Dublin is still small enough that everyone knows everyone else, and we're all related somewhere along the line. *Oh gawd, she could be your own mother!*

No, that's not the worst problem, this inability to recognise faces. It's that these very same faces expect you to know them. So-called friends thinking "Who does she think she is, the stuck-up Lady Muck ignoring us from across the street?"

They had a fancy word for it. A Greek word, the one the shrink used after she was packed off to him when she was sixteen.

"All to do with the right side of your brain," he'd said. That's about all she could remember of it now. The Greek term, and him sitting behind his desk in Leeson Street, not in a white coat but in a nasty tweed jacket with marmalade flecks, the faceless gobshite yattering on about the right side of your brain.

"You see, Niamh," he'd said, switching to his clever-clever here-comes-the-science bit, "when normal – sorry – when *most* people see a face, their brain takes a picture and develops the film. When you take a picture it's like you automatically chuck the film in the bin without bothering to develop it."

That's your problem, he said. Developmental Prosopagnosia. That's what he called it. A fancy term for a genetic disorder that was different for each patient. And incurable.

So if there's no cure, she thought, what the feck am I doing sitting here with this faceless eejit at fifty quid a pop and not even on a medical card?

The sessions stopped soon after, after she'd insisted on seeing the previous psychiatrist for a second opinion (and was told in no uncertain terms that there hadn't been a previous one or any other one in this one-man practice).

Left to her own devices, she developed her defence mechanisms. Like a Sherlock Holmes she looked for clues in what people said and did. Their clothes, hair, habits, voice, accent, gait, mannerisms. Something in their body language.

So this person is a man (good, that eliminates fifty per cent of the population), *he's middle-aged* (another thirty per cent), *medium height* (ten per cent), *standing at our front door and making no effort to be invited in. He has weatherbeaten skin, workman's hands, sunburnt neck. Behind him in the driveway is a white van and a trailer with an industrial lawnmower and gardening implements. He is asking for this week's gardening money. Aha! Elementary, my dear Watson. From what we can deduce, I do believe he must be Mr O'Leary the gardener!*

So the next time an old lady stops you in a cafe for a chat, this very fact is your first clue. It means she probably knows you. After that, engage in small talk, look out for any clues in the conversation and body language. It's more polite than saying, "Sorry, old woman, but do I know you, would you ever feck off?"

With four decades to hone her skills, Niamh had grasped how to latch onto the details that "normal" people hardly bother with. All those tiny details to tell people apart.

Shoes, for example.

Not so much women's as men's, because men often wore the same ones over and over again.

You can tell a lot about a man from his shoes: who he is, what he's like. If eyes are the window to the soul, then shoes are the Velux skylight.

Take black shiny shoes. That stood for responsible, respectable. Possibly a bit stiff and boring too. Áine's Johnny would have the same black leather shoes with almost everything – jeans even. Always shiny too. Yet you couldn't imagine him polishing them. He must have got them done by Áine, or by Mrs M who still cleans for her. Or one of those shoeshine boys in the airport. Maybe he had several identical pairs, with a spare pair in the office for emergencies.

And Terry McGann? The complete opposite. Terry was a Timberlands man. One of those laid-back, outdoorsy, drives-an-SUV types. His shoes said: *I'm business casual, Ireland's answer to Steve Jobs.* They sort of said: *I like the rap music of the kids half my age in the office, and hanging out on street corners outside pubs on summer nights drinking craft beer by the bottle, by the neck.*

Dubes, though? Dubes either literally owned a boat – like Olivia Reilly's poor departed husband – or were pseuds. Or both. Possibly into sport and pints of Heino. You'd never see Kevin Reilly in runners or trainers. Kevin often wore man-purses and overpriced sunglasses with his Dubes. Or sailing boots, deck shoes, boat shoes. Which made sense, kind of, because Kevin did have a boat. If this were America he'd probably own a beach house and boat house and spend summer in the Hamptons, wherever they were. You couldn't imagine Kevin Reilly in work clothes, in his lawyer gear. Besides, she only ever saw him outside work, at social occasions with Johnny and Terry and the rest of the crew.

Espadrilles, though? Espadrilles were for posers with sock allergies. And sandals? James Moffat in her office always wore socks and sandals. Like a Jesus with bad toenails. Niamh's secret nickname for him was Jesus James.

Or desert boots? Jarlath's younger brother Fionn had desert boots. They said little about him, just that Fionn was fairly casual. And recognisable. Suede desert boots the shade of the sand on Sandymount Strand when the tide went out, that was Fionn.

But classic Dubarry Drogue brogues? They were smart,

dependable, sweet smelling, and came with a very well-paid job. Exactly. They were Jarlath.

In the semiotics of shoes, brown brogues equals Jarlath, so file that away in your brain. On the left side of it, in its shoeshop section. Brogues equals Jarlath McElhinney.

And that wet face staring back at her in the toilet mirror in the restaurant in France? That face still glistening, with the red hair and the sensible shoes? *That equals me.*

So that was her condition. It was just her.

Over the years, after all that palaver with the Leeson Street shrink, Niamh had fine-tuned her coping strategies.

Like you no longer jump in fright when you look in the mirror in the morning. You know full well that it's a reflection (no shit, Sherlock), so you can guess who that stranger might be. It's you.

Even so, you can get fed up looking at old photos of yourself and not quite knowing who it is.

During her last year in college she'd dyed her hair a coppery golden. Two decades later it was still the same style and more or less the same shade, from the same dependable brand – though the blasted l'Oréal factory kept modifying the hydrogen peroxide and ammonia and other chemical crap, so Niamh too had to tweak and adapt to get more or less identical results every time.

With her red curly locks, her pale skin and blue-green eyes she could have passed for one of Rossetti's damsels. That's what Áine said. "You're like that painting in the Tate, *The Lady of Shalott.*"

Or Hildebrand and Whatsit in that watercolour Áine had taken her to see on the first floor of the National Gallery in Clare Street. Áine persuaded her to buy a poster of it in the gallery shop: the ill-fated lovers, the princess and her bodyguard on the turret stairs. The poster ended up on the wall of Niamh's utility room, a daily reminder of what she looked like. A bit kitsch but as good as a mirror.

Over the years Niamh's condition had cost her a succession of jobs. But her old schoolfriend Gemma Mockler took pity on her and she'd ended up at The Agency. Gemma knew all about Niamh's condition and how she was faking normal.

"When you think about it," Gemma said, "we all do it. Faking it, I mean. 'Specially in PR. But PR work isn't half as bad as you think. Trust me, Niamh. It'll be good for you."

From then on Gemma, to her credit, made everyone in The Agency wear a name badge. She put Niamh on phone work. Faceless stuff – people on the phone always say who they are straight away.

But there were media launches, which Niamh dreaded. It was like stumbling into an identical twins convention. Looking lost among identical twins isn't good PR.

After it happened twice too often, Niamh thought she'd be getting her P45. But Gemma, fair play to her, took her off the launches and press receptions. She switched her to online PR.

Strategic social media campaigns were still in their infancy back then, yet suddenly everything made sense. Facebook was a godsend: faces to names. Email was perfect too, no guesswork there. As for Twitter, you could tweet away and *Extend your brand's online relationships through our Tailored and Turnkey Solutions* from the comfort of your desk without having to see a stupid bloody face all day.

As Niamh swam away swimmingly in the new social networks – and even back in the offline face-to-face world – she began to come out of her shell.

She stopped stammering and going red with embarrassment. She learned how to socialise, to become a great mixer – like the spin doctor or sham politician who knows how to work the room and treat complete strangers as new best friends.

"How *are* you?" she'd say to her latest VBF. "What've you been up to lately? *Faaaaascinating.*"

While all that might sound terribly superficial, for Niamh it was the complete opposite.

When you can't take anyone at face value you learn to live with the uncertainty, you focus on the very essence of someone. There, underneath the surface. In fact that's how she'd met Jarlath. Through PR.

Jarlath McElhinney. He was one of Gemma's biggest clients at the time, often coming into the office, so he and Niamh kept bumping into each other, and that's when she began to notice something under the surface.

They met again, outside work this time.

Agreed to meet again. And again. Each time at the same time, same place, same table. The same context over and over until Jarlath became a familiar face.

Just the two of them. Tucked away in their slightly worn armchairs at "their" table in the corner of "their" secret place, the Library Bar on the first floor of the Central Hotel.

Back then Niamh was still in her early thirties and, thanks to Gemma, thanks to PR, thanks to Jarlath, she'd finally turned a corner. No longer lost or alone, no longer a "shelfie" stuck on a shelf. She was in her first decent relationship in ages.

After a month or so she decided to go for it. No spin, no lies – cards on the table time.

"No, Jarlath, it's not funny. That's why I had to tell you. I'm not just *bad* with faces. I mean I don't recognise them. At all. Seriously. Almost any face, including my own. Sometimes … I know this sounds daft, but … sometimes I won't even recognise *your* face. So don't get me wrong. It's not that I don't like you. Of course not, silly. I'm not being a stuck-up bitch. It's just a blindness, a genetic thing, a condition. And before you ask, it's incurable."

Jarlath was in horse feed. She thought it sounded funny when he introduced himself at work dos or dinner parties.

Me? I'm in horse feed.

So Niamh's new boyfriend would explain that he didn't actually eat horse feed or swim in it. Not exactly. His family were in the oats industry. A long line of McElhinneys who had diversified judiciously, from porridge to upmarket horse feed. It was becoming big business, particularly in the Far East.

Niamh no longer handled the account – Gemma said it might be wrong to mix business with … you know … – but she now knew more than Wikipedia about mixed grains and extruded nuggets, *highly digestible and energy-dense, scientifically formulated for speed and endurance.*

She still knew next to nothing about actual horses though. Or the racing industry. Or how to place a bet in a bookie shop. Yet through Jarlath, ever patient Jarlath and the weekend visits to his stupendously stupendous family homestead, Niamh had discovered one amazing thing: while she was useless with human faces she could easily tell horses apart.

Pity she wasn't falling in love with a horse then.

Pity it wasn't that kind of relationship. It might have made things far easier. She was falling in love with the pair of brogues of a fairly faceless man called Jarlath.

Before their wedding they'd joked about getting the word *Husband* stitched onto the breast pocket of his suit, so she wouldn't end up snogging his brother Fionn or – worse – a distant cousin from the extended McElhinney Oats clan; or end up with a complete stranger at the wrong reception entirely. She'd even made Jarlath wear his usual brown brogues on their special day, even though they clashed with his dark suit.

After the honeymoon in Venice she moved in with him, they settled down to a routine. And he was great about it, all things considered. Very patient. Made it just another small part of living with her. "Your little condition."

She could always rely on him to jump in with one of his coded phrases: "Oh Niamh, you must tell *Trisha* about that fabulous little *osteria* we found in Venice." That's how he'd casually kick off.

"Oh Niamh, you remember *Sinead,*" he'd say as a faceless face approached – his little signal that she'd met this face before and what name to attach to it: Sinead Morgan or Moran or Morrissey – a Sinead anyway.

Or, "Oh Niamh, don't listen to him, Johnny is only pulling your leg." So that must be *Johnny* again. The fat banker. Her sister Áine's other half.

"Oh Niamh … "

Jarlath was so good at it. Even when alone together in a dark cinema she could squeeze his arm and whisper, "Psst, which one's he again?" And he'd say, "Only Michael feckin' Collins, ya daft eejit."

"But he had a beard in the last scene."

"No, he didn't. Shh."

"You sure?"

"Shhhh. It's him. Liam Neeson."

"You mean Ralph … "

She could never tell Liam Neeson and Ralph Fiennes apart. George Clooney was the dead spit of Cary Grant – or was it Clark Gable? – and she hadn't a clue who Ryan Tubridy was, or any of those Kardashians. But then again nor did a lot of people.

Context was everything. If a man came downstairs in the morning that strange face had to belong to either her husband Jarlath or – you'd sometimes wonder – a burglar now wearing Jarlath's white towel dressing gown.

"Accentuate the positive." That's what Jarlath was always saying. "So I'm different every morning? You know how many men would kill for a new wife each breakfast? C'mon, gis a kiss."

Accentuate the positive.

One bonus: she stopped trying to follow *Corrie* or *EastEnders* or *Fair City*. Whenever girlfriends or workmates yattered on about this star or that celeb ("sleb"), she wouldn't know and couldn't care less. Not unless it was vaguely connected to work.

Another bonus: you hardly noticed friends and family growing older.

So Jarlath was great about it, she didn't need soaps or slebs, and she had a new man each morning.

Every morning, until one morning they both woke up and grew tired of it all, both at the same time. No big row or amateur dramatics or plates chucked in anger; they simply drifted apart.

Either of them could have had the last word, but in the end Jarlath did.

"It's like living with a stranger," the man in the white bathrobe said. "I mean a real stranger this time."

Sometimes relationships are like making caramel. Bring them to the right point and they're still sweet. Stop paying attention and go past that point and they can quickly become bitter and burnt. By then it's too late. Everything's ruined.

Thank God we didn't have kids, she told herself. Imagine not being able to recognise your own children.

Six months after the separation and divorce, Niamh was officially single again. Back to a life of ready-meals and DVD box-sets instead of proper cooking and sex, and with no Jarlath to depend on any longer. Alone again, yet it wasn't like she didn't think about going out again, sooner or later, after she picked herself up, dusted herself off and started all over again. Like the song says, accentuate the positive.

But to meet new faces, when you're hopeless at faces?

Imagine. You and your – no other word for it – your blind date. Only *you're* the blind one.

Imagine. Standing at the bar of a busy pub in town, you

turn away for a split second to pick up your G and T, you turn back to continue the conversation, *to a complete stranger because your date has just slipped out to the loo.*

Or you're in your best frock in a good restaurant, half way through dessert and you've both had too much wine to steady the nerves. This time you're the one who needs to go to the loo. Only, when you come back it will be a sea of strange tables and strange faces. So what do you do? OK Sherlock, leave a clue. Make damn sure to bring your biggest handbag, plonk it on the table when you go to the toilets, keep an eye out for it on your return. Or at least look for a strange man dining alone. Preferably a decent looking hulk waving a large handbag at you.

Or give up and tell big sister: "What's the point in looking for Mr Right? We'd need to meet a dozen times in the same place before I'd even start to recognise him."

Áine was persistent. "Oh shurrup. I wish I were still your age. Look at you, still a babe and don't even know it. Spent half your life worrying about losing weight or losing your virginity or losing face when you should just get out there and enjoy it while you can. Forget all that Catholic guilt trip crap and your bloody condition and … "

"Would you ever feck off," Niamh shot back. "We're not all like you, and don't give me all that 'How to find love later in life' rubbish. Life's not a glossy mag you know. We're not all lost without a man once we hit the big four-oh." That was telling her. "Anyway, the only thing I'm trying to attract this week is a decent offer of wine. I'm off to France. To drink vino, learn French and shag a Frenchman."

So that's exactly what she'd done of course. Apart from the "shag a Frenchman" bit.

Three

I should have seen it coming. It all started innocently enough, shortly before Chile's second goal.

A huge face fills the screen: a young man deep in sorrow. A nanosecond later he is jubilant. He's a soccer fan in a Spanish jersey who has just caught his own mugshot on the big screen. He's being beamed – beaming away – to the rest of the stadium (oh, and to a billion viewers around the planet).

I laugh. Arnaud laughs.

From here on in – I must confess I don't know it at the time – everything will begin to slide. Slowly at first, then faster and faster, relentlessly downhill.

I'm a PI, Arnaud is a chef. We've not much in common apart from football. And food of course. And getting together for a few jars and a blather two or three times a month for the past couple of decades or more.

Tonight we're in The Black Piglet. Not the greatest pub in town to catch a match but that's where we've ended up, having a bit of banter and a few scoops, with half an eye on the World Cup on the TV. Then all eyes on it as the unthinkable unfolds.

After six glorious years the Spanish brand of tippy-tappy football is unravelling before our very eyes. The footballing gods are being dragged down to earth. They were pulled apart by the Dutch in their opening game, and it's just as bad with Chile tonight.

"It's like quantum bloody physics," Arnaud says, trying to cut through the bar noise.

"You what?" I shout back.

"Him there, that bollocks." He waves at the big screen, at a slo-mo replay of the Spanish fan doing his crying-laughing thing. "It's like that Heisenberg uncertainty whatsit. Or Schrödinger's cat. He's sad, he's happy. He's sad, he's happy again. He's down in the dumps and over the moon, both at the same time."

"Maybe the director is just trying to capture the atmosphere at the game."

"Bollocks. It's all atmosphere and feck all game. See – look at that."

The camera has cut to yet more fans. "We just missed a goal-kick," he continues.

"It was a throw-in."

"Whatever."

Arnaud is in a bad mood about something and taking it out on the telly. Yet he's right. For the seasoned armchair fan, a goal-kick or throw-in isn't just a boring humdrum routine to restart play, not just an excuse for yet another crowd shot. For the armchair fan a goal-kick is part of the beautiful game's rich patterns, another tiny piece to add to the jigsaw. Is the goalie hurried? Desperate? Hoofing long balls up the yard? Or is he calm, confident, patiently passing it to his back line?

It's the full-time whistle. I order two more pints.

"Out with it. Why the long face?"

"Bloody Cromwell," he says, "that's what."

Cromwell? Arnaud Connolly is French on his mother's side but born and raised – or gently braised in his case – on Dublin's northside. And him being a chef, you might expect Arnaud to have a beef about *beef* once in a while, but not about Oliver Cromwell. You wouldn't take Arnaud to be a *tiocfaidh ár lá* type.

"Feck it, Mossie. We were counting on it."

"What?"

"The bloody film shoot."

"Ah. Gotcha."

As in the TV drama with the short but daft title *(To Hell Or),* a film about Cromwell's Irish excursion with a large army of extras. So many extras, in fact, that they had Arnaud down for eight weeks of "Lights, camera, grub", aka location catering.

"A nice little earner, all due to start next month," he

continues. "We cleared the decks for them feckers, turned down half a dozen gigs, then they shelve the bloody thing. Permanently, due to a fuck-up on the finance front."

I hold up my pint in a mock toast. "Well feck 'em."

"Yeah. Feck 'em."

We finish our drinks and grab the Luas to Smithfield. It's only a short stroll towards our respective homes in Stoneybatter (me) and Grangegorman (him and his missus, Roisin).

The tram is busy enough. I find two empty seats and sit down. "It can't be all that bad."

He sits down too. "No, Moss, worse than bad. I haven't the nerve to tell them yet."

Arnaud explains. Even under the best-case scenario he will have to lay off most of his team until August or September, till the next big job. By which time half of them will have been snapped up by other restaurants. There's a serious shortage of good chefs in town at the moment.

It's bad and sad alright, having to break up a good team like that. Some kitchen crews have a "bad boy" swagger – all shouting and swearing, kicking their oven doors shut, slapping the meat down on the counter with far more noise and force than necessary. Arnaud's crew, by contrast, are clean, calm, as tippy-tappy as those Spanish footballers in their prime.

The tram reaches Smithfield. We hop off. But as we tread gingerly across the cobbles, Arnaud halts.

"Shag it, Moss. Let's feck off somewhere."

This is a Damascus moment. Or in his case a Smithfield Square moment.

Did I say things were about to slide downhill?

I stop too. "What d'you mean?"

"Let's fly off to France."

"Hold it right there. You know me and flying. I hate the safety drills and shite snacks at thirty thousand feet, and I can't stand the mushroom farm."

"You wha'?"

"You know, the place in airport security after the X-ray machines, where they make you stand in your socks or bare feet. The mushroom farm."

Arnaud loves flying. Knowing him, he'd look at a dead old airliner – a disused DC-10, say, in an aircraft graveyard – and figure out how to turn it into a restaurant. Knowing him, he'd stick a mushroom farm in front of the main entrance, for the fully authentic experience. And Arnaud knows full well I hate flying.

"No, Moss, you daft bollix. I mean we take the ferry."

"Oh."

We begin walking again.

"Right," I say, "the ferry. That's more like it."

"And I pay the petrol if you do the driving."

"I dunno, it's … "

"We can take Tintin."

Of course. Tintin. This is Arnaud's catering truck. Or gastro wagon he prefers to call it. A gleaming silver mobile kitchen with an aerodynamic bullet-shaped roof.

"Think about it," he continues. "Tintin. It's not the worst way to check out the gastronomic hotspots around the south of France. There's enough space for a couple of camp beds. And it has a kitchen, obviously."

"Obviously. And showers, loos?"

"There's a big sink to wash in. And I could get a lend of a cassette toilet."

"What's that?"

"Look, Moss, what more do you want?"

"Well … "

He gives a big grin. "And we can stock up on cheap vino."

"Now you're talkin'."

"Put the feet up, soak up the sun, do some on-the-ground food research. Pack Tintin with lots of local wine, cheese and cassoulet and the trip will have paid for itself."

"Can I have a think about it?"

He gives a Coke tin a gentle kick. "Ah c'mon, Moss. Aren't you always saying you need the right priorities in life?"

Yeah yeah. Eat, drink and investigate, in that order. Arnaud can read me like a book.

"But … " – I'm scrambling for an excuse – "I can't just swan off to the Continent at the drop of a … "

"What's on your plate at the moment?"

"Er … "

Arnaud gives the tin another kick. "Let me guess. Wilde & Reid Investigations are snowed under. You have to wrap up the paperwork on a slip-and-fall case. What else?"

"This and that. Putting the finishing touches to a CCTV system in a polytunnel in north Dublin."

"To catch some carrot thieves."

"Actually it's aubergines and artichokes."

"Right. It all adds up to a day's work at most."

"And I have to do my VAT returns."

And, I could add, chase after client fees. The time it takes for their cheques to come through is about the same as the gestation period of the African elephant.

"So," Arnaud says. "Say another two, three days max."

"But I can't just … " We reach my turn-off at the top of the square. "Night, Arnaud. Let me sleep on it."

"*Slán.* You do that."

Four

In hindsight any sane sensible person would have left it at that. As a silly pipe dream, late-night pub stuff, the drink talking. Yet Arnaud's mad plan has begun to take shape.

He buys a couple of camp beds.

I clean up my outstanding cases.

His crew gives Tintin a shine *(Walbernize! Cleans, seals and polishes all in one go!).*

And I have to admit that Tintin's gleaming body is looking good alright.

The last time I saw his crew in action in Tintin's tight galley they moved around each other like elegant ballerinas with heavy saucepans. A great team, from Arnaud's dishpig Julie to his sous chef Aisling (that's another thing: his team are mostly women), with Arnaud in the midfield controlling the game. Such a pity to see his squad dismantled and off on free transfers.

Back in my office I think about work flows and cash flows, which are down to a trickle. Feck all cases and cheques flying through Wilde & Reid Investigations this week. The office fridge is empty, the radio has gone all silly season, with an earnest young woman haranguing me to eat less sugar. Earlier this morning an earnest young man was encouraging me to buy more Fair Trade sugar. You can't win.

Summer officially started on the first of June. That's what the weather people told us, but it's July already, in an Irish summer that's doing its best or worst to be unpredictable. Several days of glorious sunshine are followed by a week of grey skies, then another day or two of sunshine and sea fog, then thunderstorms and pissing down again, like midday today.

That's when Arnaud knocks on the door, sopping wet. He plonks a small hillock of documents and printouts on my desk. "Busy?"

I lift my feet off it. "So so."

"Yeah, looks like it." He rubs his hands and adopts the plummy accent of an English army officer in WWII. "OK chaps, we have it all worked out. *We* are here." He spreads a map out, points to a spot on it with various routes and zones highlighted in day-glo colours like it's a Normandy invasion. "And *this* is our target." The other end of France.

"Yeah but … "

"We drive south, meet a few of my cousins, catch the Tour de France in Nîmes … "

"But … "

"But what? You've no strings, Moss. You're a bachelor."

Bachelor? He has just turned me into an unloved, prissy old maid, who lives alone in his minimalist yet tastefully decorated *bachelor pad*. Said pad is either clean and tidy – a babe magnet with swish cocktail bar for my *bachelor* parties – or a perpetual tip, the toilet seat permanently up, the kitchen sink a sad reflection of my insouciant, independent yet ultimately inept lifestyle.

"No one gets called a bachelor nowadays," I tell him. "Not even a confirmed bachelor like in a Rock Hudson film. Or an eligible bachelor in a Jane Austen. Don't use the 'b' word unless it's about beans and soup and mushy peas. OK, strictly speaking that's batchelor with a T, Batchelors Beans from Cabra West but you know what I mean. I'm not the 'b' word – I'm just me. I'm not happily married with 2.4 kids, I just happen to be happily single, you're not, so get over it."

"OK OK." Arnaud puts his hands up in mock surrender.

"And don't do that thing again where you pretend you wish you were single too."

"Ah c'mon. Let's get outta here. Lunch. My treat."

"And don't be setting me up with one of Roisin's single friends either."

I get that sinking feeling again as we walk to the triangle

at the top of Manor Street. Like I'm being sucked into a dark pit with no way out.

"But I can't go to France. I've no one to look after the office."

"Bollocks," he says. "It can't be that difficult. I'm getting Aisling to hold the fort."

Aisling? Good choice. Tough as a maths test yet rarely has to raise her voice or stomp her feet, Aisling is Arnaud's frequent fort-holder. Arnaud's Roisin sometimes jokes that he and Aisling are having an affair, but it's far more serious than that: *Aisling is his sous chef.* She is super-efficient, irreplaceable and – though it's never said – a better cook than him.

Arnaud puts a hand on my shoulder. "So that's that, we're going to France."

"But one-man shows don't have second-in-commands."

"Can't you get Maggie Dardis?"

I look back in the direction of my office. "I could I suppose. She's practically living in the place at the moment."

"Anything going on between you two?"

"Would you ever feck off. She has some freelance work, her flat is a shoebox, she's going stir crazy, I offered her a spare desk."

"And your wonky broadband."

We arrive at a bright little bistro. At one time it was painted dark grey, an Italian joint called Basilico. That lasted about six months. For about ten years before that it was painted green, an Indian called the Green Chilli. Today it has a mustardy yellow exterior and is called Soulful.

Soup, falafel burgers and a glass each of a cheap but good red wine later, we've spread out the Normandy invasion plans, drawn up extensive itineraries, consulted ferry timetables and motoring atlases, checked the iPhone for local markets to plunder and possible restaurants to visit. It's all quite seductive. We're off to France.

"And no fancy Michelin joints," Arnaud says. "We stick to small family-run places, pavement cafés, good, honest, traditional stuff done well."

Bistronomy. Much like the grub he does. Classic fare and none of your posh pernickety restaurant fads. Enough of the pulled pork omelettes on trendy slate plates, with your drinks served in jamjars and your cutlery coming in tins, in an über-trendy dining room where none of the furniture matches, no two chairs are alike and the tables are transport pallets or reclaimed doors. No, none of those restos with bike-chain chandeliers and taxidermied jungle beasts, and balconies from old sailing ships, and chalkboards with inspirational quotes in delicate calligraphy from Gandhi or Brendan Behan or Bill Gates, and everything "Artisan". Which is shorthand in that context for mad prices.

Time to reveal my cunning plan. "What's the French for bag-in-a-box wine?"

"Le bag-in-box," Arnaud says.

"Serious?"

"Uh-huh." He switches to exaggerated stage French: "Zeh bag-in-box, Monsieur Mau-rees."

"You could stack a lot more wine in them. In Tintin I mean."

"Genius."

"Thank you, Arnaud."

"Bag-in-box rocks. No risk of breakages either.

"Yeah, it'll be sort of like Tetris – how to get a wine lake into a Tardis. Hold on: isn't it terrible plonk all the same?"

"Not necessarily. It's come a long way since the early days. The main problem is getting the spout thing through the cardboard hole. Worse than sex in a Mini."

Before I have time to work that one out he continues: "Anyway, before we buy shedloads we can sample some."

Sample? I like already.

Just then a tall beanpole enters. Hardly noticed until his shadow is towering over us.

"Howrya head," the beanpole says.

"Grand, how's the form?" I reply. "Oh Colley, sorry. This is Arnaud."

"Arnold, pleased to meet." Colley sits down and orders a double espresso.

I continue the introductions. "I must have mentioned Arnaud, he's a chef. And this is, um … Colley is an old client from down the road."

It's kind of true. I helped Colley to find his birth mother. How would you begin to describe him, besides being tall and thin? Fierce blue eyes, silver grey hair almost crewcut short and gelled straight up in spikes and, well, he's bloody tall. Taller and more shady than a parasol, with a permanent limp from God knows what. Colley comes from Stoneybatter's school of hard knocks, as opposed to a school of soft doorbell ringing.

He looks at our lists and atlases. "So what's the story, Reidy?"

"We're um … "

Arnaud jumps in: "Planning a holiday."

Colley rotates a map to read it. "France. Tell us more."

"A busman's holiday," I say. "But not in a bus of course. More a gastro wagon."

Colley picks up the Normandy invasion map. "Rosslare to Roscoff? Sorry lads, you're making a right hames of it. Last time we did that route we got on the ferry at four in the afternoon, arrived in France at ten-thirty the next day with half the morning gone. Rosslare? It's quicker going from Cork. See? Drive on the ferry at the same time, chill out, hit a restaurant or the swimming pool on the top deck, have a quick kip and arrive nearly four hours earlier with the whole day ahead of you."

I check a ferry timetable. "He's right you know."

"And that's all wrong too." Colley taps our route, which is in pink highlighter. "You want to take the motorway to Rennes, then down to Nantes, hit the E5 and A10, through to Saintes."

Saintes? He's right again. Arnaud is pissed off that some shady character from Cowtown who isn't even half-French knows more than Arnaud about the secret hieroglyphs of their motorway system.

"How do you know all this?" Arnaud asks.

"Ah, you know. Tour de France. Not personally, I wasn't in it I mean, but from the telly. The helicopter shots, the maps and all. You know what you need? A good navigator."

By the time he has finished his double espresso we have one. Colley has made a unilateral decision to come along for the ride. He really is incorrigible.

Did I say *a* spare desk?

If there's a direct correlation between the three variables of desk space, mess and project size, this freelance job that Maggie Dardis is working on must be bigger than the Manhattan Project. She has been here less than an hour, yet every available flat surface in my office has been taken over. Her laptops, PCs, hard drives and monitors are bleeping away.

"Hi, Maggie. I know I said make yourself at home, but I'll need it all cleared up by the time I'm back."

I can hardly complain. Four fifths of PI work nowadays depends on techie stuff. If the job had an entry exam, IT would be a compulsory subject, alongside *Data Privacy Law* and *How to Wangle A Suspect's Credit Rating Without Getting Caught*. And I'd fail miserably.

Hence Maggie Dardis, my IT consultant. Insultant more like, who forces ones and zeroes and silicon chips to do her bidding on a daily basis. And she's my office babysitter for the next two weeks.

"And I mean all of it," I continue, waving at the mess.

She nods. Like one of those noddy dogs in a car window, if noddy dogs had long dark hair with a perfectly straight fringe.

"What are you working on?"

"A B2B website that's a crock of shite. You don't want to know," she says. Her mobile gives a loud burp. "OK, mister detecty man. How many years are you away this time?"

"About a fortnight."

Another loud burp. She looks at a text message and says, "And my light office duties include … ?"

"Just make sure the place looks lived in. Let the postman in, check the email and answering machine, don't forget to put the alarm on in the evening, and there's a tenner in the petty cash box if you run out of coffee."

"So when are you flying off to France?"

"Tomorrow morning."

"I thought you had a fear of flying."

Here we go again. Aviophobia.

Avio. From the Greek for air.

Phobia. From the Greek for flying by (and doing other things in) the seat of one's pants.

Aviophobia. The fear of turbulence, take-off and landing, and TWA. Which stands for Travelling With Anxiety. The dry mouth, pale face and palpitations, the chest pains, crashes, terrorists, the mad axeman from Ardnacrusha in seat 12B.

"Actually we're taking the ferry," I reply.

"Will you be needing your laptop?"

"No. It's a holiday, Maggie. Digital detox."

Screenlessness. Maggie Dardis wouldn't know the meaning of the word. Her waking hours are spent shovelling digital snow in a hyperconnected world, and she becomes twitchy as a gunslinger when separated from her mobile for more than a minute.

"I'm joining the cult of the unplugged," I continue. "We're gonna switch off, tune out and not worry about phones and laptops for a whole fortnight, Maggie. Imagine. A whole fortnight. Arnaud has even banned Colley's PlayStation. We'll have our phones but strictly for emergencies. And to take a few holiday snaps."

To rub it in the faces of everyone back home.

"So," she says, "your laptop. Can I borrow it?"

"Be my guest. But it doesn't leave this room."

"Ta." The greedy grin of a gluttonous multi-tasker.

"And you're not to call us. Only in a dire emergency."

"But there won't be one."

"No."

As if.

Five

Niamh turned off the tap, dried her face and looked at the mirror again.

What exactly had just happened? Ten minutes ago she'd been watching the canal boats drifting by. You could almost touch them from the tables on the restaurant terrace. A peaceful sunny scene, apart from the nee-nah of a siren. And another nee-nah. So many police cars whizzing back and forth. None of the diners seemed to mind, because something far more important was happening two feet away: lunch.

She felt confused but wasn't drunk. She'd only had two glasses of the house white – chilled, cheap and very cheerful, thank you very much.

As for the other five women at her table, she hadn't bothered to put names to faces. No point. After this week she'd never see them again. Five women who were impossible to tell apart, with their interchangeable accents, similar footwear and identical blonde hair. Apart from Pauline McColl, of course. Pauline was a brunette, a nice lass from Edinburgh with a thick burr that made even her French sound Scottish.

That was another thing. Everyone at their table was supposed to speak French. *Ah oui! Maman est chez le coiffeur avec son steak haché, blah blah blah!* It was the strict rule at the language school: no English in class, not even at lunch with your fellow students. French to be spoken at all times, muddle through as best you can till four o'clock and school over for the day. They don't call it an immersion course for nothing. They push you in at the deep end.

It reminded her of being packed off to the Gaeltacht for the summer, with the céilí the highlight of the week, and getting told off by the Bean an Tí for speaking Béarla with the boys from Cork on the way to the village cinema to watch *Grease.*

But it wasn't as if Niamh's table companions were talking to each other in any language this lunchtime. Not even Estuary English or Edinburghese or their poor attempts at French. All five were miles away. In Midsomer or Musselburgh or wherever they were from, making sneaky calls and texting away, five ostrich heads ducking reality. *Mum fine how's cat XXX.*

It was enough to make you scream *Can we all fucking well look up and put those things away FOR JUST ONE MINUTE?* But she didn't have enough French for that.

Niamh never drank at lunchtime. Not normally. But what with the heat and this being France and how everyone had wine at lunch – especially the English when they let their hair down – well, you soon got into the swing of things. So it was easy enough to succumb to a third glass during the afters.

It was at that very moment, as Pauline McColl did the top ups, that Niamh spotted him across the room.

"I bloody well know that face!" she said out loud, in English, without meaning to. Four ostrich heads looked up, glaring, as though she'd just announced the arrival of a sexually transmitted disease. But who the feck was it?

She *knew* that face. A strange face yet ever so familiar. Someone she must have met dozens of times.

But where? Not here in France obviously. Was he on TV? Or one of Gemma's clients? One of Jarlath's old business connections from the racing industry? Hardly.

A distant cousin then? Someone from a wedding reception years ago? No.

Somebody from her year in college perhaps? Nope.

Shit shit shit. It's not Jarlath is it? Of course not. Wrong clothes for a start. And the man was wearing flip flops.

Try as she might she couldn't put a name to that face.

He was sitting at the other end of the terrace, at a table with a young woman.

More a girl than a woman really.

A kid who carried herself in that ever-so-French way, lots of elegant little hand gestures, brushing her hair back from her face. Her dark brown hair was in an unusual style, a blunt bob with wispy layers cut within the shape to create softness. No, Niamh definitely didn't know anyone that young with a bob like that.

But the man? Here? What were the odds of that? There was a remote possibility that she knew him, and a good chance that she didn't know him at all. Yet there was something about the way he moved. The body language, the hair, the accent.

That's what struck her first: his voice. It was like – what do gays call it? – yeah, exactly. Like gaydar. Like how, in a roomful of people gabbling away in a strange language, your antenna will always manage to pick out an English or Irish accent from the hubbub.

Yes. She knew that voice. Definitely. And his face too. But from where?

Yet that was the other strange thing: *while she must know him, he didn't know her.*

At least that's how he acted a minute ago when she walked slowly and casually past his table to the loo to splash water on her face.

It was almost as if his face were saying, *No. You don't look like anyone I know. Now fuck off and leave us alone.* Like an angry man trying to swat a pesky wasp that took a fancy to his jelly and ice cream.

As she walked to the loos she'd given a tiny smile, the kind you give when you're not quite sure whose face it is yet – whether it belongs to a close friend or sworn enemy, a complete stranger or axe murderer – and you're acting like the Queen of England, giving everyone a little wave and polite but tiny smile. Just in case.

But he didn't smile back. Quite the opposite in fact.

She felt in her handbag for her mobile.

Six

Áine Kettle would later describe it as a "flashbulb memory". Like how some people can still recall where they were when JFK was shot. Or John Lennon for Áine's generation. Or Stephen Gately for Orla's. Or 9/11 or the Concorde crash. Or, indeed, the day a light aircraft went missing over Galway Bay.

And now her sister's lunchtime call from France was one too. A flashbulb memory, deeply etched in a corner of Áine's brain.

When exactly did it begin, this memory? At home in Clonskeagh that morning? Hardly. Not while doing the weekly shop either. Of all places it began at the hairdressers (or hairdressing studio or salon or whatever they called it this week). It started with her hair.

Keeping up appearances is a time-consuming, complicated business. For a start, you need to find just the right colour to suit your skin, to cover up the grey, to stand out yet fit in. Áine always went for platinum. It had more chemicals than Saddam's secret factories. "You should try something more organic," people were always telling her. But suppose it came out a slightly different shade? Niamh would go ape.

Some women had a cut and highlights every five weeks. Five weeks was a bit much in a downturn, or even the start of an upturn. These days Áine had the works every three months. Hardly extravagant. It also made the date easy to remember: the flashbulb memory would have been on the first Wednesday of the month. Hairdresser day.

The first image in the memory was the new girl asking what she was going for this time, listing off the options like a girl in a coffee shop: "Coffee, caramel, cappuccino, mocha, honey, vanilla blonde … "

Or maybe Áine had got in first, with "The platinum please, same as always, and *come back here, young lady.* I *don't* want the foil highlights."

Behind her back the girl would probably have bristled at the very idea. That a customer might actually know more about her own hair than the full-time follicle experts? Or at least more than the new girl who was still trainee, unlike the regular girls.

So that's what must have happened. Or was that first part just something that happened more or less the same way each time at the hairdressers so her mind had tagged it onto the start of her flashbulb memory?

Who cares? Fast-forward to the next part, after her hair was done. In the next room one of the regular girls started into her nails, another began to slap on the face mask. Yes, that's exactly what happened.

Slap, slap, slap. Honey, oats and cucumber. More like a health farm breakfast than a face mask. Fully organic, freshly made on the premises each morning.

You could do it yourself at home of course, but who has the time when it takes an hour to get your nails done and half a day for the hair? Besides, it's the kind of mask that's sticky, but not sticky enough to leave on while you potter about the kitchen and put everything in the dishwasher. The kind of mask that requires time, gravity, another pair of hands and another thirty euro.

So she lay back and relaxed while the mask did its bit. Slap, slap, slap.

What next? She would have been thinking that it's well worth spending the guts of a morning and a small fortune getting your face slapped and hair whipped into shape and your nails done and varnished in case there's a lull in the conversation at the dinner party tonight.

But whose dinner party that night? For the life of her she couldn't remember. The Brannigans? Laura and Pete Fogarty? It hardly mattered, because she'd had to cancel and drive out to Trisha McGann's for their tête-à-tête.

The key thing, the only thing that mattered was what happened next. Her mobile rang.

44

What with half the mask already on and her nails in someone else's hands, Áine was paralysed. Yet somehow, for some reason, as her mobile buzzed its merry dance on the counter by her coffee mug she decided to peek at its screen.

It said *NIAMH*.

She could hardly ignore it. Niamh always rang with her daily updates from France at seven on the dot, six Irish time. Early evening, never half twelve or one in the afternoon – when Niamh knew full well that her sister would be bang in the middle of her hair-nails-and-facial.

Must be urgent so. Bloody well better be.

"Hi, Niamh?" Áine shooed the two girls away and wiped the organic breakfast gunk off her face. "Sorry, I can hardly hear you. I'm in the middle of … "

"You won't believe this," Niamh said.

"Why are you whispering?"

"It's *him*. With a young one half his age."

"You're joking. Are you in Spain?" Áine could swear there were flamenco guitars in the background.

"No silly. In a restaurant. And *he's* here. I heard him across the room and just knew it was him."

"From his face? But … "

"No, obviously not his face. His voice. You know how you can pick up an Irish accent at the other end of the room when everyone else is gabbling away in French? It's him alright."

"But … "

"No, *listen*. I just know it's him. Doesn't *look* like him, not exactly, but maybe he's had plastic surgery or something. You know me with faces."

The next minute was like an hour, as Áine tried to decipher the garbled snatches from a distant planet. The restaurant clamour was cut through by the sound of sirens. Police cars, Spanish guitars – whatever next?

A flashbulb memory. What seemed like a panic-stricken hour but in reality a couple of minutes at most. A compressed remembrance of Niamh whispering, Niamh describing how she'd gone over for a quick word ("and he said do I know you?") and she was absolutely positive (Niamh? With faces?), and how he had a neat little goatee (Johnny never went a day without shaving; he hated stubble, detested beards), and was now slim and tanned (Her Johnny? Slim? Tanned? With a goatee? Next he'll have a bloody ponytail. A banker with a ponytail?). Niamh said he was greyer too, thinning on top, as anyone his age would be, five or six years on. With not quite the same taste in clothes, "though it must be over thirty degrees this morning".

So it *was* him. And Niamh, despite her condition, was a hundred and ten per cent sure of it.

"Oh feck. Áine!" Niamh's voice was much louder.

"What?"

"He's gone ballistic. I'm gonna ask him straight up. Talk later. Bye. Yeah. Bye. *Ciao!*"

That was her final word in the flashbulb memory: *ciao*.

Your sister goes all the way to the Languedoc to learn French and ends up speaking Italian.

Áine tried ringing back. She was put through to voicemail. Tried two more times, voicemail each time. She didn't know what to do.

In a panic she rang Trish McGann. No answer. Then Olivia Reilly. No answer there either so she went ahead anyway, telling Olivia's voicemail everything.

Everything. All she could remember from that call. Everything from her flashbulb memory.

It was hard to believe, yet after all these years Johnny Kettle was still alive.

Áine's husband was hanging out in the south of France. With a goatee beard.

And a young one half his age.

Seven

How would you describe Tintin? "A vintage trailer conversion" doesn't quite do it justice.

Inside, its long kitchen galley has worktops, gas rings, a gas griddle, two fryers, an under-counter fridge, drinks fridge, freezer and – more recently installed – three camp beds. But it's the outside everyone is talking about. Its shiny body that shimmers in the early morning sun, attracting smiles and stares from other motorists as they overtake us.

Tintin is foreign, alien. It could be a 1950s sci-fi moonbase, or a slab of Americana from a bygone age.

Tintin is a symbol of a wanderlust generation, a metaphor for the freedom to roam and explore, for nuclear families on open roads. Even if you don't collect motor porn, Tintin is the kind of machine you want to touch, to run your fingers along its twenty-three feet of glistering aluminium, its body lines freshly buffed up in a high-polish finish, with all its structure and rivets on show.

Tintin was built for exploring wild frontiers in the days before trailer trash stereotypes, before of modern art museum began collecting them, these icons that are as American as a drive-in or a diner.

Tintin is a by-product of the Cold War. Literally: a silver bullet carved and bashed out of aluminum offcuts from B52s.

But not for me, not this morning. Tintin is no longer a cool museum piece or working kitchen. The sun is low, it's not that warm yet, and I'm sweating. I'm not used to driving on the right, or being chased by a lumbering hulk of aluminium in the rear-view mirror. There's no time to take in the gawping motorists or rolling French countryside. In the big towns the drivers are assertive space-grabbers; being timid or polite is asking for trouble. The motorways are scarier again. As for all the roundabouts, the French used to view them as an Anglo-Saxon ailment. The disease has arrived here too.

Arnaud rolls down the front passenger seat window to shout "Hergé's adventures of Tintin!" in a mock bombastic voice at the vehicles around us. After he tires of that he commandeers the car radio.

Every station is stuck in the Eighties. I know pop has been eating itself for years, but this stuff is gnawing away with false teeth. Arnaud wades through the jungle of old Anglo-American Eighties crap and the swamps of modern French blancmange and Johnny Halidays until he finds a civilised oasis of Belgian jazz: Melanie De Biasio.

In the back seat Colley studies maps and trots out directions. My human satnav.

On the dashboard the GPS thing is knackered and my phone keeps reminding me of its inability to perform operations. Phew, that's a relief. *Unable to perform operations.* The last thing you'd want your phone to do is to start into your appendix while you're stuck in the French motorway system.

By the time we reach Saintes I'm knackered. "Lads, can we find a café and stretch our legs?"

"Pull up over there." Arnaud points to a cluster of shops. "I'll get some things to rustle up in Tintin."

After a quick picnic in a noisy layby we inch down the map towards Bordeaux, to a land of microclimates and the luminous light of the southwest. All deep blue skies with the occasional little wisp of cloudy meringue.

"And watch out for the toll roads," Arnaud warns Colley. "Down south towards Montpellier they have one every five minutes."

The autoroutes are peppered with them, he says. Toll roads mean long queues and slow service, of the kind that would get an M50 toll operator lynched and thrown off the bridge in a justifiable homicide.

Colley guides me down to the outskirts of Toulouse, to a district called Ramonville. It's on the banks of the Canal du Midi, and we can finally begin to unwind. Twice as wide as any Dublin canal, the waterway is flanked by majestic plane trees that unfold into the distance.

But it's getting dark. Ramonville is becoming overrun by kids on scooters and loud students.

Arnaud's French contacts have recommended a local restaurant. But their information is out of date. La Pycantine is closed, as in closed for good. We end up at a little place called L'Apostrophe. The cool night air has a few diners at the outside tables and faded checked tablecloths. An elderly couple are tucking into the silky quenelles of chicken liver mousse (her) and a *boeuf daube* with slabs of polenta (him). The beef stew smells of orange peel. A young couple are having *soupe au pistou* and artichokes *à la grecque,* braised with lemon, olive oil and coriander seeds.

I take one look at the bilingual menu on the window …

At l'Apostrophe we welcome you with the relaxed professionalism. Housed in a chair on the patio-gallery with arches, your meal can be accompanied with a delicious cocktail or sample a local wine lounging under the trees. All our cuisine is local fare, and it is certain you will have an unforgettable moment of relaxation …

… and I decide hunger can wait. So much for a gastronomic adventure.

"Sorry lads. Sounds grand but I'm bushed."

I leave them to it and go back to Tintin for half a baguette, ham, cheese and a glass of red wine. I drift off to sleep to the whine of yet another scooter whizzing by. Hours later there's a vague recollection of people clattering up the steps of Tintin, snatches of conversation, a bottle being opened, Colley saying *The midges are brutal,* Arnaud saying *They're mosquitoes not midges.* More wine sounds, more male laughter, and Arnaud saying *Yeah right, and French men think Fidelity is the name of the girl who lives across the hall.*

I think Colley and Arnaud are beginning to get on.

Eight

Áine Kettle knew that look: Orla was about to give her the silent treatment.

Her daughter had been late coming down to breakfast, so Áine had said something along the lines of: "Is the shop going to open itself? There's coffee made."

Silence.

Orla's shop. Yet one more hobby to get bored with before moving on to the next. Orla was just as bad with boyfriends, clothes, college courses, husbands.

"I said there's coffee made," Áine said. "I need to pack."

More silence, another shrug. Signifying what? Disgust? Boredom? Bemusement? Áine found the body signals of Orla's generation increasingly hard to decode. Orla herself was impossible to nail down. A bit like her stupid shop.

Orla's standard reply was along the lines of: "Niamh gets but you don't get, do you, mother? *Stuff* just needs time to get a style and identity."

Stuff indeed. Bloody awful name for a shop. Yet perfect too for a bit-of-this more-of-that kind of emporium that had the kind of clothes, trinkets and other stuff that only Orla liked.

"Just give it time to get a name for itself," Orla would say. "Then you'll get."

Time was the one thing *Stuff* didn't have. After *oodles of friends* in its opening week it settled down to a few *browsers* and *just lookings,* but not many actual paying customers. Between this "temporary blip" and the rent and rates, the shop was on life support. Anyone could see that. Anyone apart from Orla, the girl who lived in a bubble. Maybe Áine should ask Niamh to have a word with her, when everything was back to normal again.

YOU talk to her because she won't listen to me. Tell your niece how it's time to pull the plug and put Stuff *out of its misery. It's like a sick donkey after a train crash waiting to happen.*

But Niamh was still AWOL in France.

"I said I'm just going upstairs to pack."

Silence.

It was bad enough when Johnny disappeared.

Áine would be on the phone to "the other two crones" (Orla's words, not hers) every time they heard a report about a dead body off the west coast. Trawling the Web for hours, only to find it was just another stupid drowned fisherman or whatever.

"You're only upsetting yourself," Niamh kept saying.

Orla kept telling her, "Why are you harping on about the past again with them two … *harpies?* It doesn't solve anything. Forget the past, let's talk about my shop idea."

After a while Áine stopped phoning "the other two witches" (Orla's words), and life went on. Johnny was gone, they'd drawn a line, she'd got over it. Grown used to it, even. If Johnny were to turn up after all this time, she couldn't care less.

But that was all before Niamh's call from France.

"Are you listening to a word I said? I'm going upstairs to pack because someone has to find out where your aunt has got to."

"Whatever."

"And whether your poor father is still alive and well."

"Yeah yeah, and having it off with a young one in the south of France."

During last night's row the bubble girl had an even madder theory. "Do you think Niamh has copped off with dad?"

Orla's own aunt. Her own godmother?

Unbefuckinglievable.

What bloody planet was Bubble Girl on?

Everyone knew Niamh couldn't stand the sight of Johnny.

Nine

We slowly wind further south, through picturesque villages and tree-lined roads among the vines. Just like the brochures and *nouvelle vague* movies.

Whenever we've parked Tintin in a quiet lane, opened its shutters and fired up the kitchen, you'd half expect the neighbourhood to descend for a takeaway batterburger and chips. But unlike Brittany they seem well used to strange camper vans the further south you go. Tintin is just a fancy shiny distant cousin of those ugly white boxy things they have, and is largely ignored.

One thing we ourselves ignore on the final leg down to the Med is a large bump in the road. But Tintin doesn't ignore it. Nor does the car's rear axle.

How was I to know what a road sign with nesting chickens means? But Arnaud does.

"Nid de poule. Chicken nest."

"What's that?" Colley asks.

"French for pothole disaster."

Arnaud rings around a few garages and finds a friendly local mechanic.

Monsieur Henri isn't quite what I expected. Young, smart, in clean white shirt and jeans rather than a boiler suit, not a drop of oil in sight. Monsieur Henri grins a lot. He shrugs, inspects the damage, shrugs again and grins.

Arnaud translates. "He says the car might be a write-off but Tintin will survive. And there's not much call for spare parts for a 1950s Airstream in this neck of the woods. Monsieur Henri can order them but there will be … "

"Oui Messieurs." Monsieur Henri switches to his serious face. *"Un grand délai."*

After arranging for the wreckage to be carted back to his garage, we go in search of alternative transport.

"Une bagnole, s'il vous plaît," Arnaud says to the woman at

the car hire.

He will later explain that a *bagnole* has a bit more character than your plain old *voiture*. A *bagnole* is a set of wheels, *une putain de bonne voiture*. "Roughly translated, a good ride."

Is it just me, is it the air around here, or is Arnaud's holiday version becoming more laddish?

The *bagnole* comes with a thick slab of documentation, and a high-vis jacket which is *obligatoire* on French roads. You see them everywhere, little yellow vests draped around the front passenger seat like a bizarre fluorescent fashion accessory.

Madame Car Hire has a long list of other compulsory items: a warning triangle in case of breakdown, spare bulbs, two breathalyser kits. Even a confirmed teetotaller motorist has to have them. Madame Car Hire has even touched upon other regulations that won't apply in our case: the spare glasses if you wear contact lenses, the snow chains if you're on snow-covered roads in the Alps.

Non, Madame, we won't be doing the Alps this summer.

We drive back to Monsieur Henri's garage, give the damage another examination, transfer our luggage to the hire car and hit the road again.

"Now what?" I ask. "Can it get any worse?"

Colley sounds anxious too. "Where are we gonna stay?"

"Of course! Yann!" Arnaud makes it sound like he has just discovered the New World. "My cousin Yann has a *peniche* around here. They won't be using it because Isabelle – his missus – is on maternity leave."

"What's a *peniche?*" Colley asks.

"A boat. A barge on the canal."

I can see it already: three men in a boat.

It was just a language thing, Áine tried to tell herself. She hadn't a word of French since her denouement in the Inter Cert (as it then was).

If the Gardai back home in Ireland had been bad enough, the French officials this afternoon were something else.

She had a French phrasebook somewhere but it was next to useless. She wouldn't want to tell the police: *This isn't the room I asked for at reception.* Or *I want to rent a deckchair.* Or *When does the parade of the bullfighters begin?*

She wanted to know the words for: *My sister is missing, you must find her.*

At least when she'd phoned the language school in the Languedoc the woman had reasonable English.

"No, of course she's one of your students," Áine told the stupid woman. "But it's not like her to disappear like that. She's always in touch twice a day, like clockwork, even when she's away. Calls, texts, emails. Something terrible must have happened, I just know it."

"But Madame, it is not unusual what your sister does, and it is not our business. Our students sometimes do not turn up for classes after a few days if they cannot … "

Cannot what? Cannot attend? Cannot hack it? Cannot escape from the white slave trade?

The woman searched for the word: " … if they cannot finish." She said Áine's sister was no model student, *and* she kept mixing up the students with the teachers.

"OK, can I have a word with the other people in her class then?"

"Non, Madame. The course is finish, they all go home."

"Then can you give us their names and addresses?"

Non, non and *non* again.

"L'informatique et libertés, the data protection, *n'est-ce pas?* Your sister was the only one from *Irlande,* the others have addresses in *Royaume-Uni."* And that's all the woman would give her.

At least the police would take her seriously, Áine thought. But the one officer at the station with any *anglais* said they didn't do missing persons.

"Your sister," he said – although she'd written it down

for him he was unable to pronounce Niamh or McElhinney – "she is, how you say, the adult? She is in no obvious danger, and we do not do missing persons any more."

"Well if you don't, who the hell does around here?"

Stupid stupid man. Didn't even get her to fill in a form with all the "Your sister's eyes and hair colour" palaver. *Niamh McElhinney. Age: 41 – Height: 5' 5"* …

And that was that. Shown the door, *bon journey, au reservoir* and you could always put her face on your Facebook page.

Which we've already done, the stupid fuckwit.

I didn't know it yet, how our paths were about to cross. All that was future knowledge. All I cared about this morning was bread. White bread and buttery substances.

This is the one thing preventing me from being fully assimilated into the post-hippy middle classes: my refusal to frown upon white bread in all its terrible glory.

Take the croissant. The Irish language has no word for croissant. And Arnaud has warned us that the French have their own problems: the traditional *petit dejeuner* is under attack from Kellogg's, and half the croissants sold in France are no longer made in a local *boulangerie*.

These are the industrial croissants: cheap, rubbery, churned out in a factory, delivered frozen, reheated on site. They are, as Monty Python might put it, an ex-croissant.

Seems the French have rules and regulations for everything from high-vis jackets in cars to how far in millimetres your postbox can jut out from the wall. There's also a rule that you can't call your shop a *boulangerie* unless you knead and ferment your own bread. But the military-industrial croissant complex has found a loophole; the rule only applies to bread and baguettes. *Viennoiseries* – croissants and pastries – can be delivered from anywhere.

Fortunately I'm in a real *boulangerie*, in *boulange* heaven this morning.

After our first night on the barge I've been sent for freshly baked baguettes and real croissants made with gallons of butter. Light, crispy, warm, fluffy, melt-in-your-mouth. And while we're at it *deux pain au chocs, s'il vous plaît.*

Pain au chocolat, a close cousin of the croissant but with chocolate in the middle. Need we say any more?

After a breakfast of strong coffee and half the *boulangerie* we unpack the rest of our gear onto the boat.

Arnaud's cousin Yann arrives again to take us through the engine's four very complex controls (Forward, Reverse, Start, Stop) in case we fancy a voyage. Then all four of us take a morning stroll along the canal.

That's the thing about these French villages. They don't bleed slowly into the countryside the way a modern Irish town or village does. They quickly dissolve into pure countryside. There's none of that sprawling inbetweenness of bungalow blitz and ribbon developments, ghost estates in the middle of nowhere.

No blots were involved in the making of this landscape, as the closing titles might say.

On either side of the waterway are regimented vines, sometimes with a red rose at the end of the row to encourage bees and pollination. Here and there is a prickly pear cactus with Mickey Mouse ears, or an occasional *mazet* – small buildings, Yann explains, for the *vignerons* to shelter and store their tools and sometimes even stay in overnight.

We ramble back to the narrow alleys and cool shadows of the village. In more open spaces the morning heat hangs thick and muggy in an invisible fog. The flies here are cheeky; they tickle and peck you on the cheek. Colley goes off in search of a suitable bar that will be showing the Tour de France.

Around the next corner is a massive old advert painted on the side of a house. It's faded, almost invisible, with faint traces of … Forvil. A sign for Forvil, a ghostly image radiating a strange aura from a bygone age.

In the main square we catch up with Colley again by

Yann's car. All four of us decide to have a game of *pétanque* on the gravel pitch.

They go mad for *pétanque* around here, Yann explains in his excellent English. Since the bowler's feet must not leave the ground it is a slow, leisurely affair. *Pétanque* is *boules* for geriatrics. Perfect for sunny climes.

Colley hasn't quite grasped all this. He thinks *pétanque* is a cousin of Irish road bowling. Road bowling is not for geriatrics. It's fast, dangerous and usually wet. A kind of *boules* for maniacs, who fly up in the air with flailing arms and whooping "*Faugh a ballach!*" – not a curse but a traditional Irish battle cry to "clear the way" – as the iron bullets shoot down the narrow country lanes of Fermanagh and West Cork.

"Keep the feet on the ground," Arnaud reminds him. "Rules is rules and never change."

"Oh but Arnaud," his cousin Yann says, "since the last time you were here they *have* changed."

I half expect him to say Colley's playing style is now permitted. Instead, Yann continues, "The alcohol is no longer on the list of banned substances. Come."

From the boot of his car he produces four glass tumblers, a bottle of Pernod and a bottle of still water.

"So you see," he continues, pouring shots of Pernod, "the players can once again enjoy their glass of *pastis*. It is sensible, *n'est-ce pas?*"

Yann passes the glasses around. He adds a glug of water to his Pernod. The liquid goes cloudy white. The rest of us add a splash of water too.

Arnaud raises his glass for a toast. "To daft rules everywhere! You can drive a car after two glasses of wine, but you can't have a *pastis* with a game of *pétanque?*"

Colley takes a tentative sip, as though expecting cough medicine. "Whoo! Nice. Imagine a game of hurling with this stuff."

Yann looks puzzled. How do you begin to explain hurling to a Frenchman? Imagine hockey played by maniacs. Or ice hockey without the ice. Sky Sports has just begun to show hurling in Britain. Bewildered viewers describe it as a cross between cricket, rugby and an egg-and-spoon race. Or a pub fight on grass with big sticks.

After a civilised half an hour our four-man *pétanque* squad is on level pegging with a team of locals. It's at this precise moment, as Arnaud's arm is poised to pitch his final ball in this major international fixture, that I get that sliding-slowly-downhill sensation again. A new case is about to walk through the door.

Well, not literally a door of course. More the pleasant shade of a village square. Our busman's holiday is about to grind to a metaphorical halt.

Ten

If this were an old B-movie she'd be a blonde bombshell in a hot number. But she isn't. Not quite. She is wearing a large straw hat and looks blonde, say late forties or early fifties and doing all the usual tricks to hide the fact. She also sounds Irish, middle aged, middle class, and prone to using CAPS LOCK when her gob opens.

"YOU-HOO! Mr Connolly? Arnaud?"

I don't mean to sound superficial or sexist or mouthist, focussing like that on big hats, big hair and big mouths. But what else is there to latch onto? The shape of her face (round)? Her height (average, say five-seven)? Nose (nosey)? Breasts (two, possibly enhanced)? Eyes (two too)?

Don't ask what colour eyes. I've problem enough with friends' and family's unless those eyes are a dazzling blue. At least I'm OK with hair. Hair, hats and mouths.

She is ash blonde. Not so much a bombshell, more a series of firecrackers going off. Quite noisy, minor damage, many casualties in *pétanque* arena.

She strides over waving her arms like a semaphore lesson. One's *pétanque* opponents are not amused.

"ARNAUD! There you are. I was looking for you EVERYwhere."

There is a touch of the Reverend Mother about her, but Arnaud still can't place her. He gives both teams a shrug and a time-out T sign.

"Sorry lads," he says. *"Désolé messieurs."*

She takes off the hat, still breathless. "I rang. Your office. Your Aisling said you were here." Dublin accent alright. "So I said … it's too good to be true but … Don't you remember? It's Áine Kettle. You did my Orla's wedding, with the croquembouche for dessert?"

A flicker of recognition. "Of course! How's she getting on?"

"She left him after six months. Kids of today, eh?"

59

Did she just say croquembouche? Arnaud's office has a couple of photos of said wedding cake: a cone-shaped tower of profiteroles stuffed with whipped cream or custard, all bound in spun sugar netting and spattered with a Jackson Pollock's worth of white and dark chocolate ganache. Any woman, any loud woman with a daft hat and Dublin 4 accent who orders such a tour de force for her daughter's wedding must be either a person of discernment or the very opposite: someone who likes to splash the cash, easily persuaded, as refined as crude oil. Someone with too many notions and no taste at all.

She shoos away a *pétanque* competitor. "Arnaud. I don't know what to do … "

No. You wouldn't use the "taste" word to describe her. "Rude" perhaps. "Pushy". "Difficult", like the cellophane wrapper on a DVD.

One of our new *pétanque* pals is trying to interrupt her in untranslatable French. Or possibly Occitan or Catalan. He gives up. Arnaud's cousin Yann does too. He gives a discreet wave as he retires to his car.

Her breath back, Áine Kettle revs up to eighty miles an hour. "My sister Niamh – you remember Niamh, Arnaud – she's gone missing and I've been here, there and everywhere and the police are absolutely useless and I can't get anyone to listen and … "

He holds up a hand. "Gone missing where, Mrs Kettle?"

"Here, Arnaud. Down the road towards Carcassonne."

Arnaud puts a hand on her shoulder. "So what can we do for you?"

Oh-oh. Arnaud always was an easy touch. Either that or he figures Mrs Kettle has further offspring requiring wedding banquets and croquembouches.

"Well, you're French, aren't you," she says.

"Half French, Mrs K."

"Exactly. I need someone who speaks the lingo. I tried to report her missing but the police here say they don't do missing persons any more. Or at least that's what I think they said. Made me look a right eejit."

Did she say missing persons? Give Arnaud a nudge.

"Oh sorry," he says. "Mrs Kettle. This is a friend of mine. Moss Reid, private detective."

"Oh!" she says. "A detective."

I'm not a detective. Maybe I would be if I were a wisecracking, chainsmoking, heavy drinking ex-cop with liver problems and six months behind in the bloody maintenance payments, while dabbling in the private sector to bump up the pension. I don't have a pension. I'm just your run-of-the-mill self-employed PI. Private *investigator*. Not detective.

"Yes Mrs Kettle, I'm a … " Fumble in pockets, must be a business card somewhere.

Wilde & Reid Investigations. What the card doesn't quite say is "One-man operation specialising in divorce, adultery, lost pets, security checks, corporate surveillance, pre-employment screening, insurance jobs where you're supposed to catch the claimant as he wheels his green bin out for collection with his 'broken arm' before going for a swim." In other words, all the usual run-of-the-mill PI stuff you can get. And missing persons of course – one of which she has.

"Oh, right," she says. "*Reid & Wilde*. Can we go somewhere quieter?"

"Absolutely," I say, already in business mode. "All four of us?"

"Why not," she says.

We trundle back to the barge – Arnaud, Mrs Kettle, Colley and yours truly. Arnaud tells her to sit down and begin at the beginning.

I wish I could read eyes properly. Sad eyes, happy eyes, angry eyes. Even bedroom eyes.

Mrs Kettle's are hard-to-place eyes, all over the shop like she's pining for something.

"Well." She fans her face with her hat. "It all started in the … I was getting my hair, nails and facial and … You wouldn't mind if I had a fag would you? I don't normally, it's just … "

"Be my guest," Arnaud says. The perfect host goes in search of an ashtray or old plate. As she lights up he opens windows along his way in case the narky smoke alarm gives out again.

"Oh and Arnaud?" she shouts after him. "You wouldn't happen to have a bottle of wine open do you?"

"Red or white?" he shouts back.

"Rosé if you have it."

"Right you are."

"And a couple of lumps of ice."

While Arnaud does his sommelier impressions I look at her long nails and think of a good opening question.

"Your sister, um … "

"Niamh."

"Yes, Niamh. Is she married?"

"Yes. *Was,* I mean. Everyone I know seems to be divorced or separated nowadays, even my own daughter. Do you have kids yourself, Mr Reid?"

I shake my head as Arnaud passes her a glass of rosé.

"Cheers," she says. "So I suppose you'd call my sister single again. She kept her married name, McElhinney. Anyway, it's all a bit complicated, because it's also about my husband. That's why I don't know where to start."

She goes on to tell the story as though she has done a dozen times. How it all seems so long ago yet was only last week.

"My sister was on a crash course in French when it happened. In a restaurant down the road from here, in a village called Mentidera. Niamh and the other students were having lunch when she sees this man across the room. Or rather, she hears him. You know when you're in a foreign country, everyone's blathering away and you hear an Irish accent at the other end of the room and it stands

62

out like a sore thumb?"

She pauses to give her fag a dramatic drag.

"Well that's exactly what happened. That's what she said on the phone. He's chatting away in English, with an Irish accent, with this pretty young thing who's maybe eighteen or nineteen – a young one anyway – and it's definitely him. That's what Niamh said."

The cigarette gets flicked out a canal-side window before she continues.

"Doesn't quite look like him – which could be down to plastic surgery – but the thing is, it sounds exactly like him. Same words, mannerisms the lot. So my sister walks up, says something along the lines of 'I couldn't help but hear you talking, where are you from yourself?' as you do. Then he explodes."

I seem to be missing something. "Why? Who was he?"

"My *husband*. That's the problem, see? He gets all hot and bothered and says something like 'Do I know you?', in French now, and pushes her away. There's a big kerfuffle but you can hear all this cos Niamh has left her phone on. So apparently he grabs this young one and they up and leave – all three of them as far as I can tell. My husband, my sister and this young flibbertigibbet."

Colley shrugs. "I still don't get."

"This is my husband we're talking about. Johnny Kettle."

All three of us look puzzled.

"Oh honestly," she says. "*The* Johnny Kettle, the banker, the one who disappeared in the plane six years ago. Look. It was in all the papers at the time."

From her large handbag come various photos, clippings, printouts of webpages. She's about to hand them to Arnaud, hesitates, gives them to me instead.

"That's her there, our Niamh." A varnished nail taps one photo. "And that," tapping another photo, this time of three men, "that's him in the middle. My husband Johnny. Piggy in the middle. She never got on with him."

None of this rings a bell yet. It's a middle-aged man with a chubby face on the deck of a boat, the kind sea anglers use. He's dressed not like a banker but in outdoor gear, a pseudo ragamuffin look that probably costs a fortune. The other two anglers are in similar gear, dark green or black oilskins.

"They were in college together," she says.

The caption says these two other faces belong to a Kevin Reilly and Terry McGann. All three grinning and holding up various marine lifeforms.

"He's not officially dead you know," she continues. "Not even 'missing presumed dead'. It's just, you'd think, after everything we've been through, well, life goes on, doesn't it? You draw a line and get on with it. Then this bloody well happens."

She waits for sympathetic nods before continuing.

"So, Arnaud. If you and your friend here could talk to the French police. That's all I'm asking. Once you explain what's going on they can get the ball rolling and find my sister. It'd be a huge favour."

The favour word should have sounded alarm bells. I should have told her something along the lines of: "Sorry, Mrs K, but either your husband's dead, missing at sea, or your sister Niamh has made an honest mistake with a doppelgänger. Or your late husband isn't so late any more, he's read all the FAQs on How-to-do-a-runner-dot-com, and he has hired a good plastic surgeon. But why, after all this time, out of the blue, is he suddenly rumbled by his own sister-in-law despite the chin and nose job? What are the odds of all that? And then for her to go missing too?"

That's what I should have told her. That I'm a PI (note: not a detective) who answers questions like "Is my hubbie sleeping around?", "Which one of my staff is the thieving scumbag?", "Who is my birth mum?" All for a modest fee, not free. And remind her that we're on holiday, and this ain't Stoneybatter any more – not my usual *terroir,* as the French say – and …

Arnaud is too quick. "You leave it to us, Mrs Kettle."

"Call me Áine."

"Of course."

"Oh. And you'll need this." From her handbag she produces a Missing Person poster. Must have cobbled it together in Word before flying out. "To put into French for us."

"OK, Mrs Kettle."

"Áine," she reminds him again.

"Look, we have a prior lunch arrangement. But as soon as we've finished, I promise Mr Reid and I will go to the police in Mentidera and sort everything out."

We walk her to her car and shake hands.

"I'll buzz you later," Arnaud says. "Does your mobile work here?"

I secretly wish it wouldn't. That her phone would be like my phone or a retired surgeon. *Unable to perform operations.*

Eleven

"What's with the 'prior lunch engagements'?"

Arnaud grins. "Ah c'mon, Moss. We all wanted to get shut of her and I'm starving."

Once Mrs Kettle is gone we take a slow gander through the cobbled alleys, passing another faded old advert on the side of a house, yet another palimpsest peeling away layers of history and commodities. Here's a Dubonnet, there's a Noilly Prat, there's a kind of chocolate drink. Faded images, faint memories.

Colley inspects the menu on the noticeboard outside the first restaurant. "Looks nice."

Arnaud frowns. "Pass." The telltale signs include the dining room with only four customers, the sad face staring out the window who's probably the owner, and the menu. It's long, too long, longer than the King James Bible. The seafood section alone lists half the species in the multitudinous seas.

By contrast, a little brasserie at the other end of the street has two plats du jour and is hopping. We grab the last of the outside tables while Arnaud goes inside to the toilets.

A young waitress with skinny tanned limbs glides up with a carafe of water and menus. Colley points to the *Plat du jour*. "Any idea what a *grenouille* is, Reidy? So. This Mrs Kettle must loaded, yeah?"

"How would I know?"

"Her hubbie." He pats the photos and clippings that she gave me. "One of the Galway Three, right?"

Where's my specs? When you reach my age you can do without sex and drugs and a large amount of rock 'n' roll, but not without your reading glasses.

LOST AT SEA

- 3 go missing in plane off Galway coast (etc etc).

"See, Reidy? So the hubbie's no longer brown bread. I

dunno if I'd bother with the plastic surgery malarkey though."

Arnaud returns from his inspection. He picks up a photo of the fat banker. "If I were him I'd have a chin job."

"How were the jacks?" I ask.

"Grand."

Arnaud treats a restaurant's loos like a canary down a mine. If they look like a CSI crime scene, imagine the sanitary nightmares in the kitchen, under the worktops, behind the fridges.

The waitress returns for our orders. Colley chances the *grenouilles* – frogs' legs with frites. She smiles and gives him a chirpy *"Bravo, Monsieur!"* as though he has just done something slightly naughty or courageous.

Everything the waitress does is a little show. More a cosy sitcom than the high drama and starched formality of an upmarket joint – those fancy places where several waiters hover or rush around you with their trays like mad robots or tightrope walkers on speed, and with their miniature brushes and pans in between courses, as if a crumb on the tablecloth might spell disaster and mess up the space-time continuum.

The waitress returns with our dishes, and a sachet of hand wipes for Colley. He looks well impressed by his dish: *"Chapeau!"* His French vocab seems to consist of stuff picked up from Sean Kelly's cycling commentaries on Eurosport.

The waitress gives him that big smile again, a smile that says: "You and me, *moi et toi?* We got a secret."

Despite their size, frogs' legs are powerful things. They can divide the universe into those who swear by them and those who can't stand the things despite never having tasted one. Judging by the nom-nom noises, guess which camp Colley is in.

"Wonder where they get them from," he says. "A frog farm?"

We both turn to our culinary expert. Arnaud scratches his black-and-white three-day stubble.

"It's a dilemma, farm versus wild I mean. Farms pollute so much that the meat ends up loaded with junk. But you can't hunt the wild ones to extinction either. Us humans aren't great at finding a balance."

The garlicky smells are killing me. "Mind if I … ?"

Colley indicates a be-my-guest. I try one. Not unlike chicken but the dominant taste is of parsley and garlic butter.

"Can I?" Arnaud asks too.

"Go ahead," Colley says.

"Um! Not exactly Escoffier but bloody good."

I look up to see the waitress giving somebody else the same special smile she gave Colley five minutes ago.

"What's an Escoffier?" Colley asks.

Arnaud sighs. "Auguste Escoffier, the first celebrity chef. Caused a sensation at the Savoy after rustling 'em up for the Prince of Wales."

"Charles and Di? Or the one who looks like a … "

"No, Colley. This would have been a century ago."

Arnaud explains in detail. Escoffier, being Escoffier, first poaches his frogs' legs in a *court-bouillon* with white wine and aromatic herbs, cools and covers them in a *sauce chaud-froid* with aspic, chicken jelly and tarragon, all coloured a golden paprika pink.

"But at the end of the day it's still frogs' legs," he says. "So to avoid upsetting his guests he called them *Cuisses de nymphes à l'Aurore*. Thighs of the nymphs of Dawn to you and me. Sometimes punters will eat anything if you get the name right."

For dessert Colley has the *île flottante* or *œufs à la neige*, snowy islands of poached meringue floating in a *crème anglaise*. I go for the *crème catalan*. Arnaud dives into a cherry soup. It's dark, chilled, and so good that he cajoles the waitress for the recipe. She brings him to the kitchen. They return eight or nine minutes later, both with a smile that seems to say "You and me, *moi et toi?* We got a secret."

The secret is as follows.

Take a pan, never aluminium. Simmer a kilo of pitted cherries for twenty minutes with a fruity bottle of the local vin rouge, a cinnamon stick, four cloves, two cardamom pods and half a lemon – sliced, with peel still on. Sweeten with sugar to taste. Get rid of the spices and lemon, liquidise most of the cherries. Chill for two hours, serve with a splash of cherry liqueur and a dollop of vanilla ice cream.

Our bill for three (including wine, tip, free tour of the kitchen and secret recipe) comes to fifty euro.

Next stop the cop shop.

She dined alone in a dowdy pizzeria four doors down from her hotel.

Áine Kettle thought about texting Simon to make sure the prodigal was still alive, still enjoying the last of his gap year of mindless fun in Magaluf or Kabul or whatever the international hotspot was this week.

She thought about facebooking Orla on the hotel's free wifi, or skypeing her if they were talking again. To tell her she was exhausted, the French police were useless, and how she'd linked up with Arnaud Connolly and his friend Mr Reid, who happened to be a detective on holiday here.

She decided instead to have a quick siesta in her room. Far too hot to be mucking about on phones and laptops and wondering how to change your FB status to single like Orla had last month.

She lay down on the duvet. Before dozing off she re-ran the scene in her head. The flashbulb memory on an endless loop.

In the hairdressers, taking the call, the face mask gunk still on her fingers; Niamh's half-whispers; the clattering plates and police sirens; her sister's final words. Ciao.

Running it over and over again. For some reason the film was black-and-white. She could swear it used to be in colour.

Maybe write everything down before she forgot anything. Every detail. If the police didn't do anything she'd write to the papers, to her local TD, to Joe Duffy, cause a right stink.

When she awoke it was still light, still mid-afternoon, still far too hot. With these kinds of temperatures, how did anybody get anything done?

In the middle of the bed she stretched out for her phone, half expecting her hand to brush across Johnny's face. Something felt odd until she remembered: at home she always slept on the right. Him on the left, her on the right.

Even after Johnny had gone. Never the left, always the right. And here she was, bang in the middle.

Twelve

I don't like guns. I had enough of them five years ago, during the big snow.

It was after a few pints in town with the lads, not that late but Dublin's public transport system is allergic to snowflakes. The buses stopped at four that afternoon, the Luas not much later, and not a taxi to be found. So I had to trek home to Stoneybatter through the slush and snow, walking slowly and cautiously.

I was about to reach St Paul's on the quays when a black car pulled in beside a white car. Normally I'm no great shakes about the makes of cars but I can remember these two: a black Nissan Qashqai and a white Opel. They were maybe less than twenty yards from me. A guy jumped out of the Nissan. Well, hardly a guy really, more a kid. He pumped bullet after bullet into the white Opel. Nobody would survive that.

When witnesses encounter a man with a weapon they tend to remember the weapon not the face, the actions not the details. Yet I can still remember the kid's face. He was gleeful. No other word for it. Like he'd just reached a bonus level in a shoot-'em-up game from the comfort of his living-room couch.

As for the weapon, all I can say is that it was a handgun. The "weapon of choice" in town these days, as they say. A high-velocity handgun rather than a low-velocity shotgun. There are hundreds of thousands of licensed firearms in circulation in the State, though I guess this wasn't one of them.

At least I didn't let the drink talk, and jump out to act the hero bollix. The drink whispered quietly; the drink said my best bet was to shrink into the shadows. Which I did. I can't remember how long all this lasted from start to finish. Two minutes? Ten?

When the kid in the black Nissan was long gone I

scarpered home and told no one. What would they call that? Leaving the scene of a crime? Obstructing official inquiries? Withholding vital information? I don't know, don't care. So I'm a guilty bystander? It wasn't my affair. Not this time.

Another thing: I can't remember if I heard really him pumping dozens of bullets into the Merc, or whether it was just two or three. Maybe my memory blanked that bit afterwards, and I simply imagined the kind of hail of bullets we've grown used to in the movies.

On the radio the next day, two words justified my decision to say nothing: "Gino" and "Beattie".

I'd just seen the latest round in the gangland wars, maybe newcomers trying to muscle in on Gino Beattie's old turf. Gino Beattie used to have the biggest and best turf in town. But Gino Beattie was locked away now.

So I don't like guns. Strictly speaking, though, if guns kill people then I guess pencils misspell words and spoons make people fat. No, it's not guns per se I don't like. It's the big men behind them. And the gleeful kids.

At least there are no sign of guns in this room this afternoon. Not yet anyway. About the only sign of life is the groan of the air conditioning.

"C'mon Moss," Arnaud says in a low voice. "You're the private detective man, it'll be a doddle."

The reception desk is unattended.

"Hold on," I mutter.

It's not exactly my *terroir* around here, is it? I don't even know their regulations for private investigators. And I don't like all those guns.

No, a French copshop isn't exactly my *tasse de thé*. On top of the language, I don't understand their postal codes, their telephone area codes, how to decipher a French licence plate, how to tell if a Frenchman is lying through his *dents,* and whether PIs need a licence.

We've been in France less than a week and I've seen

more guns on cops' waists than all the weapons I've ever come across in Ireland in my entire life, even counting drive-by shootings in the snow.

The French State is highly policed, highly armed, and *les flics* are organised into a bewildering array of forces. I guess Arnaud would prefer to start with the *Police Nationale* and the heavy gang, their belts bulging with pistols and tasers. Or the CRS, the riot squad, with an armed Inspector Maigret type hovering over everything.

Instead, in Mentidera we've started with the local *Police Municipale* – the lowest of the low apparently, one step up from car clampers and traffic wardens. They redirected us to the *gendarmerie*, which seems empty.

Eventually a short-sleeved shirt emerges from a basement area. He has a gun in his holster and a pile of important papers, including *L'Équipe*.

After two minutes of his paper shuffling, Arnaud interrupts him with an *"Excusez-moi? Bonjour monsieur l'agent."*

The cop looks up. He beckons us forward. There's a passing resemblance to a dalek, if daleks had Alain Delon's floppy dark hair.

The subsequent high-speed interchange is about – Arnaud explains afterwards – *porter disparu* (we'd like to report a missing person), *une enquête* (investigation), *un enlèvement* (possible kidnapping), and *les témoins* (any witnesses). Oh, and *pas de pièces à conviction* (feck all evidence of any of that).

I've OK restaurant French. I can ask for *l'addition* at the end of the meal or say *bon continuation* and where are the toilets. But I don't do French bureaucrat copshop French.

Seems Arnaud isn't faring much better.

"It's like talking to a flamin' dalek," he mutters.

"I know."

He addresses the cop again: *"Excusez moi, vous parlez trop vite pour moi."*

"Mais une Rif, Monsieur?" the cop slows down. *"C'est pas*

possible." EX-TER-MINATE! EX-TER-MINATE!

I tap Arnaud. "What's a *Rif?*"

"Recherche dans l'intérêt des familles. A search in the family's interest. French for a missing persons case."

"C'est compliqué," the dalek continues. *"Il n'est plus possible de déposer une demande de recherche dans l'intérêt des familles. Cette procédure a été supprimée."*

"What's he say?"

"Pas possible. It's like they told Mrs Kettle. They don't do missing persons any more."

"Flamin' Nora."

While the dalek takes an urgent phone call – probably Mrs Dalek wanting to know what time he'll be home for tea – Arnaud explains how the *Rif* dates back to the first World War, to help families find missing relatives. Last year the authorities decided that *Rifs* were old hat in the social media age.

"So much for a doddle," I tell Arnaud. "Now what?"

The dalek has finished his call. *"Messieurs.* As I have said." So it *does* do English. "The Ministry of the Interior advises us to direct the public towards the social network of the Internet."

Arnaud also switches to English. "Can't you make an exception? I mean this woman isn't just missing. She disappeared with a man who is supposed to be dead, if you know what I mean."

"Messieurs, that is the rule. The only exception is the minors, or the individual who expresses the desire to commit suicide. Has this woman expressed the desire … "

"But I thought you said … " Arnaud turns to me. "He said they can investigate if there are signs of foul play."

"Exactement, Messieurs." He consults a ledger. "I can say with all certainty, there is no foul play." Which he elaborates at great length in more high-speed dalek French. Arnaud translates again …

On being contacted by Mrs Kettle, they did indeed investigate a minor altercation at a local restaurant, Le

Moulin de Mentidera. It involved two English people. Or, to be more specific, let's guess that means two English-speakers. None of the staff could identify Niamh from the photo Mrs Kettle has provided the police. Nobody could recall anyone answering the description of Mrs Kettle's dead husband either, or recognise his photo. Some said the row was over in seconds, others that it lasted minutes. Which could mean anything of course. Witnesses often overestimate events of short duration.

But Monsieur Le Dalek has one final twist.

That same morning there was a bank robbery at the local branch of Crédit Agricole. Roadblocks on every route out of town for forty-eight hours. All very thorough. Even buses were searched.

So that would account for all the sirens Mrs Kettle heard over the phone.

The gang holed up in a backstreet garage. They were eventually nabbed, though not before a large database of vehicle registration numbers and motorists' and passengers' names had been amassed (both male and female names, because these days armed robbers are equal opportunity employers). There was no one remotely like Niamh McElhinney among the notes and names.

So that's that, the dalek says. Madame Kettle's sister may be missing but there is nothing more they can do unless we can produce concrete evidence that Niamh McElhinney is suicidal, has been kidnapped or owns a magic invisible flying machine that can skip over roadblocks.

"Feck it, Arnaud. Let's go, before I start shouting a load of French four-letter words."

"Yeah. Like *merde.*"

"That's five letters."

"See? I told you they're treating us like bloody eejits."

Áine Kettle sounds like she could kill someone. In the still night air every other barge on the canal can probably hear her.

I feel we've done our bit. Wasted half the afternoon with a pigheaded dalek, honour has been served, we *are* on our holidays, and it's not as if we're being paid for all this.

"You might be better off hiring someone local," I suggest. "You know, like … like a French detective. Someone who knows the lie of the land, the ins and outs of their system."

Arnaud pours her another glass of red. "Like Maurice says. Best leave it to the authorities."

"For what? They've done feck all so far," she says.

"OK," Arnaud says. "What about the Irish embassy, our Department of Foreign Affairs people?"

"You can't be serious. They said they *may* be able to provide consular assistance. From their office in Cannes. That's about as far away as bloody Belfast."

All our faces show concern, mainly because Mrs K has made serious inroads into the EU's wine lake. She still needs to drive twenty miles back to her hotel.

"Mr Reid, you're the detective. Can't you find out?"

"Give it time," I tell her, "she's bound to turn up."

"How can you be sure?"

She's like a stray dog or cheap perfume that won't go away. So I do the two things you should never do: pat the dog, smell the perfume.

"OK, Mrs Kettle, how about this. I won't tell you to stop panicking or give you empty promises. Maybe it's nothing serious, but you can't sit here doing nothing, I can understand that. Why not give us a couple of days to see what we can dig up? We can try that restaurant and where she stayed, and possibly clear up this mystery about your dead husband while we're at it. So you go back to your hotel and …"

Arnaud jumps in: "You sure you're OK to drive, Mrs K?"

Thirteen

Last seen. That's what they say: this is where Niamh McElhinney was last seen.

The restaurant is easy to find. Le Moulin is a pretty spot on the canal near the centre of the little village of Mentidera, in the Aude department of Languedoc-Roussillon. The canal boats putter by yards away from the outside terrace, soft gypsy music wafts out from the dining room.

Simple decor, scenic outdoor seating, flamenco guitars, top-notch grub. What more do you want? So before making inquiries we need to interrogate a lunch menu. The midday sun is a killer; instead of the terrace we opt for the cool dining room indoors. I order the caramelised lamb shank, Colley the gigantic prawn *gambas,* Arnaud the golden *paella de maison.* All washed down with *un demi de rouge* – half a litre of the house red – and a couple of glasses of white. Once dessert is out of the way we can quiz the staff.

Onlookers often avoid becoming involved in a crime or a big row. Psychologists call it bystander apathy. I call it looking after number one. Maybe that's what I came down with, that night with the gleeful gunman in the snow: bystander apathy.

All the restaurant staff we talk to seem to have succumbed to it too. All, it seems, until we try a young waitress called Gabrielle Laforet.

"So where did it happen?" I gesture around the room. "Can you show me which table?"

"Not *ici.*" Gabrielle speaks a sort of blend of Frenglish. *"À l'extérieur,* on the *terrasse."*

"OK." I wave towards the terrace. Arnaud and Colley get up to follow but I give Colley a little shake of the head – four's a crowd. He's not needed.

Sometimes you take a witness back to where it all

happened. To let the surroundings speak to them and trigger a memory. Or at least you get them to think back to the place and what it was like. The fancy term for this is Context Reinstatement. I call it *A Bit Like Retracing Your Steps When You've Lost Your Car Keys.*

The terrace, fierce busy on our arrival almost two hours ago, has been whittled down to a few stragglers here and there.

"Where were they sitting?" I ask.

Gabrielle walks over to an empty table for two.

"Ici."

"Good. Now, in your own time and own words tell me what happened. *Parlez français* if it's easier, and Arnaud here will translate. OK?"

She nods.

"Describe what happened that lunchtime," I continue, "everything you can remember, even if you think it's trivial or irrelevant. *D'accord?*"

Another nod.

"Begin as soon as you're ready."

PIs and shrinks have much in common: listening to people's memories and secrets, letting them talk, nodding a lot while taking notes and keeping an eye on the meter. Normally I charge fifty an hour.

Or it's like a GP trying to sieve out a patient's real symptoms from their everyday aches and pains and anxieties. Listen patiently, say nothing, don't interrupt the flow with too many questions. And try to catch any unusual words that Arnaud mumbles when he thinks my French isn't up to it.

Gabrielle remembers the row at the table. It was quite loud. She has already brought their main course. The young woman and old man have also ordered a bottle of wine.

She stops. Sometimes the pauses in the story are half the story. Time for a gentle prompt: "An old man. How old is old?"

"Old."

"Would he be fifty? Sixty?"

Sometimes we don't have enough words to describe someone's age or face. Or we lack common definitions. A twentysomething waitress and someone my age will apply different parameters when describing someone as "young" or "old". Same words, different definitions.

"Maybe forty-five," she continues, "fifty-five? The girl, she is very young. For a time I think she is his daughter."

"Describe her."

"Jeune et jolie. Maybe eighteen?"

"So you see or hear a disturbance. Where are you at that moment?"

"At the bar." She gestures towards the opposite end of the terrace. *"Oui.* I am waiting for a drinks order."

Gabrielle had gone from the bar towards the table to see what the row was about. Another customer, a woman, is standing at the couple's table. This woman and the man are talking loudly. Shouting really, *en anglais.*

L'argument dure une minute. All over in a minute. Gabrielle wants to ask them what the problem is, but the old man and young girl are already getting up to leave, even though they've hardly begun their main course.

"The angry woman, what does she do?"

"She returns to her table. No. She departs with them too, I think. The three of them go inside, to the dining room. Then they all leave."

"How do you know they all leave?"

"Because I do not see them again. Oh, and the man leaves the *monnaie* on the table."

"This older woman. What does she look like?"

"Her hair is in the … "

She has problems so Arnaud translates: "Long curly red hair, maybe thirty-five to forty-five. Niamh is forty-one isn't she?

"Shh!" I turn back to the young waitress: "What is the older woman wearing?"

A shrug of her shoulders. Gabrielle can't remember.

"What about her face?"

She's not sure.

You can't blame her. Some people are lumbered with an unphotographic memory, or their creative side takes over and fills in the details. Or you tell yourself something along the lines of *Glasses, clean-shaven, short brown hair, green T-shirt*. Afterwards what you remember isn't the picture of a face any more. It's that list of words you've just told yourself. Which you then use to recreate the image in your mind. It can be messy alright.

"Can I show you this photograph?" It's of Niamh McElhinney. "Is this the woman?"

"Perhaps."

"How tall is she?"

"My height maybe? I can't remember."

"And the man. How tall is he?"

"I do not know. It is – how you say? – *très occupé* that day. Busy. And most of the time he is sitting."

"Did he look like this?" Show her a photo of Johnny Kettle this time.

"No. I don't think so. The man is older, more … "

She switches to French, Arnaud translates: "No joy, it's nowt like him. Though she may have seen the young girl before."

"Gabrielle, you said the girl was young and pretty. What do you mean by that? What did she look like? If you don't have the English words just say it in French."

More French, more translations by Arnaud: "White blouse or shirt, white jeans, a dark blue jacket that she wasn't wearing. Can't remember what her shoes were like."

Funny how female eyewitnesses are so much better than male ones at describing clothes and colours, and knowing the brand names and fashion words. And young people are far better at recalling details if the person is around their own age.

"And the hair is quite short," Gabrielle continues.

"And dark." She mimes its shape – a short bob.

"That's very good. Can we go back to the argument? They're talking loudly. What else are they doing? Could you show me?"

Gabrielle gives another little mime. The older woman, the one with the red hair, is standing across from the man. He stands up, waggles his finger, tries to shoo her away.

"What's the young girl doing in all this?"

"She stays sitting, like this." Gabrielle gives a good impression of a petulant girl shrugging her shoulders.

"OK. Now slow down, close your eyes if you like, picture the scene. Is there anything else you can remember? The food, the customers, the colours, sounds, smells even. Get a clear image in your mind, then in your own time and own words tell me everything you remember."

Gabrielle remembers them ordering a *formule* – a main course and dessert. Yes, definitely a *formule*. Lunchtimes are always busy and although it was well over a week ago she is certain. Because she was surprised at the time: they didn't stay for their dessert. She also remembers the smell of saffron. So the *plat du jour* would have been *paella de maison*. Which would make it Wednesday. Oh, and many police cars were going by.

"That's excellent, Gabrielle." The same day as the bank robbery and the roadblocks. "So you've gone over to their table. What are the other diners and staff doing?"

"I cannot remember."

"There is a row. What do you think the guy is thinking?"

"The man from Dublin?" she asks.

"We never said he was from Dublin."

"Maybe he tells her he's Irish," Arnaud says.

"Shh," I tell him in a low voice, *"let Gabrielle do the talking."* Back to the questions: "Why do you say he was from Dublin? And the woman with red hair, where do you think she was from?"

More high-speed French.

Arnaud shrugs his shoulders: "He had a foreign accent. *Rosbif,* English. They often have English diners. Tourists, boat people. But I doubt she can tell the difference between an English and Irish accent. She thinks you're a Yank, Moss."

The language school often block-books tables, its students are supposed to speak French during lunch. She says the *rosbifs* are always breaking into English when teacher isn't looking. But she can't remember anyone else with a *rosbif* accent that day. Just the old man and the woman with the red hair.

"Fine. But Gabrielle, you said he was from Dublin. Why Dublin?"

She gives another Gallic shrug – the full works this time: raised shoulders, hands held up with palms out, lower lip stuck out, raised eyebrows. As if to say *Bof!* – the French equivalent of "whatever".

"Maybe another girl tells me," she says eventually. *"Oui, Monsieur,* that must be it. Angélique!" She calls a slightly older waitress over from the bar, a petite woman dressed in black from head to toe.

Angélique has no English. She gabbers away with Gabrielle and Arnaud. More photo inspections, more shaking of heads and *peut-êtres.*

Arnaud says, "Angélique doesn't remember Mrs Kettle's sister either. Or the man in the photo."

"She's sure it's not him?"

"Fairly. But she says the guy from Dublin was a regular customer."

There's that *from Dublin* again. "How regular?"

He translates back and forth. "Say once a month?"

Time for a hunch. "So he's probably not from the village. If I were local, Arnaud, I'd be dining here twice a week, right? Not once a month. Ask her how tall he was. Not feet and inches, get her to show me."

Besides, she probably thinks in metric, and in my day

we were taught and thought in feet and inches. I still have to turn metres into yards for it to mean anything.

Arnaud translates once more. Angélique raises her hand a foot and a bit above her head. Like I said, she's petite.

"I'd make that around six foot, Moss."

"Yeah, give or take. Take her over to the door to show me how tall he was when he came in. Use the door like a measuring stick."

Again she demonstrates. He's about six foot alright.

"Ask her why she thinks he's from Dublin. *Pourquoi Dublin?*"

She explains. Arnaud translates. "Because that's what the police told her."

"*Les gendarmes?*" I ask.

She nods. I'm about to go ballistic when another woman scurries over.

"*Messieurs,* there is something wrong?"

She introduces herself: Madame Agnès, the proprietor. I outline our missing person case and ask her about the incident.

No, she says, she was off that day. Doesn't recognise the Johnny Kettle photo either.

As Madame Agnès and Arnaud chat away I go inside to the dining room for a sneaky peek at the reservations book. From his table Colley gives a cheeky little thumbs up as I run a finger down the bookings. No obvious Irish or English surnames that day. The language school booked three tables. Plenty of *rosbif* then. But no individual names, just an elegant scribble: *L'école de français, 3 tables x 6.* Take a discreet photo on the iPhone.

That gives me another idea. I sidle back to Arnaud and Madame Agnès.

"Madame, do you have CCTV?"

"Sorry? *Je comprends pas.*"

"Arnaud, what's the French for CCTV?"

"Er, *la télévision en circuit fermé, la vidéosurveillance, caméra de surveillance …* "

"I don't need the whole flamin' dictionary."

"The camera?" she says. "*Bien sûr!*" She bundles us outside. "*Et voilà.*" A camera above the entrance. Back inside she shows us a screen by the till.

"Can we see the footage from that lunchtime?"

She goes into a long spiel in French, no doubt about data protection, customers' privacy blah blah blah.

"What's she sayin'?"

"The police took it."

"*What?*" I lower my voice to Arnaud. "The same cops who said they couldn't open a missing person file on her?" I turn back to Madame Agnès: "Did you or your staff ask the police to come, or did they come unannounced?"

"They just arrive. We never demand them to come."

"And did they say why they were here?"

"No. We thought it was about the bonk."

Bonk? Oh, of course, the *banc* heist.

"When was all this?"

"The day after the *banc* robbery."

And several days before Mrs Kettle turns up in France to make a nuisance of herself.

"When they questioned your staff, were you there?"

"*Oui.*"

"Did they interview you one by one, or all together?"

"*Ensemble.* Together."

"Can you remember the questions they asked? One second." I hand Arnaud my pen and notebook. "Write down everything she says. The exact words."

She explains, he scribbles away, I get the gist.

"Arnaud, this stinks. It makes no sense."

"I know. C'mon. Let's look at where she was staying."

"Thank you *Madame, Mam'selles,*" I tell her. "*Merci beaucoup.*"

We thank all three women for a delightful meal, and I leave a business card and my mobile number in case anything else jogs their memories.

Fourteen

We grab Colley to hit the road to the next village. But guess who forgot to park the car in the shade?

Open all the windows, give everything five minutes to cool down. Everything including me.

Now I wouldn't be the greatest fan of the State and its enforcers. Of its frontline cops and backroom bureaucrats, its pen pushers and parish priests, its prison goons and politicians, its taxmen, judges, robbing bankers, censors, the spin doctors and the hacks they feed and the counsel for the prosecution. Have I left anyone out?

I operate in the private sector, but the State is never that far away. Sometimes Wilde & Reid Investigations has to earn a crust from one or other branch of this very same State. Needs must. And from these dealings I've learned to my cost how incredibly easy it is to alter and shape a person's memory. That might sound like science fiction but it's far from it.

As we drive to the *gîte* where Niamh McElhinney stayed I give the lads a lecture – angry diatribe more like – on the standard procedures for taking witness evidence. You have to know these best practices, this way of doing things. Often it's the only way to do things.

Suppose a lawyer asks you to get a witness statement. You're collecting evidence. It might end up in court. So everything must be played strictly by the book. Any one of your questions might contaminate the witness's memory. It's a bit like how the behaviour and emotions of, say, a football fan can be fundamentally altered simply by pointing a camera and a big screen at him.

Ask a witness a leading question, and the other side's barrister will pick holes in it in no time. Big holes in what you've done and how you did it. *A suggestive question, your honour.* A begging question, a loaded question, a rhetorical question, a statement superficially phrased as a question but not a true question at all. So many holes that it's a colander. *Have you stopped beating your wife?* And me not even married.

No, you don't want to be near a loaded question when it goes off in court like a loaded gun. That's like grabbing scraps of DNA and other evidence with your sticky fingers – no gloves and evidence bags of course – and popping everything in your jeans back pocket to ferment away for a week or two.

So you try to follow the procedures that the cops use: interview witnesses separately; avoid leading or suggestive questions; aim to maximise their recall while minimising any damage you might do to their memories. All this you learn the hard way.

And French cops should do it in much the same way.

Which gets me angry and suspicious. When the cops round up witnesses, interview them *ensemble,* and Inspector Maigret's opening question is *"Parlez-moi de l'homme de Dublin ce jour-là",* their memories are already contaminated, their evidence next to useless.

"For feck sake, can't you see where I'm coming from?" The lads can tell I'm angry. Arnaud has made me swap seats so he can drive.

"The police arrive at the restaurant," I continue. "Why were they there in the first place? Nobody asked them to come. And I know Hercule Poirot sometimes likes to assemble all of Lord Babbington's staff in the library to ask them in one big group whether they saw a six-foot Dublin man in the east wing on Tuesday last having a loud argie-bargie with a forty-year-old Irish woman with red hair, before revealing that it was in fact Mephisto the Great Illusionist who done it. But for feck sake. It's like having a police line-up and telling the witness that another witness has already told you the suspect is five foot two with Arab features, *and can you pick him out from this lot, the wee Arab lad third from the left in the loud shirt?* Their interviewing techniques broke every bloody rule in the book."

La Vigne Bleue isn't a little *gîte* or cottage. It's a tall townhouse a stone's throw from the canal. From the outside it seems abandoned, locked up, its old stone weatherbeaten, its faded blue shutters blistered by the sun. The only signs of life are a lattice of white roses around the front door, red geraniums spilling out of a pot on a ground-floor windowsill, a lean tabby cat ambling by in search of shade.

The shutters are deceptive. Most of the houses around here have them, not just for security or privacy but to keep the heat out and coolness in. It's an eco-friendly form of air-conditioning, for insulation in the winter and outsulation (word just invented) in high summer, on hot days like today.

Arnaud rings the buzzer. A dark-haired woman opens the door. At the same time an upstairs shutter creaks open, though there's no sign of anyone behind it.

Madame Véronique Le Guen has no English. Arnaud translates as she ushers us into a cool open-plan room with high ceilings, thick wooden beams and not a radiator in sight. An ultra modern wood-burning stove has pride of place. She brushes her hair back behind her ears, opens a bureau, takes out a large diary and flicks through its pages. *Et voilà.* Yes, the guest from Ireland was called – Madame Véronique struggles with the name – Mam'selle McElhinney.

The Irish Mademoiselle wasn't much of a talker. Paid in advance, left without saying goodbye. Left quite suddenly in fact, days before she was due to, and lost part of her deposit because she forgot to leave her keys back.

Madame Véronique does the French equivalent of tut-tutting. She couldn't tell the police much either, when they asked about the Irish Mademoiselle.

So the police were here too?

Yes, she says, the day after the bank robbery.

"You'd almost think the cops thought Mrs Kettle's sister had something to do with the heist," Arnaud says.

Now that would be plain daft.

Perhaps, Madame continues, her daughter might know more about the Irish woman?

She calls upstairs. "Marie?"

She says Marie is in *le grenier* – the attic. This ground floor used to be a *cave,* an old winery. La Vigne Bleue is their family home, with two *chambres d'hôtes* or guest suites in the attic and in *l'ancien pigeonnier.*

"What used to be a dovecote," Arnaud translates. He needn't have bothered.

A tall teenager with long fair hair bounces down the stairs.

"Ma fille Marie," Madame says. *"Elle parle anglais."*

Marie smiles. *"Un peu."*

Arnaud does his *Enchanté, Mam'selle* routine, gives Marie a quick recap and she shows us up to the guest suites.

The girl has been cleaning windows. While most Irish windows open outwards, these ones open into the room, so the outsides can be cleaned without having to get up on a ladder. It kind of sums up life in the Midi, a world of shutters and the outside windowsill for the geraniums, the glass of wine and the neighbours' cat.

"This was her *chambre,* Monsieur," Marie continues. "It is empty now."

"Mind if I … ?" I point into the room. She nods.

Spotless.

Drawers, wastebasket, wardrobes all empty apart from fresh linen. No luggage or handbags, no stray clothes, not one sign that Áine Kettle's sister has ever been here.

"Did you see her much?"

"No. She had her own keys to come and go."

"Which she forgot to leave back. Did anybody see her leaving on her last day?"

"No. Nobody. It was … *une surprise.* She must have departed at lunchtime, when we were all out."

"Did she leave anything behind?"

"Par example? Has the lady lost a bag?"

Stick my head in the en-suite bathroom. Nothing to see there either. "No, nothing like that. We're just looking for any traces she left behind. What about her cleaning clobber? I mean makeup, moisturisers, that kind of thing."

While the average male has five items in his bathroom – razor, soap, towel, toothbrush, toothpaste – a typical female has four hundred items, of which a typical Irish male wouldn't be able to identify more than eight.

"Yes," she says. "Many things. *Très cher* I think."

"She left them behind? In the *salle de bain?*"

"Yes, but we throw them away."

"Why not keep them, if they're *très cher?*"

"C'est compliqué, parce que … "

I can't follow her explanation. Arnaud translates: "She didn't understand the labels and she doesn't need red hair dye."

"Right," I say. "Did you tell the police any of this?"

"They did not ask," she replies. "They talk to Maman, not to me."

"So you binned the lot?" Marie doesn't understand me. "Arnaud, what's the French for bin again?"

"Poubelle."

"Ah! Bien sûr, Messieurs!" she says.

The narrow back yard has a line-up of *poubelles* in all shapes and sizes: a grey wheelie bin for general rubbish; three plastic trays for recyclables; a compost bin for the garden.

Young Marie purses her lips – hard to tell if it's in distaste or disapproval – as she picks out bottles and jars, many still with the bulk of their contents. L'Oréal this, Boots that, cosmetics, sun creams, hair dye. The labels and instructions are mainly in English.

"You're sure these were all hers?"

She nods.

"Can we take them?"

"Yes, of course."

She goes indoors, returning with a large plastic Lidl

bag. I don't know what taking all this makeup stuff back to the barge will tell us, but you never can tell. These jars and bottles are my first truly tangible evidence of Niamh McElhinney's presence here.

"One last thing. Can you remember what she was wearing the morning she left?"

Long silence. I'm about to give up. Or maybe she is struggling with her English.

Then out comes a long list of clothing: white short-sleeved blouse, faded jeans, the exact colour of her shoes. It's not quite down to her underwear, but most of what Niamh was wearing when they last saw her leaving for breakfast in the little café around the corner.

We thank Marie and her mother and retrieve Colley.

"What's with the make-up, Reidy?" he says as he looks in my shopping bag.

"I don't know. What kind of woman would do that – leave all her clobber behind?"

As we stroll back to the police station, Arnaud advances his theory. *Les hommes viennent de Mars, les femmes de Vénus.* Boys grow up in a world of drill-bits and the offside rule, and Action Men not Barbie dolls (we're generalising here). Boys absorb a vocabulary culled from boys' games and dads' DIY manuals, and wouldn't have a clue what taffeta is, or découpage or wisteria.

Girls grow up in a word-soup of petticoats and gardening gloves. It's like (more generalising) a different planet, based on a Victorian salon that has earnest discussions during the needlework about Mrs Beeton's cookbooks and whether future husbands will take notice of one's domestic goddess skills.

Maybe men our age will never understand how there can be at least fifty-seven different varieties of moisturiser.

Colley's theory is simpler: Áine Kettle's sister must have left in a fierce hurry.

Fifteen

He's called Giradot. Fabrice Giradot, an older, fatter dalek lodged behind the counter in the copshop this afternoon.

Giradot begins with the same line about how they don't do missing persons any more. He sounds as sincere and genuine as a radio ad by my caring sharing bank.

"They're fobbing us off again," I mumble to Arnaud. "Ask him what they did with the CCTV footage from the restaurant. Why take it away if there's nothing suspicious? Tell him we have to see it."

Arnaud explains in French.

Giradot puts hands on hips, like he's already tired of us.

"Our country is exactly like yours, Messieurs. We too have regulations about data protections. Maybe you should talk to the Irish authorities. I believe the video has been passed on to them."

"What do you mean? Can you give us the email address where they were sent?"

"Mais non. You do not understand. They were collected in person."

"By courier?"

"Non." He opens a large ledger, consults a page and says something quickly like he is reading the price of hoggets on *Mart & Market.*

"Run that by me again," I say.

"It was collected by the Detective Superintendent Coleman from Dublin," he replies.

"Can we get this straight? You keep saying it's nothing, not even a missing person case and – as you all keep reminding us – you don't do missing persons any more. Yet you quiz all the staff in the restaurant, you interview Madame Véronique at her *chambre d'hôte,* you call the Irish police to collect evidence or liaise with you, and you …"

"And it is not for you to question our *logique.* Besides, your missing lady may have returned to Ireland."

"What makes you think that?" I say.

"No more questions, Monsieur. My officers have made inquiries at the place where she stays. All her belongings are no longer there. Her *passeport* is gone. So. *C'est logique.* She must have left. The investigation it is finish, *terminé."*

"We're getting the runaround," I mutter to Arnaud.

"I know," he mumbles back. "We won't get any more out of Fat Boy Slim here."

At normal volume again Arnaud thanks *Monsieur l'Agent* and gives him a *bonne journée.*

Back at the car we fill in Colley.

"Maybe it's like your man says, and she's left town," he says.

"So how did she slip through the roadblocks? Even the bank robbers couldn't do that."

Arnaud gets into the passenger seat to let me drive again. "The cops are talking bollocks, Colley, and everybody knows it." He thinks for a moment before putting his seatbelt on. Obviously a grand plan is being hatched. "Feckit lads, let's go shopping."

The kind of French spoken around here – in the bars, shops and cafes – isn't the French you learned at school. Even a fluent speaker like Arnaud can take days to tune in to the strong southern accent.

Take bread and wine: *le pain, le vin,* the stuff of life. In the Midi they don't drink *vin* – they prefer something that sounds more like *veng.* And *peng* instead of *pain.* Or sometimes there's a hint of an extra vowel at the end, such as *una* (rather than *une) baguette.*

We leave the plastic bag of cosmetics back at the barge and drive to Narbonne. At its large covered market we stock up on *veng* and *peng* and *pintade* (guinea fowl) and veg and a large bush of parsley and a string of sweet pink garlic and a bunch of tomatoes.

Tomatoes. These ones come in all shapes and sizes and wrinkliosities. You can forget what real tomatoes smell and taste like, thanks to that devious Hispanic plot to export scarce water from the Costa del Package Hols to northern Europe in identical thick-skinned spheres that have been force-grown in polythene prisons.

Arnaud inspects a serious display of *coquillages* – local shellfish – and at the next stall goes all philosophical about its colourful display of spices.

"Look at these. Spices are the food of the soul, the punctuation marks in a dish. They give it rhythm and reveal its hidden side. *Une poignée s'il vous plaît, Madame."*

The spice girl scoops out *une poignée* – a fistful – of red powder. It could be cayenne pepper, paprika, chili or rouille; but it's ras el hanout, a spice mix with robust flavours, subtle nuances and a big hint of the Maghreb.

At the *supermarché* on the outskirts of town our trolley is filled with industrial size tins of cassoulet – "No, Colley, it's not just posh beans and sausages" – and big jars of *soupe de poisson* and spicy mergez sausage and bottles and boxes of wine and tins and jars of pâté and a large metal drum of olive oil and more wine.

Back at the village bar Arnaud orders a draught beer – *un pression.* A large one, *une grande?* No, *una granda,* see? More Languedoc French, he says. It's a zesty mix of sounds, with hints of Occitan, Catalan, Spanish, Italian even. Sometimes all this is at the level of overtones, akin to how the Irish language leaves its lingering imprint on Hiberno-English, like a ghost sign on a village gable.

In the *boulangerie* or at the benches in the village square where the old folk gather for a chat, people switch from French to Spanish and back again in mid-sentence, in a shared soup of languages and accents. This is a cultural crossroads, from bullfights to flamenco, a shared history of migrant labour and refugees and border crossings.

I thought Arnaud was half French. Over lunch at the bar he explains how he's a quarter Spanish. He speaks softly as he tells how his grandfather arrived here from Spain.

They called it *La Retirada. La Retraite* in French – the retreat of half a million people from the Spanish Civil War, a mass exodus over the border after the fall of Barcelona. It was January 1939, the depths of winter, as they came on foot across the Pyrenees to France. That's when Arnaud's grandmother Josefa died. They had to leave her body in the mountain snows.

You'd think the republican refugees arriving in Languedoc-Roussillon would be welcomed with open arms? Far from it. The women and children – including Arnaud's mother and uncle – were sent to accommodation centres, the men herded into temporary camps on the beach at St Cyprien and Le Barcarès. Arnaud's grandfather ended up at Argelès-sur-Mer near Perpignan. He called it a concentration camp, a hell on sand, an ocean of pain and death.

One night seventeen men died of exposure. Mounted French guards beat up the dying men. Arnaud's grandfather said the troops from Senegal were the most brutal. The prisoners were buried where they lay.

Thousands died of dysentery. Those who survived were later moved to concentration camps scattered across the South of France. During the Occupation they were joined by other "undesirables": Jews, Romany families, gays, communists.

Arnaud's grandfather was moved to a camp at Agde, from which he managed to escape with two other men. They sat out the war in a small farm in the Black Mountains. Afterwards he couldn't return to Spain. He had nothing to return to. He found a job in Montpellier, where he was reunited with his children.

Arnaud says his grandfather was never angry or bitter. Not until his final years, when he gave out about God and Franco and Hitler and France and God knows what. Most of all he gave out about the snow. And Senegal. Arnaud says his grandfather was quite a racist bollix in his old age.

After lunch, after all that dark history, we have a gander down the Canal du Midi, under the shade of its plane trees.

The canal is an engineering marvel. A century older than the French Revolution, it is the strategic link between the Atlantic and the Mediterranean. The canal system is a unique combination of aesthetics, nature and functionality, from its locks and bridges to its oval lock-basins, artificial lakes and lines of trees. Forty-five thousand trees were planted, mostly planes with a few cypress, umbrella pines and chestnuts. An endless parasol to shade the water and reduce evaporation in the harsh summer sun.

Yet along many stretches – particularly at popular mooring spots – we come across raw gaps where the diseased planes were recently cut down. They were victims of a canker that arrived down the coast in Provence at the end of the war. The microscopic fungus was carried by – of all people – the liberating forces. The GIs' ammunition crates were made from infected trees.

Some six decades later the disease spread to the Canal du Midi. It was transmitted not only by water – the plane trees dip their thick roots into the canal – but also by the comings and goings of the boats. As they stop and squeeze against the bank you get thirty metres of hull rubbing harshly against the roots, mooring ropes against bark. Cross-contamination ensues, and hence the canker is able to travel upstream too.

The very people who have taken most pleasure from the canal have added to its slow destruction.

OK, I know there are far worse things going on in the world at the moment, from Ebola in West Africa to the carnage in Syria. Or, indeed, in the roads of shameful memories of the Retirada. Even so, I find the whole thing quite sad.

When we return to the barge we are surrounded by police uniforms. Well, by two of them. The boat has been turned over. Clothes and papers are scattered everywhere, a

Georges Simenon is floating cover-side up in the canal.

One cop quizzes Arnaud while the other takes notes.

"He wants to know what's missing," Arnaud tells us.

In the cabin I poke through the stuff with Colley. I'm surprised to find my mobile phone among a heap of papers on the kitchen table. I'm sure I left it on my bed this morning. How could the thieves have missed it?

"At least they left my iPhone. Shit – they took the bag."

Arnaud and the cops look flummoxed.

"What bag?" he asks.

"The ... " I'm about to say bag of makeup ... "oh, nothing."

Two more cops drive up. With Giradot in the back seat, the fat old dalek from the copshop.

"I hope that not much is stolen," he says. "I came to tell you that Madame" – he struggles with her surname – "Madame McElhinney is in Paris."

"I don't get," I tell him. "Was she seen there?"

"No, Monsieur. But she has reserved the seat on the TGV this morning."

All three of us fire simultaneous questions at him.

What's she doing on the fast train to Paris?

Did anyone see her?

C'mon man, what's the story?

Giradot holds up his hands to push our pesky questions away. "She bought a second-class ticket in the *Gare*. I thought you might like a copy." He hands it to Arnaud, who looks at it and passes it to me.

"As you can see, Messieurs," Giradot continues, "the ticket office asks for her name, *prénom,* date of birth ... "

I look at the lads and shake my head. "This could mean anything. Did the ticket office recognise her?"

"And why go to Paris?" Arnaud asks him.

"No more questions." Giradot walks back to his car. "I will call if there are any developments. You will be staying here for the moment, in the *bateau?*"

"Oh yeah," Arnaud says. "We're going nowhere fast."

Sixteen

After supper we were having a beer in the village bar when a loud English accent waddled in.

"Arnaud Connolly! Talk of the devil."

"Dave!"

The English accent belongs to one Dave Smedley. Arnaud knows him from the film business back in Dublin. The guy is on his own. Arnaud has invited him to join us.

"Dave, this is Colley – we're on a sort of busman's holiday – and this is Moss. Moss is a private detective." I wince. "Long story short," he tells his film director chum, "we're looking for a missing woman. Moss, show him the photo. She's from Dublin. I don't suppose you … "

I take out the pic. Dave shakes his head. "Nah, can't say I do."

The telly has a footie match with the sound down. One of those meaningless pre-season friendlies for mega clubs to milk overseas markets and give the reserves a run-out.

"Who's playing?" the Englishman asks.

Colley shrugs. "Sorry Dave, we're only half watching."

Arnaud gives me a sly wink. "I think it's Heisenberg v Schrödinger."

"Do wha' mate? Is that Germans or Scandis?"

The stadium is half empty, the tackles tame, the football boring. For want of something better to do the TV coverage keeps cutting to the fans.

"Flamin' Nora." Arnaud winces. "There's more of it."

Dave takes a sip of his lager. "More of what?"

"All them shots of fans instead of the actual football."

"No harm? innit? It's only footie tottie. "

"No, Dave, it's only faking it," Arnaud says. "It's like … like … a film about a musician, where the maestro sits on his piano stool tinkling his ivories … "

"Ooh err missus."

"Shut up Dave." Arnaud sounds slightly irritated. "And

the camera cuts from his hands – I mean from a real musician's hands – to a wide shot. Now it's the actor's fingers and they are all over the place cos he can't play the piano, then they cut back to the real musician's hands … "

"Oh," Dave says. "Gotcha. What's that to do with footie?"

Arnaud's friend from the film biz seems slow on the uptake about cuts and shots. And how come he's such a famous film director yet none of us have heard of him? Does Dave Smedley make smutty films with *Carry On* jokes? *Debbie Does Darndale?*

Seriously, though, I've nothing against the English. The Brits give us the BBC, the Open University, Newton's laws of gravity and most of Monty Python. But Dave is a certain kind of Englishman; the kind whose flat satnav accent seems to drain the life out of everything it touches, replacing it with embalming fluid and double entendres.

This Dave sounds like the kind of prat who makes lawn mowers sound alluring – and probably has an innuendo about that too. "See her, mate? Bet she keeps *her* lawn mowed." He also does that annoying English thing of impersonating your Irish accent. Badly. *Because begorrah that's the Arrish, twinkly-eyed leprechauns with a pig under an arm.*

"All I'm saying is," Arnaud goes on, "the fans are hamming it up for the camera. Like the guy on the piano. Faking it."

"OK," says Dave, "talking about faking it, how come all you lot follow the Premiership and … "

Here we go. Eight hundred years of it.

"What lot?" Colley jumps in.

"You know," Dave drones on. "The Arrish kids with their Man U jerseys and their Wayne Rooney pyjamas, and half the Arrland team play for English clubs. But when it comes to the World Cup, well, it's like the Arrish are all prayin' for England to lose."

The three "Arrishmen" from "Arrland" at the bar look at each other. Who should tell him first?

"Yeah, Dave," Arnaud kicks off. "Funny that. We pray to Saint Anthony that Ingalund are losing ten nil."

I take up the ball: "At half time."

Colley shoots: "And Wayne Rooney gets a red card."

"Yeah. Bloody mad, innit?" Dave misses our sarcasm, finishes his lager and checks his watch. "I could stay all night but I've an early start in the morning – a trade show thing in Barcelona. Where you off to yourselves?"

"Oh, hanging around here I guess," Arnaud says.

We do all the "see yous," "good lucks," and "maybe catch up again when I'm back from Barcleonas," and once he's out of sight it's Colley who gives the first verdict.

"He does drone on a bit."

"To put it lightly," I say.

Arnaud smirks. "Funny that."

"What?" Colley and I say it together.

"That's what they call him. Dave the Drone."

The next morning we have our first big row. It's over breakfast. I mean it's both *during* breakfast and *about* breakfast. Maybe everybody is still pissed off about the strange break-in on the barge.

Our deal on the trip was this: I do the driving, Arnaud cooks the main meal – usually supper because eating out is cheaper at lunchtime – Colley does breakfast and navigating, and we all share the washing up. It's only fair.

But Colley has gone all bolshie this morning. "So what does Monsieur Escoffier fancy?"

Arnaud gives a sour look. "Scrambled eggs is fine."

"Yeah, I'm easy," I say. "Poached, boiled, fried, sunny side up, *en cocotte* … "

Colley opens the fridge. "Eggs it is then, no problemo. Sure anyone can scramble an egg. Where've they got to?"

Arnaud points to a cupboard. "There. You never store eggs in a fridge. Or tomatoes."

Colley mutters away as he assembles his bits and pieces.

Arnaud gets up. "Maybe I'll do it, Colley."

"Ah feck that for *un jeu de* soldiers. It ain't rocket science. It's only scrambled eggs."

"No, Colley. I'll do it."

Arnaud is a reasonably reasonable man. The one time I've known him to really lose the head – this comes via his sous chef Aisling – was when a commis straight from catering college told him, "Anyone can scramble an egg."

You don't go there. Not with Arnaud Connolly. When Arnaud is hiring, the candidates can have the fanciest CVs, flashiest knives and done snail porridge ice cream and lobster caviar frittata for Heston Whatshisname, but Arnaud tells them to do one thing: *Make me scrambled eggs.*

So. Do they do it the proper old way or the geeky way? The geeky way involves immersion circulators, water baths, two eggs and an extra egg yolk (for the perfect fat-to-protein ratio), which are whisked and poured into a Ziploc bag, which is plonked in the water bath at exactly seventy-four degrees for exactly fifteen minutes.

You can tart them up as much as you like with your bacon and chives, smoked eel, grated Gruyère, chanterelles, sliced sausage, truffles or trout caviar. But scrambled eggs, pure and simple, the traditional way?

Some cooks use the double boiler method, like a bain marie over simmering water, or a sous vide. Others lace the curds at the end with chunks of butter and cream, or crème fraîche. Then there's the seasoning. But forget all that. Simply concentrate on the scrambling.

That's all that matters, if you want your curds to be creamy and smooth, in varying sizes, just cooked yet still soft and tender. So why don't we define "scrambling"? It sounds simple, insouciant, careless even. A scramble: I can't help thinking of dozens of young men lolling around in deckchairs in a field of England, then – a siren, bells, clamour, panic stations – a mad dash to their Spitfires to repel the latest waves of Luftwaffe. That kind of scramble.

Arnaud waited as the young commis chef did his worst, then showed him the door.

Back to this morning in the barge, and Colley too is about to get the sack.

"No, no, no. Scramble *AN* egg?" Arnaud continues. *"ONE* egg? Wrong, Colley. A minimum quantity is required and always more than one egg." Arnaud can get nitpicky when narky. He's right though; a solitary scrambled egg will set too fast for the human hand and human eye and all the other cheffy senses.

"It's virtually impossible to scramble *an* egg," he continues. "You need at least two per person, five for two people. Otherwise it's like making bread dough with an ounce of flour, or boiled eggs with half an egg."

He breaks eight eggs, one after the other, one-handed out of habit rather than to show off.

"Beat them lightly, see? It's not an omelette. I'm adding a teaspoon of water for a lighter finish. Get me a pan. Too big, no, that small one there. Grease it lightly – we're not making fried eggs. Turn the gas down, and find a wooden spoon or spatula."

The mixture goes into the pan.

"Watch. Already beginning to stick. So you push and scrape like mad, curl the curds from the bottom and corners. It's starting to set. We take it off the heat when it's still ever-so-slightly underdone. Too early and you've raw runny bits. Too late and the curds will be rubbery, separating like curds and whey. *Anyone can scramble an egg?* Yeah right.

"So that's the secret: slightly undercooked to allow for how it continues to set in those remaining seconds, between you taking it off the stove and the eggs hitting the toast."

Shit. Did he just say toast? *Simply make some toast?* Toast is another day's work.

"OK," Arnaud says, "just make do with them baguettes."

Áine Kettle arrives shortly after our breakfast on deck.

Arnaud fetches her coffee as I fill her in on our progress – or lack thereof – in finding her sister.

What Niamh was last seen wearing.

How her luggage and passport were gone from her room, yet someone forgot to check the bathroom cabinet – all those cosmetics which, Mrs Kettle agrees, her sister would never leave behind like that.

How an Irish cop called Coleman was given the restaurant's CCTV footage to take back to Ireland.

Then there's the restaurant's reservations book, the shots on my iPhone. And the waitresses' descriptions of Niamh and of a young girl and a much older man who may or may not be Mrs K's missing husband, and how no one can recognise him from the photograph, and how he's quite tall and speaks French with a *rosbif* accent, so he may be English or Irish, and someone thinks he's from Dublin.

Áine Kettle raises her eyebrows. "I don't get. You said he was about six foot. That must be a mistake."

"The waitress was pretty sure," I say. "He was sitting most of the time, but she said he was a regular. She must have seen him standing a good few times."

"But he's never six foot," she says. "Five six, five seven at most."

"I can't think of an explanation."

Because I can't. Ask a witness to recall someone's height and weight and they can make a mistake. If anything, though, they tend to underestimate it, not overestimate. And I didn't ask the waitress to give me feet and inches. Or centimetres even. I did the standard trick, getting her to compare his height to an external reference point – a doorway.

"I guess some things are hard to disguise," I continue.

"Even with plastic surgery," Colley says. "Tell her about the train ticket, Reidy."

I show her the copy of the rail ticket and say we're unlikely to get access to CCTV footage from the railway station. "The police say she took a train to Paris but … "

"And that's all wrong," she interrupts. "Her birthday." She taps the copy of the ticket then crosses her arms. "Right year, wrong day. Should be the twelfth, not the twenty-first. And May, not April."

"Maybe they made a mistake," I say.

A long silence. I for one feel awkward.

Arnaud gets up. "Look, Mrs Kettle. At least we have some idea of where she's got to, but I can't see much else we can do here. Why don't you go back to Ireland and wait for her to fly home from Paris or wherever she is."

"Yes," I say. "She's bound to turn up."

She picks up her handbag to go. "I guess so."

"I think I got it," Colley says shortly after she's gone. "The ticket office asked for her date of birth. Maybe it's a typing mistake, or she's crap at French numbers."

"Sure," Arnaud says, "but there's a world of a difference between saying *vingt-et-un* and *douze.*"

"And they typed April instead of May," I say. "Nobody makes that many typing mistakes. And no one messes up their own date of birth like that, not even in a foreign language. Arnaud, how do you fancy a trip to the railway station?"

"OK," he says. "But only if Colley does the washing up."

Seventeen

La Gare is your typical French railway station. A ticket office with three hatches, an information desk, a newspaper kiosk, an abandoned café, arrival and departure signs, not enough seating, and the yellow "composting" machines to validate your ticket before going through to the platforms.

"How do you fake a train journey, Arnaud? Or more precisely, how do you fake a train ticket?"

He gives me a what-do-you-mean look.

"Well," I continue, "if I had feck all French I'd use one of them touchscreen ticket machines over there. No need to speak to anyone. Just press the Union Jack for instructions in English."

"But she didn't."

"No, she hit the ticket office with her schoolgirl French. Or so the cops say. So that's what you're going to do. Queue up and buy a ticket to the next station."

"Aller simple?"

"Yep. One-way. Give them any old name and date of birth if they ask for one." I hand him a fifty euro note. "Don't spend it all at once."

Arnaud returns ten minutes later with a big grin and a ticket made out to Dustin Turkey, date of birth Christmas Day. I grab it from him, walk towards the platforms and "compost" it in a ticket machine. Twice, because the first time I put the ticket in the wrong way.

Instead of continuing to the platform I turn back and head out to the station's car park.

"Hey," Arnaud says as he catches up. "What was that all about?"

I try to explain as we drive back towards the canal. "Pre-booked seats are nothing new on French railways, right?"

"They've had them for as long as I can remember," he

says. It can be mayhem when you get on the train though. Seat numbers mean nothing. Half the passengers ignore them. It's even worse than the Irish system."

"Yeah, but once you have your ticket for seat six in carriage fifteen, you can use your ticket to prove to any interloper that that's your seat, right?"

"Where are we going with all this?"

"Not to Paris, that's for sure." I pause to find our bearings as we reach the intersection to the motorway. "But having your name on the ticket, and your date of birth too – that's a relatively new thing, yeah?"

"They've been doing it on and off for a couple of years now."

"Exactly. Tickets with names on them. And dates of birth. But it's not like you're asking for a discount as a student or a pensioner, is it? It's yet more stuff for the ticket office person to type, like your one just did. Yet one more layer of bureaucracy and useless keystrokes. Now, apart from this brief transaction at the ticket office, and any CCTV footage they might have, what evidence is there that *you* took *this* train from *this* station this morning?"

Two motorcycle cops appear in the rear mirror. Check the speedometer, best behaviour Mossie.

"The ticket inspector only cares about you having a valid ticket," I continue. "With has a timestamp from the composting machine, and a seat number so you can argue with anyone sitting in your seat. That's all they care about: that you have a valid ticket. There's no real record of who paid for the ticket – it was paid in cash of course – and no evidence of whether you actually took the journey or whether you … "

"Walked back out of the station, like we just did."

"Exactly. No evidence of whether you swapped tickets with someone else, swapped seats, ordered a coffee from the sandwich trolley, had your passport checked at the border, whether you went all the way to the destination on the ticket or got off and changed trains, or whether you took the journey in the first place."

"So if she's gone to Paris … "

" … I'm Napoleon Bonaparte."

That's when the motorbike cops flagged us down.

"Vos papiers!"

So two heavy looking dudes with gun holsters start hassling you for ID. What would you do?

"Contrôle de papiers, Monsieur!"

In France they can stop you and demand identification at any time. Without your papers you can be arrested. They even used to have a law that you had to have at least ten francs on you to avoid a vagrancy charge.

"Et vos éthylotests!"

Besides your *papiers,* French motorists must have various other compulsory items – your *éthylotests chimique* for a start, your breathalysers – or risk an on-the-spot fine.

The breathalysers come in two kinds: expensive electronic ones which can be re-used; or cheap disposable chemical kits. The hire car crowd supplied us with a pair of breathalysers – you'll need two at any one time, at least one of them unused. We also spent a tenner on a dozen of the one-off kits in the *supermarché.* We figured we'd hardly need them but they'd be a bit of crack back home in Ireland. As in, "Moss, take the test – that's it, you're officially pissed." Irish supermarkets don't sell disposable breathalysers.

"Vos éthylotests!" he barks again, arms crossed, feet wide apart.

Arnaud gives me a stern look as I fumble around on the dashboard. "Try the glove compartment."

"Nope."

"That's where they were last time we looked."

"No."

"Shite and onions."

The cop orders us both out.

"Now what's he want?"

"Your *gilet jaune.* The hi-viz jacket."

"It must be in the back somewhere."

Although we've left our own reflective vests back in Tintin, I could swear the one from the hire company was in the *bagnole's* back seat. It definitely was when we hired it.

"Then check the boot."

"Not there either."

No jacket or warning triangles or breathalysers. Am I losing my mind? Were they stolen from the car? At the same time as the break-in at the barge?

After a brief discussion with the cops, Arnaud gets back in the car. On the driver's side this time.

"What did they say?" I ask. " On-the-spot fine?"

"No. They're confiscating the car. Get in."

"They can't just … "

"They just have. We're to follow them to the cop shop. I think we're under arrest."

"I don't understand."

"Nicked, collared, lifted, arrested. From the French word *arrêter*, meaning 'to stop'."

"Fucksake."

It's one big *cauchemar,* as the French say. *Un nuit blanche.* In the *gendarmerie* we are relieved of our mobile phones and made to empty our pockets. We are fingerprinted, photographed and taken to separate interview rooms.

I can be kept in custody *("garde à vue")* for twenty-four hours without formal charges, a young cop explains. After twenty-one hours they might let me see an *avocat* if they feel like it. I'm breathalysed and escorted to a cell. It has a rock-hard bench for a bed.

Fifteen minutes later a bell rings loudly. Pandemonium, loads of footsteps. A clatter of cops arrive with Arnaud. His grin is bigger than the Laughing Cow's.

The same two traffic cops have a sour look as they return our phones and other possessions and escort us – I'd almost say "frogmarch" but I'm not in the mood – to the car park. They get on their bikes.

"C'mon," Arnaud says, "we're out of here." He throws me the car keys. "You're driving."

"OK, what's the big joke?"

"You know my cousin Yann?"

"The one who lent us the boat?"

"Yeah. Whose wife Isabelle happens to be a *gendarme?*"

"So she got us out?"

"Not quite."

Seems Yann was stopped a few years back for a minor traffic offence. It was shortly after lunchtime. The police ask him to do an on-the-spot breath test. He refuses. They take him to the local nick to force him to take it. Now, his missus being a *gendarme,* Yann knows his rights. He only agrees to the breath test if every cop on duty does one too. In the end he passes and half the station fails.

"And you did that? Arnaud, you cheeky beggar."

The traffic cops escort our car to the nearest *supermarché,* refusing to leave until they've seen us buying ten more breathalyser kits, a high-vis jacket, the lot. After that we stock up on more provisions.

The greatest mystery of French supermarkets is where they keep the tinned anchovies. Not in an obvious place among the other tinned stuff. Instead, they are in the chiller compartment, alongside the smoked salmon, tubs of prawns and so on. Chilled tins of anchovies.

Back in the *bagnole,* although it's roasting I don the yellow jacket. It's not leaving my sight. That's when I notice the dark blue Renault in the rear-view mirror. It was following our convoy when we arrived at the supermarket with the traffic cops. It's tailing us again as we leave the supermarket's car park.

"Mind if we take the scenic route?"

Arnaud checks the mirror. "The blue Renault?"

"Yep."

It is still following at a distance as we reach the village. We park by the barge and take a circuitous walk through the alleyways to the bar.

At the counter Colley has made new friends: Keith and Patsey, an Aussie or Kiwi couple – I'm not great with accents – who are taking their big old barge down to Sète. Patsey looks like a sixties hippy chick, as in a hippy in her early sixties. Keith has a grey ponytail and thick, gingery-grey handlebar moustache. The kind of whiskers that wouldn't look out of place in an Astérix comic, if the Roman legions had invaded Adelaide.

Arnaud joins them on a tall stool by the bar. "Colley, you won't believe the morning we've just had."

I grab another stool. The bar's owner comes to take our orders.

"Bonjour Monsieur Gérard."

"Bonjour Arnaud."

"Deux cafés Calvas, s'il vous plaît!"

A couple of minutes later Monsieur Gérard returns with two steaming hot coffees served with a snifter of Calvados on the side. In a showy gesture, he half-stoppers the bottle with his thumb and sprinkles a splash of Calvados over the hot coffee.

We fill Colley in on our escapades at the copshop. Colley in turn advances his latest theory.

"Suppose this Johnny Kettle guy is still alive and on the run. He kidnaps Mrs whatsit's sister. He grabs her luggage and her passport, but forgets half her makeup stuff. She's drugged or killed or both. But he can't simply drive out of town with a body in the boot, what with all the roadblocks after the bank job. So me theory is: *he went by canal.*"

"He could be onto something, you know," Colley's new mate Keith says. "We were moored up in Mentidera that day and saw the roadblocks. But here's the thing: nobody checked the boats."

Arnaud laughs. "Even if you break the canal's speed limits, you still wouldn't make a fast getaway on it."

Keith grins too. "See, they don't have canal patrols, do they? That's what makes it so appealing. You wouldn't need to do a ton on it to be fifteen, twenty miles away in a couple of hours, and you'd soon be in the wop wops."

Wop wops?

"Once you reach the woods and mountains and the *garrigue*," Keith continues, "well, it's scrubland, miles from anywhere. You could hide anything out there. You tell 'em, Patsey."

"It's like this bloke was arrested the other day for growing cannabis," she says. "Thousands of pot plants in the *garrigue*. The wop wops."

"It's flamin' hot out there," Keith continues, "so he finds a well in the field and rigs up an irrigation system. Only, how do you power a water pump in the middle of the wop wops? He lays a long cable to the main road." He slaps his thigh. "To a *speed* camera. Sheer bloody genius."

"I woulda used a solar panel meself," Colley says.

I'm only half listening when I jump off my stool. "That's *him.*"

Everyone else is puzzled, apart from Arnaud. "The blue Renault. It's been following us."

"Fuckit. Let's find out what he's at," I say.

So we run after him, Arnaud and I, with Colley hobbling behind. Not sure if the guy has seen us yet, as he briskly turns a corner.

Seconds later the dark blue Renault drives off, leaving us all puffing away. I feel twenty again, but with arthritis this time.

"Arnaud – licence plate." I dig out a biro for him, and the train ticket to write on. "Scribble it down."

"I think I got it," he says.

"You know your cousin Yann, whose missus is a …?"

"No, Moss. She's on maternity leave."

"But she could ask a colleague."

"For a vehicle check? Don't be mad."

The two of us walk back towards Colley and the bar.

"Oh shit." Arnaud has just thought of something. "You know Colley's mad theory about making a getaway along the canal?"

"Uh huh?"

"And the waitress in the restaurant – the one with no English?"

"Angélique?"

"Yeah. She said she thought the regular customer, our man who might be Johnny Kettle – had a *bateau.*"

"She said all that, did she?"

"Didn't I tell you?"

"No."

"Sorry, Moss."

"What kind of boat? A barge? Canoe? Speedboat? Viking longship?"

"I forgot to ask. Does it matter?"

That evening Keith and Patsey entertain us on their barge with chilled wine and beer and tapas. Keith turns out to be from Taradale, in the Hawke's Bay region of North Island. Patsey is from Wellington. So they're New Zealanders, and good eggs.

Despite the heat we're forced to stay indoors, with all the windows closed to keep the smoke out – and the distant sound of one or more helicopters as they flutter, growl and rattle away. There's a big fire out there somewhere.

Arnaud's mobile rings. Mrs Kettle says she's flying back to Dublin tomorrow. No point in telling her about today's events.

His mobile rings again. Monsieur Henri the car mechanic has tracked down the spare parts for Tintin.

"It could take a whole week?" says Colley. "What do we do for a whole week?"

Early signs of cabin fever. We can't stay here a week.

Áine Kettle took a shower and packed her bags. A heavy smell of smoke filled the air.

The woman at reception said there were fires in the

garrigue. Huge tracts of scrubland and forest up in smoke, a hundred firemen trying to fight dozens of outbreaks. And the airplanes – *bombardiers d'eau,* water bombers. It was a red alert because strong winds were expected.

The woman at reception was angry about it. She said a French Foreign Legion drill instructor had been suspended. An "imbecilic" shooting practice had started one of the wildfires.

I don't like flying, but last night I had a pleasant dream.

I'm swimming through the air, flying over sand dunes, vineyards and fields of poppies. I'm lucid. I know it's a dream. As long as I keep flying I'll be safe and happy.

Perhaps it signifies something deep. Like rising above the situation, soaring to new heights, finding a new perspective, finding a place where no one can tell me what to do.

Or maybe it's symbolic. All very Freudian and about to involve umbrellas, lobsters, penis envy and a psychiatrist's chair.

Or it just means I'm about to lose control and crash.

Then I'm driving a fast car, with Tintin behind it swaying from side to side, and a dark blue Renault on our tail.

The following morning we have a plan.

We have a week to kill. So dump the *bagnole* at the nearest car hire and head down the canal, east towards the Med, in a convoy with Keith and Patsey's barge.

Eighteen

After a hotel holiday it's the little things you notice. How your house seems emptier than usual. And more dusty.

That thin layer of dust on the washing machine. That mildew on the shower room tiles. That suit still hanging in the bedroom wardrobe, between his two tweed jackets.

That stupid suit. His board meetings and business conventions suit.

Friends and relatives would pop round in the weeks after Johnny disappeared. Hover around more like, the ghouls and gawkers. "Oh you must miss him so, the house must feel empty without him."

It was far from empty. It was full of reminders. All those photos staring back at you, and his clothes. Those terrible sky-blue shirts with white collars. If you packed them away or got shut of them everyone would call you a callous bitch in a cold empty house. You couldn't win.

Áine took the suit jacket off the hangar and laid it on the bed. It was too small for Simon, who was taller than his dad. Besides, Simon had a healthy allergy to suits. Who on earth would want a double breasted old suit like that, with its ugly fat pinstripe?

In the flashbulb memory, what was Johnny wearing in France again? What did Niamh say he was wearing? Not a suit of course. Niamh said he was in something different. For the life of her Áine couldn't remember.

The master bedroom was clean, far from dusty. Though it could do with a lick of paint. She would prefer to do it herself. That's something Johnny would never understand. How you become far more attached to your home when you do it up yourself, when you leave your own mark on it. When it's *hands on.*

Johnny must have handled some of the biggest property deals in the State, yet he was never really in touch with his own property, his "principal residence" as they call it for tax purposes. Not properly. He never became intimate with each nook and cranny, never knew which corner of the dining-room floor had been a devil to polyurethane; or the shape of every groove in the French windows as you prepped them, washed and sanded them; and as you washed them again with white spirit, dusting and wiping them dry, massaging with saddle soap before applying the undercoat and two further coats.

Coats. His coats and jackets, suits and shirts. Maybe sell them. Flog the lot, give it all to Oxfam, throw the whole wardrobe away. Downsize your memories once and for all.

Would it be tasteless to give his pinstripe suit to Orla to sell in her shop?

Poor bubble girl. She couldn't sell a piss-up in a brewery. Orla was just playing at shop.

No, don't be all the time so hard on Orla, Áine thought. Hadn't she herself only been pretending too? Playing the perfect wife, the perfect mother, the perfect doormat. Then, after he disappeared, the perfect widow, though it's hard to do that properly when you've no body to grieve over. A body that didn't exist yet kept coming back to haunt her, with its stupid bloody suits and shirts.

What would Niamh say? What would she do? Niamh would probably come swanning back from Paris and say, *Don't be daft – of course get shut of it. Try eBay or Gumtree. There's bound to be some sad soul out there who still likes that kind of …*

Áine put the suit back, closed the wardrobe, closed the bedroom door and walked downstairs.

Surely it doesn't take that long to fly back from France?

Nineteen

Our convoy putters along at a leisurely pace, the two boats' pistons snoring and snorting away. The canal's speed limit is eight kilometres an hour, not even a brisk jog. Who cares? Neither boat has a speedometer and we're in no hurry.

Whenever we come across a local winemaker near the canal, all five of us descend for a *dégustation* or two. Colley initially thought it sounded disgusting.

"No, Colley, it's a free wine tasting, you gobshite."

Soon Colley is well into the *dégustations*.

Each morning we wake up in a new village, to fresh tastes, fresh sights and sounds. The churchbells and creaking shutters, the *coq du village* with its dawn *cocorico* (in France they don't do cock-a-doodle-do), the cheeky ducks on the canal, the swallows swooping and shrieking around the treetops in the evening.

Once in a while there's the old-fashioned nee-nah of a police car or fire truck. Out on manoeuvres or off to another big fire in the *garrigue*. Or then again they could be dashing home for lunch.

By midday, twelve on the dot, we will have found the busiest bistro or café in our latest village. A noisy circus as the staff shout orders back and forth in three-part harmonies.

"Deux cafés au lait!!!"

"Un demi de blanc!"

"Una tassa … " A cup of something (in Catalan).

All very raucous to make themselves heard above the lunchtime crowd. It's loud, it's life, you can't beat it.

We settle down to Midi time. The shops all close at midday; the locks are shut by half seven each evening, even in high season, so that the keepers can have their supper undisturbed.

Sometimes for a change we avoid villages altogether

and moor up by a distant field for peace and quiet.

Like our *peniche,* Keith and Patsey's is a proper wooden barge, a world away from the noddy boats that pootle past, They bob up and down like plastic ducks in a bath, horrible white plastic Tupperware tubs that a travel writer once likened to a one-piece injection-moulded bathroom fitting.

We have become flaneurs on glossy thick green water. Either in complete isolation, or mad busy as the towpaths become infested with bicycles, anglers, walkers with little smiles and waves and *"Bonjour Monsieurdame!"* greetings.

Dawdling, strolling, stopping to soak in the sights between the plane trees in the dappled light.

If Johnny Kettle made his great escape along here, it would have been one of the slowest and most tranquil getaway routes in the world.

Áine Kettle and her elusive husband and missing sister are becoming a faded memory, as distant and remote as footprints on the Moon. Footprints long forgotten yet left there for an eternity, even when there's no one there to see them any more.

Slowly nudging east we reach Béziers. After mooring and an early supper it's time to hit town.

A lazy evening heat swirls through Les Allées, its main thoroughfare. It's far wider than Dublin's O'Connell Street, maybe five times longer, far more pedestrian-friendly. Leading off Les Allées are cobbled alleyways of peeling buildings with rusty terracotta roofs, shuttered windows and ornate balconies with satellite dishes and laundry lines. The washing lines are empty because the right-wing mayor has brought in a ban on outside laundry.

As if to piss the mayor off, Arabic music and rap reverberate from car speakers into the bistros and boulevards, where old men play pétanque under palm trees in a dozen languages (including French).

Béziers is a slow-cooked stew of a place, with exotic

Mediterranean ingredients: French, obviously, but with spicy hints of North Africa, Spain, Romania, Catalunya. Gypsies haggle with gendarmes and Halal butchers, while bemused cowboys and debonair young students look on.

Keith's barge has a TV. Tonight we break the digital detox rule and turn on the evening news.

Have we missed anything? It could almost be a re-run from years ago: the Kurds in Iraq are calling on the US for help; North Korea is getting ready to nuke the White House; a virulent contagion in Africa has Europeans and Americans worrying about when it will reach their shores; another Clinton has begun a presidential campaign; there's a further massive shift in the political tectonic plates of the Middle East; and, in a re-run of a re-run, the Israeli military machine is trundling into Gaza again with its tanks, jets, drones and missiles. We're in for another long summer of broken ceasefires, shuttle diplomacy and rising bodycounts.

Sometimes the news feels less like journalistic reportage and more like a modern twist on ancient myths, as the TV people try to shape the stories into something more eternal than pure information. Even the latest schoolyard killings, hurricanes and airline crashes have a whiff of deja vu about them, as the news empires milk their mythic qualities.

Russian separatists in eastern Ukraine have shot down a passenger plane. It's an international air disaster in a war zone. Viewers are warned about shocking scenes.

Every so often Arnaud gives us a quick translation as the camera pans across fields of sunflowers and smouldering debris; a giant white tail-piece with the Malaysian Airlines insignia; more plane parts, passenger seats, passports, handbags, suitcases, beach sandals, poolside novels, toiletries, charred souvenirs, guidebooks, comics, magazines, stuffed animals and other toys.

We are told that many passengers were naked. Some were still strapped into their seats, some wearing in-flight headphones.

This is the vast area where the bodies rained down. Strips of white cotton flutter from wooden stakes and tree branches. Each stake marks a victim or body part. There are a lot of stakes. Some three hundred passengers and crew were killed, the death toll almost as high as in the opening days of the assault on Gaza.

We arrive at Agde. The same town where Arnaud's grandfather made his wartime escape.

Keith and Arnaud go ashore in search of a couple of barge poles. Colley, Patsey and I stretch our legs at an inland harbour and a round lock where boats can turn around to access three outlets: the canal back to Béziers and westwards to Toulouse; the town of Agde via the Canalet; and the Bassin de Thau via the Hérault River.

You can't avoid the Étang de Thau if you want to cross from the Canal du Midi to the Canal du Rhône à Sète. It's a vast lake, the second largest in France, twenty kilometres long and technically inland though full of salty water. It will take a good two hours to cross the Étang, Keith has warned us, and that's under good conditions.

Conditions this morning aren't great.

Our two barges set off. At the entrance to the Étang we pass a white lighthouse with a red top, Les Onglous. Several pretty villages come into view on the northern shore to our left. If Arnaud had his way we'd stop at every one of them, starting with Marseillan, the home of Noilly Prat, the legendary vermouth. But time is against us so we head for the little harbour at Bouzigues.

We down platters of its famous oysters with the local white wine, Picpoul de Pinet. I'm Picpoul's number two fan in Ireland – Arnaud is number one. After lunch we move our barges next to three small fishing boats and wait for a break in the weather.

Unlike the straightforward canals, these open waters can be hair-raising. Hence the lighthouses.

The geography is flat, open. There are no channel markers, just millions of oyster beds to guide you. The lagoon is relatively shallow. Large areas around its fringes are less than three metres deep. Hence the bargepoles.

We're making good headway when the winds kick the surface into a choppy soup, lashing our boats from side to side. Judging by the thumps, bangs and clangs, everything in the cabin below is being thrown about too.

As we try for safer waters our barge hits a sandbank. Stuck.

Keith tries to shout across from his barge. He's thirty yards away, impossible to hear in this gale.

He calls Colley on his mobile. Do we want him to radio for rescue? A rescue operation would cost us several hundred euro. We decide to sit it out while Keith and Patsey head back to the harbour at Mèze.

We take turns to keep watch, with Colley on the first shift in a thick old lifejacket. Arnaud and I retire to the cabin. Time to buckle down and break out the brandy.

"If you were Johnny Kettle," I ask him, "how would you do it?"

"Disappear you mean?"

"Yeah."

"The old autopilot-and-parachute trick I guess."

I give him a seen-too-many-movies look.

"No, really," Arnaud continues. "Stick the plane on autopilot, point it at America, and by the time it runs out of fuel I'd be long gone. You jump out on your parachutes, and woosh!" He has put his hands together in prayer then pointed them straight ahead. "The plane carries on and what's there to see? Even if they scramble the fighter jets or rescue helicopters it's just a ghost plane with an iced-over windshield."

"But you'd need to know how to use a parachute."

"Always a first time," he says.

"Oh come on. And jumping out of a moving plane, far out to sea? I wouldn't even parachute into this." I point down to the choppy waves lapping our hull. "And you'd need a dinghy or something to keep you afloat. Way too messy."

"So swim ashore in your life jackets."

"Forty miles out to sea? In mid-November? It would be bad enough trying to swim ashore here in the *étang*. No, if Johnny Kettle is alive and well in the south of France there has to be some other explanation. And if they did do the autopilot trick the plane would have to turn up eventually."

"I dunno," he says. "It's not an *étang*, not a nine-foot-deep lake, is it? It's the whole bloody ocean."

By dawn the winds die down to a tolerable level. We manage to bargepole off the sandbank. Colley has a kip, I make breakfast, Arnaud takes the wheel, we head to Sète for fresh supplies and water, electricity and brandy.

Colley is woken by another phone call: we're about to lose Keith and Patsey. Their throttle cable has snapped so they have to find a workshop with a spare cable.

The Canal du Rhône à Sète is a relief as our barge navigates a series of smaller lagoons south of Montpellier, past seaside resorts towards La Grande-Motte.

Arnaud's words from last night echo in the wind. "Not a lake, but the whole bloody ocean."

All that ocean. It covers two-thirds of the planet. Finding something lost at sea is like, well, looking for a needle in a haystack. Needles and haystacks, clutching at straws.

But an airliner's black box isn't black. It's orange. And a small light aircraft like a Beech Duchess wouldn't have a little orange black box, would it?

Even if it did, say the box measures two feet square. By comparison a needle would be, say, two inches long. And say a haystack is six feet tall, six wide. But this is a crash at sea, so the needle isn't in the *middle* of the haystack – it's at the bottom of it.

A small plane in a vast ocean must be a billion times harder to find. Like looking for a tiny needle in a big haystack in a vast field.

A haystack that has been put on the dark side of the Moon, under a hundred feet of water. Deep dark waters, far out in the Atlantic.

The whole bloody ocean.

Twenty

Monsieur Henri our young mechanic has performed miracles. Tintin is due back from the motor hospital. And the car will live. Give it a couple more days and it will be hobbling around again.

Meanwhile Yann has offered to drive us up to Nîmes to catch the Tour de France.

While Colley is in his element I'm only half following the Tour this year. I've stood and watched the Dublin stages of a few big races in my time, including this year's Giro d'Italia, though being stuck on the roadside at the same spot for hours can be very bitty. Give me the telly coverage any day. All those swooping helicopter shots — they even have mini cameras in the riders' bikes this year.

I've only seen Le Tour at first hand once before, the one that started in Ireland in 1998, a year before the Armstrong era began. Even then the cycling world was being shattered by dope cheats, though most of us didn't know it at the time.

It was the twelfth of July, the start of the economic boom, the ink still fresh on the Good Friday Agreement. The twelfth. The Orangemen still strutting their stuff on the streets of the north, half the streets festooned in union jacks, while Dublin in the south was decked out in the red, white and blue of the French tricolour.

The roads were closed at dawn. Thousands were already lining the streets as we set up camp near the finish line in the Phoenix Park, the crowds six deep in places.

The advanced party arrived. Not the race proper but the *caravane*, a convoy of sponsors and advertisers, vans and lorries whizzing by, honking, whistling. Young women in yellow T-shirts standing on the floats, throwing caps and water bottles and sweets to the crowds. Party time.

Then another long wait.

The helicopter in the far distance was the first sign that

the riders were approaching. A phalanx of motorbike cops turned into the park gates, followed by the race officials' red cars and more motorbikes.

Then the first glimpse of the lead bikes and the chasing pack.

In a flash the multicoloured river of riders flew by, surrounded by motorbikes with cameramen riding pillion. Claps, cheers and children's shrieks, the grown-ups shouting *"Allez allez allez!"*

The river was followed by a trickle of team cars and vans with a forest of spare bikes on their roofs. Finally the race doctor's car, the media cars, more cops, more support vehicles.

The whole thing took less than a minute. Dazed onlookers lingered for a good quarter of an hour, unable to believe it was all over.

Two days before the start of the race an official from the Festina team was caught with a car full of drugs in France. He was on his way to catch the ferry to Ireland. The arrest in turn started a drug-fuelled panic. After the Irish stages, as the ferries took the convoy to France to resume the race, there were mad stories of teams chucking bags of drugs into the Irish Sea. Like dancers in a disco raid chucking their contraband to the floor.

That year's Tour went on to be known as the *Tour du Dopage*. The Tour of Dope.

We don't care. We're off to Nîmes.

There are only two things the film star Michael Caine asks when offered a job.

"Where is it?" and "Who's doing the catering?"

Arnaud's only two questions are: "Have you ever cooked tellines before, Mossie?" and – not really a question – "Colley, you're on the lentils, right?"

Arnaud has invited a few relatives around for supper after the Nîmes stage of the Tour. A mere forty or fifty of them, sixty at a push. All those children of the Retirada, three generations of them.

He makes feeding sixty sound a cinch. All you need is a sensible plan, everything chosen by what's local and in season, what's easy to do, and what to avoid.

For a start, don't bother with fecky little *amuse-bouches* (gob ticklers to you and me) for your starters. Begin with a dish done quickly – tellines (that's my job) and hunks of bread from the *boulangerie*. No point baking it yourself.

Then a main course, done long and slow. Arnaud was toying with the idea of a bistro classic, *poulet aux quarante gousses d'ail*. Roast chicken with forty cloves of garlic. Sounds excessive, but sometimes when you take things past their tipping point (as the scientists say) a magical transformation takes place.

It's not forty cloves of *raw* garlic, which would be a terrible shock to the system. And not garlic fried in thin slices in hot fat either until it verges on the bitter. It's forty cloves of garlic cooked whole, cocooned in their protective skins, slowly simmered with the chicken until the bulbs become intensely mild, mellow and so sweet and creamy that you'd be tempted to make ice cream out of them. Seriously.

The barge doesn't have enough oven space for that many chickens, so Arnaud abandons that idea and settles for tellines (me) followed by *joues de porc* (Arnaud) with lentils (Colley), then assorted cheeses and a choice of *tarte de citron* (from the local baker) or *affogato* drizzled with a raspberry couli (Arnaud again).

Begin with the tellines.

"You get them everywhere along the shore around here, from Montpellier to Arles," he says. "Simply dig your hand a couple of inches into the wet sand and dredge them up between your fingers like a sieve. It can take ages to gather a decent haul."

I don't like the sound of that. "Can't we bribe some small children to do it?"

Colley goes one better: "And tell 'em if you don't get at

least five hundred of these pretty little shells Harry Potter will die!"

Arnaud laughs. "Don't be daft. We call in the professionals. The *telliniers*. They have fancy net contraptions to dredge them up."

At the village market he scoops up a handful of the tiny yellow shellfish. Tellines are a bit like clams but with much smaller shells. So smooth and small that you'd probably use more energy opening them than you'd get from the flesh in each shell.

"I grew up on them wee lads on my summer holidays. I'll get eight or nine litres, yeah?"

That's the other thing. Tellines are sold by the litre.

Back at the barge we soak a small test batch with sea salt and a pinch of flour for two hours to purge them. The residual sand comes with the territory, as it were.

"Give them a final rinse and that's basically all the prep work," he says. "Not half as bad as all that scrubbing and de-bearding with a bucket of mussels."

He picks up a shell that is slightly open. He gives it a quick tap. It closes.

"It's exactly like mussels. Don't cook any that don't close. Then don't eat any that don't open. We're doing something that's quicker than *moules marinières* and far easier. Watch."

The gas goes on. He adds a fistful of hazelnuts to a dry pan. While they toast away he makes a persillade with chopped parsley, finely sliced pink garlic and the zest and juice of a lemon. The nuts get roughly crushed with a rolling pin – "that's the only hard part". A large pot goes on the heat. In with the tellines, persillade, olive oil, half a glass of dry white wine. The shells open in seconds.

Tellines à la Camarguaise, sprinkled with the crushed hazelnuts, served with a glass of chilled Picpoul and lashings of sliced baguette to soak up the seriously serious sauce. You could grow addicted to fast food like this.

"See, Moss? *Très simple*. Simply multiply the ingredients

by ten, do it in batches and you'll be rockin'. What you think, Colley?

"Mmmm. Nice one."

"Now put your apron on," Arnaud says to Colley. "We're making *joue de porc*. Pig's cheek in red wine sauce to you and me, with creamy lentils. The lentils are your bit, but we need to prep the meat first."

How come you find pigs' cheeks everywhere in France but rarely in an Irish butcher's? It's not as if pigs in Ireland are cheekless – we probably have the cheekiest pigs in the world. Do they all end up in the sausage factory?

"It's a cheap cut," Arnaud continues. "We need to break down all that tissue and collagen, cook it slowly until the meat melts into … OK. We're doing it in the typical *daube* way, a bit like stewing. But first the marinade. Find me a dozen glass dishes. Oh shit."

He realises we're not in Tintin's fancy galley any more.

"OK, make that twenty ziplock bags, you know, the plastic bags with the … That's the ones. We'll make a line cook out of you yet, Colley."

"But I didn't go to cook school."

"In my kitchen I don't need someone with fancy notions and qualifications. Give me a dish pig any day."

"But I'm not a … "

"Just say 'Yes, chef'."

"Yes, chef."

"Right. Watch. Put the cheek in the bag, add a glass of red wine, a splash of balsamic and the zest of an orange. See?"

"Yes, chef." Colley works away. "Now what?"

"Do it again in the other twenty bags then let them soak away. We'll slow-cook it later with a bit of this and that. But that's the only real secret: time."

Later on he will fry *lardons fumés* in four large pans, drain the cheeks from the marinade, turn up the heat and brown them. Fry sliced onions until softened, add roughly diced carrot, celery and leeks. Finally, deglaze the pans with the marinade, transfer everything to four huge stockpots that he has cadged from a new friend in the local bistro, add sprigs of thyme, rosemary, black peppercorns, bay leaves, chopped garlic, chicken stock and several spoons of sugar, and leave everything to bubble and gloop for five and a half centuries.

Twenty-One

The next day's weather is rotten. We skip the race proper and retreat to a bar, watching the action on the TV, overdosing on caffeine and *citrons pressés* to stay sober for tonight.

By half three it's pissing down. Raindrops smear the helicopter cameras. The roads are slippery, the peloton nervous, the skies in a foul mood.

The only Irish rider to shout for this year is Nicolas Roche. Nico was never going to be the big winner that his dad Stephen was, but that's all the more reason to get behind him. Nico is not a team leader, the queen bee, but one of the selfless worker ants in the peloton. An underdog with a brave heart.

About fifteen kilometres from the finish the camera cuts to Nico.

Shit! He's had a puncture.

Damn damn damn damn damn.

The cousin Yann gives us a lift back to the barge, where Arnaud reheats the pigs' cheeks for half an hour, removes the tender meat and reduces the sauce to a glorious thickness.

As the guests arrive, sixty or so in dribs and drabs, the evening sun returns. Our Kiwi friends Keith and Patsey turn up too – they've managed to fix their boat. Yann and his wife Isabelle are on their first night out together since – and *sans* – the new baby.

By dessert Arnaud has plenty of time to natter with relatives as he plates up. The lemon tarts are ready-mades from the bakers, the *affogato* a simple Italian classic: scoops of ice cream in scrounged coffee cups, bobbing in a sea of strong hot coffee and topped by streaks of an intense raspberry syrup that Arnaud made last night.

"Here, Mossie." It's Keith with a tinnie from the chilly

bin. "Did you find your missing banker bloke?"

"Johnny Kettle? No, Keith. No joy."

"Why would a rich banker need to do a runner?"

"Who knows? Half of them were crooks back then. If he were still alive he'd probably be banged up in jail by now."

Colley takes off his apron. "Or strung up outside it."

"They were strange times," I go on. "Before the crash these people thought they were invincible, indestructible. But what gets me is why they'd all need to do a runner, all three of them, all at the same time."

Colley plonks himself down with a glass of wine. "And none of them taking their wives or kids."

"Maybe they fancied the quiet life," Keith says.

The meal, everyone agrees, is a triumph. Especially Colley's creamy lentils.

The main talking point of the evening is *la vendange* – the forthcoming harvest and how 2014 looks *like "moins de raisins mais du bon vin"*. Fewer grapes but a good wine after two years of miserable harvests. Yann and another cousin, Pierre, are debating the main differences between the *Juilletistes* and *Aoûtiens*. Trust the French to have words for people who holiday in July or August.

Somehow Colley and I end up in the cabin quizzing Isabelle about what police work must be like around here. She gives nothing away but we push her anyway. So she grabs a couple of old *Midi Libres* to give us a quick tour of the typical local crimes. Most of the misdemeanours on these mean streets seem to involve drink or iPods. Or both.

Pour un Ipod, une dizaine de mineurs tombent sur un garçon.

A dozen minors descend on a young lad for his iPod.

Ivre, il provoque un accident et prend la fuite.

Ivre. Pissed.

Deux hommes suspectés de quatorze cambriolages.

Two men, fourteen burglaries.

The headlines follow a formula so different to Irish newspapers. While the *Skibbereen Eagle* might say "Man bites dog", the *Midi Libre* prefers "He bites dog". It would also say "Drunk, he provokes", while an Irish paper would go "Drunk man causes minor altercation and flees".

Next story: *Dérangé par le bruit, il poignarde ses voisins.* Noisy neighbours, GBH, stabbings.

Other stories are about fraudsters, embezzlers.

Sa victime meurt, elle émet des chèques.

Her victim dead (in nursing home), a conwoman uses the dead woman's chequebook.

Then in this morning's paper, page eight: *La femme retrouvée noyée dans le canal.*

A body has turned up near Aigues-Mortes.

"Le cadavre d'une femme d'un certain âge a été découvert jeudi matin … "

"You what?" Arnaud appears out of nowhere to grab the paper from Isabelle. "Did you just say canal?"

He reads and translates.

"La victime était chauve et en partie dénudée. A woman, about forty … *n'a pas encore été identifiée … elle aurait séjourné dans l'eau pendant plusieurs heures.* Wearing only her underwear, no ID, in the water some time. *Une trace de coup à la tête.* Possible blow to the head, could have been done while falling." He turns to Isabelle. "Have you heard about this?"

"Arnaud! I am still on *le congé de maternité.*"

He carries on reading and translating. *"Ce sont des promeneurs qui ont aperçu la victime flottant entre deux eaux. Un batelier qui franchissait l'ouvrage a été appelé par les passants afin de porter secour aux noyé, mais il était trop tard."*

"Some walkers see her floating in midwater. Passers-by call a boatman. Clothes discarded at the scene: white short-sleeved blouse, jeans, and" – he looks up from the paper at Colley and me – "before you ask, the 'right' colour shoes."

Colley says it first: "Are you thinking what I'm thinking?"

I'm next: "We have to go there."

Arnaud hurls the newspaper at us. "You mean right now? Give me one good bloody reason."

"Because it sounds good."

"No, Mossie. There's a world of a difference between a good sound reason and a reason that sounds good. It's getting dark, we've no car, Yann has had a bottle of vino. And Isabelle – no offence *ma chérie* – you're not far behind him."

"Yeah, but" – I'm trying to think – "the barge has two bicycles at the back."

"You can't cycle. Aigues-Mortes is miles away, *and* you've drink taken."

"What about Keith's bike?"

The big motorbike on the back of Keith and Patsey's barge. *La nécessité est mère d'invention* and all that.

I go up on deck to find Keith. "Have you had much to drink?"

"Just this. Still on my first tinnie."

"Great. Can you give me a lift to Aigues-Mortes?"

"Right away?"

I nod.

He nods too. "No trouble mate."

Arnaud shouts after us: "What do you hope to find? They'll never release the autopsy information to a small-time detective from Ireland."

"Arnaud, would you ever feck off? I may be small-time but that's my business. Being nosey, I mean. C'mon Keith."

In the dusky distance, Aigues-Mortes sits in a flat wasteland of sand and monotonous marsh. A fortress within symmetrical, crenellated walls, the old town's streets laid out in geometrical grids.

By the thirteenth century it was a major port. Semi-religious nutters set sail from it to conquer Jerusalem and slaughter infidels. Later it became a watery version of a major motorway junction: a crossroads of canals, *étangs* and Mediterranean inlets.

As we approach a bridge on the outskirts there's a feeling of déjà vu, as a pair of motorcycle cops drive up behind us and flag us down. Keith stops his bike, I step off. The cops take out their weapons. Black truncheons dangle from their belts. I stand there, hands outstretched. Getting shot isn't on my to-do list tonight.

A car pulls up. From a back door. man in a suit gets out. Not the dark blue Renault again, but it's that same stocky guy who was tailing us before.

"Where do you think you're going?" The accent is Irish, Cork or Kerry. He's more stocky too, now that he's standing in my face. Keep calm, don't provoke them.

"Sorry?" I ask. "And you are?"

His ID says: *Aonad Speisialta Bleachtaireachta.* Special Detective Unit, *An Garda Síochána.* Detective Superintendent Sean Coleman.

Special Branch?

I tilt my head to do the humble-and-polite routine. "What seems to be the problem, Guard? My friend and I are just sightseeing."

"At this time of night, Mr Reid?" Shit. He knows my name too. "Looking for bodies in canals is not what I'd call sightseeing."

"What makes you think we're looking for a body?"

"I don't think, Mr Reid. I know. That's my business. We know everything about you. When you arrived here, what kind of laptop you use, where you live, where you work, your passport number, PPS number, how much tax you paid last year and who's your accountant. We know your IP address when you booked your ferry tickets, the credit card number you used at the garage outside Toulouse, even how many litres you bought that day."

He might as well be saying: *we can track you in ways the Stasi and KGB could only dream of.*

"And you've a smell of drink off you," he continues.

"Now on your bike." He points back the way we came. "Go, before they throw the book at you under some obscure Napoleonic law. Feck off back to Ireland before they bang you up in the Bastille. And you can tell your old Hell's Angel pal to fuck off back to Australia too."

"But he's not from … "

Keith grabs me and makes me climb back on the bike. He revs up and kicks the bike forward off its side stand.

Twenty-Two

Coleman stood at the side of the road, watching the light of the motorbike fade into the distance.

As the French police drove him back to his hotel he had a strong temptation to nod off in the back seat. It had been a very long day.

"Monsieur Coleman? Sean?" Giradot's words drifted in from the front seat. "Do you wish to see the body?"

By rights he should go. It was, after all, an Irish tourist, an Irish citizen. The French would expect him to go. Dublin would probably want him there too.

Should he make excuses? Hint that he was squeamish?

"Monsieur Coleman?"

"I can't see her tonight," he said. "Tomorrow perhaps."

Squeamish? And him a senior officer? Don't be daft. Dead flesh and blood ran in his family.

Coleman's dad had been a butcher, and what a butcher did wasn't that far removed from an autopsy.

You'd need to know about decomposition and rigor mortis for a start. How the muscles clench in the stiffness of death, so the meat would be far too tough to cook like that. His dad would know the exact point at which rigor set in. Anyone who grew up above a beef and lamb butchers' shop would. At least the approximate times. Say an hour for lamb, pork or chicken. Two and a half to three hours for a side of beef. About the same for a human corpse.

When the muscle fibres ran out of energy their control mechanisms failed. This would trigger a contracting movement of the protein filaments, locking them in place. So his dad and uncle Padraig would hang the carcasses out the back, in such a way that the muscles were stretched by gravity, until the protein-digesting enzymes within the fibres began to eat away at the structure.

His dad and uncle Padraig, when they were both still alive. Wiping their hands on their aprons, joking with the kids, gossiping with the customers, patiently explaining how long the meat was aged, the marbling and fat, the muscles most used, the difference between red and white meat, how the more active muscles had a higher concentration of what Sean Coleman now knew to be myoglobin. The times and temperatures for maximum juiciness, the proportion of fat and connective tissue in a particular cut. All their waste-not-want-not tricks for the offal and less popular cuts. And all those things you could do with all that blood.

No, Sean Coleman would never describe himself as squeamish.

He knew dead meat was just trying to tell a story.

He knew that bodies talk and he was paid to listen. Listening to the body language of the living and the dead.

Even so, there was always something about a corpse on an autopsy table. A naked woman's corpse that is.

He'd never forget his first one. The murder inquiry down in Cork.

The Prof arrived – this would have been years before he retired – and was handed an apron and a set of notes to read. For a minute or two the Prof was wrapped up in these notes, hardly noticing the body behind him, already naked on the table. Hardly noticing the young detective from Kerry either.

The next part, the butchery part if you like, was easy enough to handle. The Prof made a neat "Y" incision from the shoulders to the pubic bone, peeling back the skin to take the organs out, one by one. Weighing, slicing, looking for signs of injury or disease.

All done with such a matter-of-factness that you'd half expect the Prof to parcel everything up in greaseproof paper and a *Colemans the Butchers* bag, hand it across the autopsy table to a happy housewife and lean over to the till for change.

No, Sean Coleman wasn't squeamish. It was all very clinical, as they say. No need to keep reminding himself how a corpse wasn't a person any more, just a collection of evidence. Even the weirder stuff didn't faze him, the signs of violence, the morgue humour, the daft rumour of how a body's decay rate changes if the deceased has eaten too many hot dogs. All those preservatives you see.

Most of the time you wouldn't be there at the slab anyway. You'd be at one remove, back at the office among the reports and photographs.

After all these years Coleman still didn't know half the medical terms, the maths or physics involved, the equations and footnotes and references to lab experiments where someone somewhere had already worked it all out, ages ago, down to the last gram, degree or minute.

But in a way he did know too.

He was still wet behind the ears when the Prof's assistant told him about one particular experiment that ended up in the footnotes. The one with the corpses. Not human ones of course but dead pigs.

Pigmeat. So like human flesh, so perfect to show the effects of drowning and being submerged in water for X amount of time.

This particular experiment involved dumping the awkward carcasses of three whole pigs into three separate tanks – fresh water, chlorinated water, brine – to compare the decay rates in three different scenarios: canal or lake, swimming pool, sea. A fourth pig was the "control group", the one left out in the wind and the rain.

White coats could blind you with science, with all their talk of ambient temperatures and fat distribution, larva activity, stomach contents. But the physics of a body in a canal wasn't that complicated. The body of a human – or a pig – has roughly the same density as water. Bacteria consume its flesh at a particular rate. When the lungs deflate the body becomes denser. It sinks, but much faster in fresh water than salt water, which has a higher density. Even a young Sean Coleman could grasp that.

As for the biology, it was basically about seeing the dead body as a complex, interlocking ecosystem. The bacteria produce gases. These in turn make a body in, say, a river or canal rise like a balloon. A lake, though, would be a different kettle of fish. A cold lake or deep *étang* might act like a fridge, slowing down bacteria growth or stopping it altogether. In such cases the corpse doesn't decompose, gases won't form, the body stays submerged.

But this particular body didn't, did it? It bloody well had to turn up again, in Aigues-Mortes of all places.

No, he decided, their reports could wait.

Yet that wasn't what he wanted to avoid, was it? An autopsy, the clinical butchery of a human body?

No. It was the moment just before, when you first saw the corpse, out of its body bag and already stripped by the technicians and laid out on the table.

A woman's body, still largely intact. And completely naked, like that woman on the slab the first time in Cork.

In the Catholic Ireland of the early Eighties he was not long out of garda college; porn was banned, lapdancing clubs didn't exist, the graphic muck on the Internet still a decade away or more. Seeing a woman's naked flesh in a public place was a rare thing, unless you counted the paintings in the National Gallery. Even his first girlfriend would undress in the dark.

So that must be what disturbed him all those years ago.

Something he would never talk about, not to colleagues or even his wife. Something far more unspeakable and embarrassing than mere squeamishness. It was about seeing a strange woman – albeit a dead one, a cold and lifeless one – completely naked and completely still.

It was like ... it felt ... it made him feel ... *transgressive.*

Yes, that was the word.

"On second thoughts, Monsieur Giradot," he said at last, "I think I'll give it a miss tomorrow."

"At least you will stay to read the report?"

"Sorry, I'm stuck for time. Send it on to me in Dublin."

The car turned the corner to the street of his hotel.

If the French were anything like the Irish, it would take at least a week for the tox report to come back. No, Coleman told himself. He had far better things to do.

Besides, the files were bad enough in English. They would be in French, bogging you down in detail and measurements when all you wanted was a simple "who", "when" and "how". A main conclusion, those two or three final sentences about how the person was shot, drowned, strangled or whatever. When and how she met her end. And maybe even who had helped her meet it.

After he told Giradot he needed to stretch his legs, they dropped him forty yards from the hotel. He walked back along the jetty to look down at the waters one last time.

There was a time when the Mediterranean was more than a glorified paddling pool for German tourists. It was a cradle of civilization, it fashioned language, art, trade and alphabets. But he'd be glad to see the back of it.

The lads back home didn't know the half of it. *The Super's back! How was the sun, sea and expenses? You jammy bollix. Was the weather good? Hey guys – he's back! You must have been on the pig's back.*

Under the glossy surface of the tourist brochures, the Med was not all idyllic canals and long sandy beaches, endless holidays with miles of naked flesh soaking up the sun. It was a rotting sewer of dead meat.

Twenty-Three

Nobody is talking much. Not even when Yann drives us to Monsieur Henri's garage to hitch up Tintin. Not even after we hit the long road home.

Colley is pissed off that we shot down his plan to follow the Tour into the Pyrenees. Arnaud is still convinced we're being followed. And me? I'm knackered from the driving, and glad to be back in Roscoff.

On the ferry crossing I go up on deck for a breather. The waters are choppy, the dull skies hint at an approaching storm. The Irish coast is due to appear any time soon.

So what is an Irish cop – and not any old cop but a senior man from Special Branch – doing in the south of France on a missing person case – or quite possibly a suicide, abduction, rape and murder case – involving an Irish tourist? More importantly, why was he looking into me?

Arnaud has crept up behind me. "A penny for them?"

"Ah nothing," I reply. "Just something Keith said on the bike ride back."

Said, or rather shouted into the wind. *You couldn't make it up,* Keith said. *Aigues-Mortes means dead water in Occitan.*

The coastline appears. Cork, Spike Island, Cobh. After the ship docks at Ringaskiddy we're down the ramp and about to take the road to Douglas and the motorway to Dublin when a uniform in fluorescent yellow vest pulls us over.

"Oh shit, customs." I automatically reach for my own high-vis jacket. "We're all under the limit aren't we?"

In the back seat Colley peers through the rear window at Tintin. It has been recently packed to the rafters with food and drink.

"All for personal consumption, Reidy. They can't prove otherwise so they can just feck off."

The three customs officers couldn't care less about our Tetris walls of wine boxes. They spend hours taking Tintin apart, as if they were looking for ten kilos of cocaine. Or at least their sniffer dog is. It takes even more time to put everything back together again. By the time I get home to Stoneybatter the evening news is already half way through the *And in other news* ... bit.

Flop on the couch with a glass of wine from one of the bag-in-boxes. The red is not bad, not bad at all.

A minor news item near the end is about an Irish tourist who has drowned in the south of France. Further investigations, post mortem and so on. Her name isn't being released until her family are contacted.

It hardly matters. We all know who she is already.

Twenty-Four

The next day is a scruffy wet Dublin morning, the kind that wants to mitch off school at lunchtime to tear off its school tie, jump in puddles and make mud pies.

I pull into the drive of a detached house in Clonskeagh, on an affluent southside patch of the city. The house isn't much: slightly smaller than Áras an Uachtarain, with only a double garage. So this is how the other five per cent live.

It's pissing down as I dash to the porch, ring the bell, glare at the CCTV camera.

A twentysomething answers my bing-bong. She's in a light green top and blue jeans, unnaturally blonde with a hint of her mother's genes. Must be Orla Kettle, Áine's eldest.

"Before I see her, can I ask you something about your father?"

She nods.

"How tall was he?" I have his passport details, but passports don't give height and weight any more.

"Is."

"Sorry?"

"Is he. He's not dead you know."

"How tall *is* he then?"

"Around my height." So, say around five six. "Though I thought he was starting to shrink. Or maybe grown ups do that as you get older. They seem smaller. Know what I mean?"

"And his weight?"

"What about it? D'you need numbers?"

"How would you describe him? Thin? Heavy?"

"A lost cause. Too much butter and bad stuff."

"What about his accent?"

"What about it? Dublin I guess."

"What kind of Dublin?"

As in more the Ross O'Carroll Kelly type, or more the

"real Dub, story bud" kind of accent.

"Ordinary. Just ordinary."

What's ordinary to her? Put it down as middle-class Dublin then. Like her accent, minus the creeping Americanisations of her generation.

"You really think he's still alive?" I ask.

"I just know it." Yeah right. And I read palms in Fossett's Circus. "What's your name again?"

"Moss Reid."

"Stupid cow has only got herself to blame."

"Your aunt?"

"No, Mum. They were always arguing. He was always saying he was going to leave her, so that's what he must have done."

She escorts me into one of the living rooms. Leather and upholstered furniture is arranged around a HDTV. It's slightly smaller than the scoreboard in the Aviva Stadium. Áine Kettle gets up off a couch.

"Mr Reid. Good of you to come."

A tall man rises more slowly from his armchair. He is mid- or late-forties, expensive clothes, nice brogues.

"This is Jarlath," she continues. "Jarlath McElhinney, Niamh's ex. They were married for … three years wasn't it?"

He nods. "We were talking about the funeral arrangements. Or trying to."

Have I interrupted the grieving ex and grieving widow? Strictly speaking not legally a widow, though, and not in black this morning but a sleeveless white top, cream slacks, brown shoes. Looks like she has recently had her hair done.

Some people might call Mrs Kettle attractive; I find it hard to tell, what with all the botox and peroxide and cosmetic debris orbiting around her. Yet as the song says, there are some things you can't cover up with lipstick and powder. Or distracting jewellery and all the exercise balls from all the gyms in the world. Or maybe you can. Maybe that's why older women really do look far younger than my Nana's generation. The ones who can afford to.

I try to find something to say that's not a cliché, not one of those *We share in your suffering* bullshit expressions a funeral director would give a customer. All I can come up with is a lame *Sorry for your troubles.*

Jarlath McElhinney has sat back in his armchair. Mrs Kettle gestures for me to join her on the couch. No sooner have I sat down than she makes to get up again. "Can I get you a drink?"

A red and a white wine are already on the coffee table, both nearly drained.

"No thanks. A bit early for me and I'm driving." I sink into the couch. "I hate to ask, Mrs Kettle, but are they absolutely sure it's her?"

"Yes. It's Niamh alright. Isn't it?"

Jarlath McElhinney nods. "The divers found her passport in the canal, and she fits the description and … Sorry. I've just flown in from New York, so apologies if I fall asleep in mid-sentence."

"I'll try to be quick. When did you last see her?"

He exchanges glances with Mrs Kettle. "A couple of years ago?"

"That would be about right," she says.

What's the body language between these two? Informal. What else would it be? Reserved? Antagonistic? This is simply a woman and her sister's ex preparing for a wake – a real one, with a real body.

"And your divorce," I ask him, "if you don't mind me asking. Was it … ?"

"Civilized. We simply drifted apart, as people do. She said let's not waste a fortune on the legal eagles, so we kept it short and simple. We sold the house, split the proceeds and that was that."

"But you kept in touch?"

"Sure. An occasional email or phone call. The last was

maybe three or four months ago."

"Can we talk about the days leading up to her death? I'm trying to build a picture of what she was doing."

"Like I said, we hadn't seen each other in years. I've been in the States."

And I'm running out of questions. What motive could a man have to kill his ex when they're happily divorced, they've already divvied out the proceeds and he has a damn good alibi on the other side of the planet?

Plod on anyway. "Did she have any enemies?"

"Absolutely not. Even if she did she probably wouldn't know it."

"What do you mean?"

"He means," Áine Kettle says, "half the time she probably wouldn't even recognise them."

I don't get. "But your sister said she'd seen someone in the restaurant in Mentidera. Someone whose face rang a bell. Someone she thought she definitely knew."

Jarlath McElhinney looks at me as if I've just called him grandma. "You can't be serious."

"What do you mean?" I ask.

He turns to Áine Kettle. "You haven't told him, have you?" More a statement than a question. He looks back at me. "Niamh ... had this condition."

"That's an understatement," she says. The understatement word gets slightly slurred by a hiccup.

"Some people have a problem with faces," he continues, "and Niamh was a severe case. Sometimes she wouldn't even recognise me. Her own husband."

A pause. I don't interrupt.

"I knew what I was letting myself in for. When we did the weekly shop she'd make me wear this horrible red old thing. She called it my supermarket jacket."

"That puffy jacket yoke?" Áine Kettle says.

He nods. "Made me wear it come rain or shine, so I'd be easy to spot in a shopping aisle."

"*And* your brogues," she reminds him.

"Yeah. Always brown brogues. Never trainers or anything else if I could help it."

I still don't get. "Are you saying she'd find it hard to recognise Mrs Kettle's husband?"

"Possibly. It's hard to say," he replies. "Like Áine says, he may have had plastic surgery."

Damn. Áine Kettle must have already filled him in on all the details of her final phone call. I know they say it's good to talk, but each time she tells that story she's polluting her memories, adding a few minor elaborations here and there as various details begin to leak away.

"OK. What can you tell me about Johnny Kettle's friends?" I ask him. "The ones who went missing in the plane."

"I never really knew them. Niamh would have met them dozens of times – *and* their wives, Olivia and what's the other one?"

Áine Kettle reminds him: "Trisha. Olivia Reilly and Patricia McGann. Absolutely. Niamh was a great socialiser, despite her condition."

I notice his shoes. Black rather than brown brogues this morning. "And you never met the husbands?"

"Maybe. Did I?" He turns to her for a clue.

"Don't ask me. Hold on." She goes to the next room and rummages in a bureau for something.

"How did they get on," I ask him while she's away, "I mean Niamh and Mrs Kettle's husband?"

"Like a house not on fire, if you know what I mean. Badly."

She comes back with a shoebox and photo albums. Family snaps of a chubby husband. Clippings of presentations and photo ops. Johnny Kettle's mugshot in a dark pinstripe suit in the business pages and in the bank's staff magazine.

"That bloody suit," she says, rustling through the pictures and handing one to Jarlath. "That's them. Kevin and Terry, the three musketeers.

He shakes his head before passing the pic to me. "Can't say they ring a bell."

Out with the reading glasses. I've not seen this particular picture before. The gang of three are in sweatshirts or rugby jerseys, unshaven, tanned, a world away from business suits.

She tries to jog his memory. "The one on the left, that's Kevin Reilly, Olivia's husband. The other one is Terry, Trisha's."

"No, sorry," he says. "I can't place them."

A doorbell rings.

He gets up. "My taxi. If you don't mind I really need to head back to the hotel and get some shut-eye."

We shake hands and exchange business cards.

While Mrs Kettle shows Jarlath out I browse through the envelopes and photograph albums. More pictures of Johnny Kettle. Stuff on holidays, stuff with the kids, stuff with his mates, stuff with pints, stuff with dead fish.

One photo keeps dragging me back: it's of the three amigos in mufti, arm in arm, like a scrum's front row with Johnny Kettle as the hooker.

Johnny, Kev and Tel. Inseparable buddies. In the background is a yacht. Don't ask what kind. I wouldn't know the difference between a sloop and a ketch, a mizzenmast and a spinnaker.

Mrs Kettle returns with a fresh bottle of white wine. "He's still in shock. We all are." She wiggles the bottle. "Sure I can't tempt you?"

I decline.

She opens the screwtop, refills her glass. "It's all so bloody vague. The French say it's an ongoing investigation, and can't say when they'll release the body. Which is why we can't make arrangements … "

Investigations. Arrangements. Nice, clean, businesslike words. Not like autopsies, DNA swabs, dental X-rays.

"They told you nothing more about how she died?"

"A possible drowning. But they mentioned suicide."

"She left a note?"

"Of course not. Niamh wasn't the suicidal type. They said the initial toxicology tests point to a drugs overdose so they can't rule out suicide just yet. Before you ask, Niamh was always dead set against drugs. Not unless you count a bit of this." She waves her glass, nearly spilling the wine. "So. Who knows?"

She reaches for a box of tissues and blows her nose. I half expect the waterworks.

Silence falls. Seconds pass. She does begin to cry. Quietly, no melodrama. Sometimes, no matter how cool you think you are, the memories sneak out of your eyes and roll down your cheeks while your back is turned.

What can you tell her? That things will get better, when everyone knows they won't? That murder investigations would be far easier if only the dying victim could leave a decent clue about who killed her?

She settles down again. I give her a summary of everything we found out in the Languedoc after her return to Ireland.

"At the time of his disappearance did your husband have any problems?"

"No more than the next man. If the boom had carried on we'd have been laughing."

"But it didn't, did it. He never mentioned any money worries?"

"Not that I can remember, and I've an excellent memory Mr Reid. You know the last thing he said to me, his very last words? Not 'I love you' or money worries or 'Should we get the box set of *Father Ted*?' It was 'Don't forget to pick up the dry cleaning'."

"Would you happen to have his passport?"

"Hold on."

She goes off to that bureau again. Maybe it's like our old family desk. Our mum and dad would horde everything from old bills and bank statements to passports

– both current and old ones, because there was a time when they'd return your old cancelled passport with your new one. Passports were common enough in Ireland back then – unlike, say, the States, where they say most people don't have one. They were common because each successive generation would emigrate en masse.

"Here you go." She hands me a passport still valid for another three years.

Why and how would Johnny Kettle go abroad without his passport?

Pick up the photograph of the gang of three again. Check for scribbles on the back. Nothing.

"Where was this picture taken?"

"I can't remember."

Other snapshots show the three anglers holding up their spoils of the sea: little cartoon-like red gurnard; larger pollock; mullet; striped mackerel; conger eel; a shark. It's not exactly *Jaws* but in Kevin Reilly's awkward embrace the presumably dead shark is still nearly six feet long. They are like a pair of tired drunken dancers.

None of the photos has a date or location on the back.

"Hold on." She digs around in the shoebox. "There was a film somewhere. Here."

A DVD case with a blank cover, no label or writing. Inside is a shiny disk, with green felt-tip scribble: *Kinsale, Aug 2007*.

"Mind if we watch this?"

She points to a DVD player under the widescreen TV.

"It won't upset you?" I ask.

"No."

Hit play. It's the three men again, larking about beside the same yacht, on a quayside or marina with other boats in the background. Shots out to sea, mucking around with dead fish, fat cigars, a champagne bottle. Snatches of conversation. Johnny Kettle's accent is middle-class Dublin alright.

Three men, at least one murder, and everything has a

reason, a purpose. Even if you can't see it at the time.

"They did a lot of sailing together?"

"They did everything together."

"Whose is the boat?" I try to make out its name. "The *Mona B* … "

"The *Nora Barnacle*. A yacht not a boat. It's Kevin Reilly's. He loved that thing."

They say money can't buy you happiness but it can buy you a big fuck-off yacht to help you spend a lot of time trying to find happiness.

"Where is it now?"

"Stolen, slipped its moorings, God knows where. He used to keep it in Kinsale. They noticed it wasn't in the marina about a month after the plane went missing."

"Did the guards investigate?"

"They said they did but they said they did a lot of things at the time. It was all very vague. I asked for a written report – you need one for the life insurance and pension, you know? But they said the papers went missing. So I lodged a complaint about the officer in charge."

"What happened?"

"The complaint went missing too."

"You wouldn't happen to remember the officer's name? It wasn't Coleman by any chance?"

"No. He was a Mac Something."

"Look, I've given you everything I know from France. What exactly do you want me to do, Mrs Kettle?"

"Get him. Get my husband. Find the fucker, whatever it takes. He killed my sister and I'm gonna kill him. Not literally but … "

I bring up the touchy subject of money: fifty an hour, cash preferably, no discounts (not even for grieving widows or grieving sisters).

She doesn't flinch. Goes upstairs, comes back down with a serious handbag, out of which comes a large envelope. A big bundle of fifties.

"He always had a bit of spare cash lying around the

house," she says. "Rainy day money. And it's a rainy day now, isn't it?"

A banker who doesn't trust banks, and prefers cash under the mattress?

"There's one thing I have to warn you, Mrs Kettle."

"Yes?"

"For some reason I'm persona non grata in France at the moment. I can only do things from here."

"But you will take it on?"

"Absolutely. You'll have my undivided attention."

Because at every stage in France we've been hampered, fobbed off, misled, terrorised. In the restaurant, train station and cop shop. On the canal, on the road to Aigues-Mortes. Because this time it's personal.

"Before I go can I have a quick word with your daughter?"

"Orla? She's already gone to town for a party."

Orla Kettle, a fully paid up member not Generation X or Generation Y but Generation TBA. To Be Announced. The generation that still hasn't quite figured out what it wants to be yet, and in the meantime it's going to *parrrrty*.

I'm about to give out yards about the insensitivity of the girl when Mrs Kettle explains that it's a wake of sorts. One of those going away dos that kids in their twenties have grown used to. Another couple of Orla's friends are about to try their luck abroad.

Because they are GFE. Generation For Export.

Twenty-Five

Yeah yeah, I know there's Google and all kinds of online databases nowadays, but much of the material I'm looking for is a good half a decade old. Half of it is offline, another half behind firewalls and I'm not made of money. Hence I'm camped in the National Library in Kildare Street.

Where to start? With the ghost flight, the crash that never was.

Dublin, November 12 (Reuters) – A search was under way last night after a light aircraft carrying three leading Irish businessmen disappeared off the west coast of …

So hubbie and two best mates fly off in a light aircraft six years ago, leaving three widows up shit creek without a pension. No inquests, no inquiry, no closure.

The newspapers say there was no distress message.

That if there was an incident several miles up, the winds at that altitude would be, well, many knots. I don't do knots. I prefer good old mph.

The reports say that at that altitude and at those wind speeds, fragments of a small plane would be thrown to the winds; they could end up anywhere. Heavier pieces – engines, landing gear – would plummet straight down. Aerodynamic sections – wings, tail – would be buffeted about by the wind like a paper bag. Aviation fuel, instead of leaving a neat oil slick directly below, would be scattered too. The debris field would spread over several miles, in a huge ocean. Nigh on impossible for air sea rescue to spot anything in the water unless they were directly over of it. A needle in a haystack on the far side of the moon.

But how can two tons of metal and fuel simply vanish in thin air? We live in an age when the pre-teens of rich nations have GPS in their pockets, US agencies can track anyone anywhere, spy satellites can spot an aircraft explosion, and search engines can find your classmates from three decades ago in five minutes.

Commercial aircraft have an emergency locator beacon. The crew can trigger it in an instant. Or it self-activates under certain circumstances, such as hitting water. The Beech Duchess didn't have such a beacon.

Then there was the transponder. Even I've heard of transponders. They are used for communicating with air traffic control as you fly near an airport. Some articles say the plane had one. Others – some in the same edition of the same newspaper – are adamant that it didn't. Or that it could have been switched to standby or disabled.

Why would anyone disable a transponder? Wouldn't it be on all the time? Not so, another aviation expert is wheeled on to explain. Pilots might switch it off when the plane is parked, to avoid interfering with airborne aircraft.

Yet another expert says the transponder issue is a red herring. The aircraft disappeared over the sea, well out of range of the ground radar the transponder uses to communicate.

Later stories are peppered with "search parties", "hopes fade", "lack of closure" and more psychobabble "Ambiguous loss": that's where the relatives are left in the dark about whether the loved one is dead or alive.

In all that browsing you inevitably soak up the other main stories of the day. Car crashes, bad storms, the banking crisis in full swing. Belfast riots, celebs getting engaged, well-known high-street businesses closing down, a nationwide pork recall due to a dioxin scare.

Unconnected events and themes in a country awash with property crashes, drug raids and shootings. Angry pensioners and students marching on the Dáil. The MoD seals off a large field in Fermanagh after a suspicious object is found. In a case of mistaken identity a rugby player is shot dead outside his home. Gardai seize a huge haul of heroin and – "in a related incident" – the subsequent arrest of one Gino Beattie.

Gino Beattie. There's no escaping him. The ex-paramilitary who financed his private army with drugs money and extortion rackets.

Another thirty kilos of heroin with an estimated street value of €4.5 million are recovered in west Dublin. Martin Kane, Gino's bagman, is found dead in a prison cell. More drug busts, property scams and zombie banks. A tabloid says Gino has gone vegetarian. He'll only eat salad and non-processed food in case his meals are laced with poison. That's how paranoid Gino has become.

There is a major search of Donegal Bay after a red flare is spotted out to sea. But it's a couple of weeks before the plane's disappearance, and the search is stood down when the distress flare turns out to be an early Halloween fireworks party.

That was autumn 2008 for you: newspapers brimming with fireworks and crime stories, celebs and scandals, economic warnings and emergency meetings, all signs that a nation had developed "notions". Notions that would become its downfall.

And I'm getting nowhere.

Frank Ferriter is a hack you can trust. I give him a call. Does he know anything about the story?

"The Galway Three? You bet. I was on the newsdesk that day. Coffee in my sub-office in half an hour?"

His sub-office is the bar of the Black Piglet.

"If Twitter had been big back then," he says in the pub forty minutes later, "imagine all the smartarses comparing the ghost flight to *Lost.*"

Twitter would have been full of joky one-liners, merging a supernatural drama about fictional characters trapped on a mysterious island with three real-life missing people in a lost little aircraft. I think Frank hates Twitter.

Although Twitter was still a baby at the time, the rumour machines of the fourth estate cranked out their expert evaluations and speculations for several days after. Frank gives me a good summary of it all.

That there must have been a fire on board.

Or engine failure due to low oil pressure.

Or pilot fatigue could have been a factor.

Or that said fatigue would have played a part in a miscalculation regarding fuel management or a series of events following a possible engine power loss.

Or that experienced multiple bird strikes, although less likely so far out to sea.

Or that the pilot, Terry McGann, could have had a heart attack. Even that he was suicidal. Or that it was a suicide pact between the three men.

Or a hijacking, an act of terrorism. Stranger things have happened.

And that the aircraft would have remained largely intact after hitting the water but would have sunk eventually. Or that search and rescue were looking in the wrong places.

There was even speculation about their mobile phones. On whether you could still use one at such and such an altitude and distance from a cell tower, and the scientific experiments conducted along these lines after 9/11.

Six years later, what was left? No wreckage, no bodies, no inquest or coroner's verdict. Just a few faded clippings, scratchy microfiche films and Frank's own memories about "three tragic deaths".

That's the one thing the speculators and commentators could all agree on: that it was tragic. Tragic and mysterious.

Like I said, I'm no aviation expert. The black box and transponder stuff has got me nowhere. Same with all that empty speculation and contradictory evidence. The media could have been chasing sci-fi aliens and UFOs instead of hard facts.

It reminded me of how TV detective shows always seem to begin at the wrong place: the murder. The murder is never the start of it. The end of it more like.

Yet you have to start somewhere. So start again, this time at the middle. Work backwards if needs be, backtracking to more solid ground: the "Final Hours

Before Tragic Flight" angle.

I order refills of our coffees. Frank continues to fill me in on what he knows.

"The twenty-four hours before seem normal enough," he says. "Nothing out of the ordinary, so everyone kept saying."

"So start with the banker, Johnny Kettle," I say.

"The day before the flight he has a long meeting with clients of their asset management division about a property investment in Budapest. Nothing untoward apparently. After work he meets the wife in town and pays for a meal by credit card."

It's the day before the three businessmen disappear off the face of the earth. At least they make the hacks' jobs easier by leaving a credit-card trail in their wake.

The next morning, Johnny Kettle takes a taxi from his Clonskeagh home to Weston Airport outside Leixlip. Presumably paid in cash, presumably cost an arm and several legs.

Next: Kevin Reilly, the lawyer. The day before the flight he too is with clients all morning. Spends the afternoon researching an upcoming case. Gets a call at the office from his ex-wife Olivia, to clear up some final minor details in what everybody agrees was "an amicable divorce". His credit card transactions that evening include groceries bought at a convenience store near his home. He orders a Woodie Allen box-set from Amazon at 8:46 pm. Nothing else until late the following afternoon when his car is discovered in the airport car park. So he must have driven there the morning of the flight.

Finally: the dot com entrepreneur, Terry McGann. He spends the morning in conference calls with three separate sets of investors. His car, too, is located in the airport car park the following evening.

"But here's where it gets interesting," Frank continues. "At first we all thought Terry McGann left his office around six the night before, and went home to the wife with a bottle of Châteauneuf-du-Pape. Then there was this."

It's a clipping from a tabloid, from two weeks later, which I must have missed in the library: "EXCLUSIVE! LOVE RAT NIGHT BEFORE FATAL FLIGHT".

The night before, Terry wasn't at home in Dublin after all. He drove down to Waterford for supper with one Mary Buckley – why didn't Áine Kettle mention any of this? He must have declined the Châteauneuf because he would be driving back to Dublin early the next morning and couldn't risk flying while over the limit. How did the tabloids know all this? Ms Buckley "refused to comment", the story went on, and "She is believed to be staying with relatives."

That could mean anything, Frank says. Even that the paper never actually talked to her.

The double-page spread shows separate photos of Terry McGann, Mary Buckley ("his mistress"), and a semi-detached house ("their Waterford love nest"). It also has quotes from neighbours and from her local wine shop where McGann's credit card had bought said Châteauneuf-du-Pape.

"That would have been how they tracked her down," Frank says. "His credit card."

In my line of work you come across a mistress or two. Always made out to be a sad creature, the outsider, a parasite, the homewrecker, a shallow sexual fantasy made flesh. As if the Other Woman is the only guilty party, as if she was ensnaring him, and it wasn't the husband who was shagging around.

But in my job you're not paid to judge others. The mistress usually remains just a name, a blurry face, a piece of info that you may or may not pass on to the client. Or am I kidding myself?

Anyway. That's what the Galway Three did the twenty-four hours before, and it's beginning to sound like a bad joke: *Three men walk into a bar – a family man, an amicable divorcé and a love rat …*

We've had too much coffee so we switch to pints of stout and move on to the next morning.

They fly from Weston to Galway Airport at Carnmore. Taxi into town to dine in the Park House Restaurant on Forster Street. "A bit of an institution", Frank says, "popular with business types and attached to a four-star hotel."

They have three courses from the menu of "classical French cuisine with modern Irish influences" and a €50 bottle of Domaine Charbonniere. We know all this because Johnny Kettle paid for everything, again by credit card. A waiter later recalls that only two were on the wine; McGann the pilot would have stuck to the sparkling water.

In Eyre Square they are seen grabbing a cab outside the Hotel Meyrick. The taxi driver isn't interviewed or mentioned again, though someone from the airport staff recalls a cab driving up shortly after lunchtime.

Several news stories have a library shot of the airport's khaki green terminal, where Johnny Kettle pays the €20 landing fee, again by credit card. Cards that are never used again. After that they take off and fly west.

So that was their day, and that was mine: frittered away on desk research and Frank's background info, and on too much bad coffee and too many other news stories that wheedled their way into my brain. All that sex, drugs and celebs I've never heard of.

After leaving Frank I make one last call to Olivia Reilly and Patricia McGann to set up interviews. Neither is answering so I call it a day.

Text Arnaud: *"Fancy a pint?"*

Twenty-Six

"You've been to the barbers." That's an understatement. Arnaud is no longer the Byronic man. His long grey-and-black locks are seriously shorter.

Some men do that when they hit a certain age. Not to look more "respectable", just that time has caught up with them. You're greyer, thinner on top, can't quite carry it off with the old swagger and panache any more. Or maybe a big mop of hair is becoming a pain in the kitchen. Maybe Arnaud can't stand the heat. He's not twenty or even thirtysomething any more.

I'm filling him in on the Johnny Kettle case, but trying not to shout it to the world either.

We're at the counter of the Dice Bar on Benburb Street. It's not your typical Irish pub, more a dive bar, the kind you could hoist up and set down comfortably in New Jersey or Kreuzberg in Berlin. Think dark and loud, fun and serious, grunge and grot. Low ceilings, black paintwork, red lighting, dripping candles. The "distressed" seating is patched up with black tape, which is "cool". If this joint were any cooler it'd be in the freezer cabinet.

It's busy tonight. Tonight's clientele are as eclectic as ever, including us two old fogies.

"I still don't get why all three of them would want to disappear," Arnaud says, brushing back the remains of his fringe. "All at the same time, without the wife and kids."

"I know. The banker has two kids. The lawyer guy, Kevin Reilly, has none. *And* he was as good as divorced – 'very amicably', everyone keeps reminding me. His ex would hardly need to knock him off and he has no need to escape her."

Arnaud nods. "And Terry McGann had no kids."

"Yeah. But he had a mistress."

"He never!"

"Tucked away in Waterford. God knows where she

ended up."

"But if she's still with him, and if … "

"Too many ifs," I say. "What if three leading businessmen all gain something from doing runner. What if they dump their wives and families, what if all three are now waltzing around the south of France with their mistresses and young women half their age. It's far too many ifs."

We both take a swig of beer.

"What are the odds of all that, Arnaud, without their wives – or their passports?"

In the States they say you're eight times more likely to be killed by a cop than by a terrorist. Eleven thousand times more likely to die in a routine air accident than a terrorist plot to down an airliner. And ten times more likely to die from a pink poodle jumping out of a twelfth-storey window and landing on your head than in a terrorist attack.

So what do we do? Lock up the poodles in Guantanamo Bay? Besides, we don't have many twelve-storey buildings in Dublin. Or that many pink poodles either.

"The trouble with this case is that there are too many what-ifs and improbables and poodle talk," I continue.

"Poodle talk?"

"Look at the main ingredients in this case. Put yourself in their shoes. It's six years ago, the banks are beginning to unravel, you're a banker, a highly successful one yet you want to do a runner. What's the first thing you'd do?"

Arnaud scratches his head. "Squirrel away my assets."

"Exactly. Put them in the wife's name, in Zürich or the Caymans. Get her to do the asset stripping. But Johnny Kettle doesn't. Not unless you count a large wodge of cash under the mattress. His missus has no widow's pension, no income from her interior design business which went belly up ages ago, her daughter's shop is a disaster too, yet Mrs Kettle is seriously loaded."

"What about the other two wives?"

"I don't think the wives are the common denominator. It's the husbands. Has to be. They're lifelong friends from college, but what else do they have in common?"

Arnaud studies his pint. "A dark secret?"

"Sex? Money? Nine times in ten it boils down to one of the two."

"So follow the money."

We both sup away and think in silence in the noisy bar. Johnny Kettle is well-off, Dublin middle class. Kevin Reilly hails from Kerry, his family moved to Foxrock when he was fourteen. Again, well off. Terry McGann is from Enniskillen. Went to the same posh school as Neil Hannon and Samuel Beckett, though not at the same time of course. What do they have in common? The same well-off, well-monied middle-classness.

"No, I say eventually. "From their late teens they share everything. Same university, same holidays, share their boats and planes and wives for all I know. But I still don't buy the 'three men doing a runner at the same time' theory."

"You said the lawyer had a boat."

"Yeah. A dead fancy yoke."

"If I were doing a runner, I wouldn't bother with all the ghost flight rigmarole. I'd use my big bloody yacht."

"Good point. And here's something else, Arnaud. Our chubby banker isn't the tallest of the three. Yet all our witnesses in France make him out to be around six foot. Is he on stilts or what?"

"Maybe it's like Colley says." Arnaud puts on his joky voice: "Maybe he got a discount from the plastic surgeon to throw in some leg extensions."

"As if. There's still too many ifs and maybes."

The place is getting mighty crowded; nearly time for the DJ and the dancing. The "people ping pong" games are about to begin.

Arnaud gets up. "Fancy some proper music?"

"Why not."

We walk past the Market Café, a derelict one-storey building on the east side of Smithfield Square. If there's one certainty in life it's death. And if there's one certainty in retail and catering life it's a business death.

Around our way you notice those kind of things, as shops and restaurants come and go, change hands, get new tenants. Or don't get them, in the case of the Market Café.

Even a place like that, once lovable in its own little way, with its breakfast fries and builder's tea, and cheery Maureen behind the counter with the huge metal teapot. The boom came and went, construction ground to a halt, the cranes were taken down, the builders lost their jobs, and the city was frozen in amber. Places like the Market Café somehow avoided the Celtic Tiger's wrecking ball, yet were passed by, lost, left to rot like a beached whale. A greasy spoon in a world that doesn't do greasy spoons any more.

We reach our second bar. Arnaud grabs a table while I get in the pints.

The decor, dark furniture and dark wooden floors have all the charm and musty elegance of a quiet old country pub. But the Cobblestone isn't musty. Rarely quiet either. It's a well-defended bastion of Irish traditional music.

To the left of the main door, in a corner permanently devoted to them, a bunch of musicians are at full tilt. It's a "sesh". A session. A young guy is belting out a tune on a tin whistle, chased by two fiddle players and a bodhran. Notices on the benches behind them say "Reserved For MUSICIANS". On the walls, among the posters and photos of performers, is a sign saying "LISTENING AREA: PLEASE RESPECT MUSICIANS". Proper order too. High above them a large banner says "Cobblestone – temporary sign". I forget how long that slightly surreal sign has been here.

The music stops. Someone announces "Hardiman the

Fiddler". It's a slip jig, slower, more complicated, weaving in and out of itself like one of those ancient runes of strange animals chasing their own tails.

On the musicians' tables are the usual assortment of capos, tuners, plectrums, flutes and whistles in different keys, pint glasses and paraphernalia from a more modern age: car keys, beermats, mobiles, an iPad, a mug of tea.

A couple more lads arrive and unbuckle boxes. Out come a banjo and accordion. You can't beat a good box and a banjo. Everybody who is anybody has played the Cobblestone, including Ireland's greatest banjo player: the Beethoven of the Banjo, Banjo Barney from Donnycarney, the late Barney McKenna of The Dubliners.

When I last saw him in the Cobblestone, one of Barney's "Barneyisms" came when he played a mandolin duet with guitar accompaniment. As Barney prefaced it: "It's an Irish duet, so there's three of us going to play it."

The slip jig over, a flute breaks into a slow air. Probably about (a) a pretty young maid who proceeds to lose her true love after roving out one morning in May (always May, never March or April) or (b) Perfidious Albion.

Arnaud returns from the bar with two creamy pints of stout. After letting mine settle I take a sip.

"Trouble is, I don't know anyone who flies a plane and knows all that aeronautical palaver."

"Me neither," he replies. "About the nearest I'd get to a pilot is the voice on the PA saying 'Doors to manual and crosscheck, and the weather in Dublin is four degrees and wet again'. Or then again … "

"What?"

"Not quite a pilot but the next best thing. You met him in France, remember? Dave Smedley. Dave the Drone."

Oh yeah. The Englishman, Dave the Drone. It almost sounds like an old music hall act. *Ladies an' gennilmen, apples an' pears, put yer 'ands togevva for … Dave the Drone!*

"I thought you said Dave was in the film business."

Arnaud takes a glug of his pint. "Exactly. Aerial work –

planes, drones and helicopters. He's a flying cameraman."

"What d'you mean, 'drones'? Like them things the superpowers use to bomb the peasants back into the stone age?"

"Nah, you daft eejit. Those little helicoptery things with a camera, all controlled from your iPad yoke. I thought of getting one myself, a basic starter kit. Anyway, thing is: Dave Smedley is bound to know loads of pilots."

"And he has a drone."

"Yeah."

"He does drone on a bit."

"Mmm."

We settle down with the jigs and the reels and polkas and pints.

Twenty-Seven

"Morning, Alan. How's tricks?"

I'm trying to get a free consultation from Alan Brennan, my solicitor. From behind his messy desk he points to a chair with a stack of files on it. I plonk them on the carpet and sit down.

"OK, Moss. What is it this time?"

"You sound like a paid-up member of the Cynics Club. Didn't I do you proud in the Jimmy Brennan case?"

That's a reference to a Missper case, my admittedly slightly botched attempt to find a missing person for him last year.

"Oh go on then," he says. "Five minutes. After that the meter's running."

"Grand. I've only three questions anyway. Maybe four."

"Shoot."

"Question one. What happens to a missing person's estate if everyone thinks he's dead but there's no body?"

"A Missper? How come?"

"They went missing in an aircraft in the mid Atlantic."

"Lost at sea? Don't tell me, the Galway Three." He waits for a nod. "Their assets and property would be frozen. Unless it's jointly owned of course, or someone has power of attorney."

"Ta. Question two: if the Missper has life insurance, what happens to it?"

"You're not thinking it's a life insurance scam? No death cert means no life insurance. And no pension either. Not unless there's strong evidence that your Missper is actually dead."

"But if there's no inquest?"

"There wouldn't be. Not normally. An inquest usually needs a body, Mossie. But the coroner can ask the Minister for Justice for one – an inquest I mean, not a body – if he

… hold on."

He taps at something on his PC. "It's here somewhere … 'Death in abstentia' … shit … " Half a ton of paperwork has fallen off the desk. "Ah. Here goes: if he (or she) has reason to believe that a death has occurred in or near his (or her) district in such circumstances blah blah blah that an inquest is appropriate even though the body may have been destroyed – for example in a fire – or is unrecoverable – for example after a drowning et cetera et cetera … "

"Suppose they can't even get to the inquest stage."

"Wait, I know this one." More keyboard tapping. "The seven-year rule. Once they're missing seven years you can make an application to the High Court."

"Seven years." I do a calculation. Still a year and a bit to go. "Then what?"

"Oh, 'Milord' weighs up the balance of probabilities, goes for a long liquid lunch and comes back with a ruling on whether your Missper can be legally presumed dead."

"Good stuff. Question three … "

"You mean six." He checks his watch. Better push on.

"Right. Question six: when a lawyer dies, what happens to the client files?"

"A solicitor? Not Kevin Reilly you mean? They'd end up with his partners if the practice is still going. If it isn't, they'd be passed on to another practice, or some clients would find a new solicitor by themselves."

"What kind of work did he do?"

"Kevin Reilly? Mostly civil stuff when he started, but from the late 1990s he began doing more criminal law. Pays better apparently. It's hard to do both because in criminal law you're mostly stuck in the courts, while in civil law you have to be … "

"Can you get a list of his former clients?"

"I'll think about it."

"One last question."

"That's question twelve, Mossie."

"Can you find out about his will? I tried contacting his ex but she's not answering."

"You're not saying the ex did it? You've been watching far too many movies."

"Can you do it for me?"

A long, loud sigh. "I'll see."

"And Johnny Kettle's and Terry McGann's? Their wills I mean."

"Also in that flippin' plane crash?"

On the walk back to my office I try to call a few other numbers Mrs Kettle has given me.

Getting anyone from the bank to talk about Johnny Kettle is nigh on impossible. Seems many of our former respectable business heroes have become the unspeakables. The lawyer's ex wife, the elusive Olivia Reilly, still isn't returning my calls either. She's turning into – pardon the expression – a dead end.

At least Dave the Drone has agreed to meet me. And Patricia McGann – Terry's wife Trisha.

I put the key in the office door. It's not locked. Inside, signs of my office-sitter are everywhere. Maggie Dardis has colonised the desk, chairs, floor, corkboard, the lot.

Maggie is a developer. These days that usually means a software developer rather than a property developer, reflecting the fact that the smart money is speculating on Java, C and PHP instead of bricks and mortar.

"Hiya. It's pissing down again."

"Mmm." She doesn't even bother to take her eye off a screen.

"Made yourself at home I see."

"What has you all grumpy, mister detecty man?"

"Where do I start?"

The weather? A wild goose chase around in France for a dead man? Tintin getting turned inside out by customs and excise?

I reclaim the cork noticeboard and begin sticking up

my photos and clippings of the Galway Three. I'm not sure if it'll solve anything, but it's what they do on TV.

Maggie looks this way and that at the rogue's gallery.

"New case?"

"Yeah, kind of."

"Oh. I think I know him. Well, kind of."

I'm only half listening as I boot up the laptop to catch up on my email. One important message via my website's contact form says: *I have read your webpage and its is [sic] obviously that your [sic] a foggot [sic] you homo.* There's a lot of [sic] stuff out there on the Internet. Then it's off on the trail of Terry McGann's mistress, Mary Buckley. Losing myself in yet another sea of old news stories. Twenty minutes later I've reached another dead end. Literally.

A couple of months after the Galway Three's flight, five short news items appear within days of each other about Mary Buckley. This time none of the articles connects her to the missing plane story. No references to mistresses or love rats either. The five reports – they have no byline but probably have a common source because the wording is almost identical – are about Mary Buckley's "tragic death". Are all deaths in newspapers tragic now?

The death is wrapped up in a thick Foxford rug of crimespeak.

The remains of the deceased were discovered at a property in Waterford.

Crosscheck: the same road as in the earlier love-nest story.

The scene was sealed off by members of the Garda Technical Bureau.

And: *The body was examined at the scene by the pathologist before being taken away for a postmortem.*

And: *no obvious injuries.*

And: *… are still awaiting the results of toxicology tests, but foul play is not suspected.*

Toxicol reports? A suicide then?

So that, in a few paragraphs two months apart, from

love nests to toxicology tests, was the beginning and end of Mary Buckley.

I'm trying to find any follow-up stories about her inquest when Maggie butts in. "Having fun?"

"Sorry. I was miles away." I look up. "Is it just me, or is there something about the room this morning?"

"What do you mean?"

The furniture isn't quite right.

Everything has been moved around. Half a centimetre here, half an inch there, but definitely moved around. You can tell from the dust marks. And the smoke detector is slightly crooked. I never touch that smoke alarm. The framed Mondrian print is crooked too.

"Did you move that?"

"Nope."

"Nice," I continue, picking up a shiny new clock-radio from the desk. "Yours?"

"Ah no. That's your free gift with the Viking office stationery."

Hold a finger up to my lips.

Grab a notepad.

Scribble: *I DON'T use Viking.*

Back to a nonchalant voice: "Fancy a coffee?"

Turn on the kettle, and my real radio, and the battered old vacuum cleaner. Find a screwdriver. Open up the new radio.

It's not from Viking. It's a Trojan. An eavesdropping device.

Maggie's face makes a question mark.

Now I could go round checking light switches and wall sockets, looking for dust and debris on the floor directly below them. But there's no point when you already know the answer.

"On second thoughts," I say – possibly too theatrically while grabbing all the Galway Three material – "let's go out for coffee. My treat."

Twenty-Eight

One thing about Manor Street: turn your back on it for five minutes and there's another little change.

Like this new coffee shop. It used to be a florists, and a Polish grocery before that, and a ...

"What the heck is going on?" Maggie half-whispers as I sip my coffee. "Are we being bugged?"

"Seems so."

"Something to do with your latest case?"

"Maybe."

"How d'you know all this?"

"You tend to notice those kinda things in my line of work."

I slip open the file of clippings and photos of the Galway Three before continuing.

"Paranoid people pay good money for someone to check for bugs. Mind you, I don't do phone tapping. It's against the law, Maggie. Unless you are the law of course."

"Oh. Him again," she says, glancing at one of the photos.

"Do you know him?" I pull out a photo of Johnny Kettle.

She shakes her head.

"Nearly six years ago this Johnny Kettle guy disappears in a small plane over the Atlantic."

"Yeah, I know," she says.

"Now I'm confused. I thought you said…"

"No, not him. I meant that one." She grabs another photo from the pile. "Him I know."

"Terry McGann?"

"I used to work for him."

"The tech entrepreneur?"

"Entrepreneur my arse."

"So you wouldn't trust him to fly you to Greenland?"

"I wouldn't trust that shyster as far as Capel Street. He

was daft as a brush."

"What d'you mean?"

"Mad, bad, a bit of a creep."

"Mad as in mad suicidal?"

"I don't think so. The company was in fierce trouble but he was never there. Always swanning off in that fancy plane of his."

"Where to?"

"Cork, Galway, here and there once or twice a month. And off with his mistress of course."

"You knew about the mistress?"

"Everybody did."

"So these two other guys," I show her a couple more photos. "Johnny Kettle and Kevin Reilly. You've never seen either of them?"

"No. Not in work anyway."

"They're the Galway Three. You've heard of the … "

"Yeah, but I only knew Terry, as my boss."

I have a good look around at the other customers. She does too. Paranoia is infectious.

"Apparently this Johnny Kettle has turned up again," I continue, "in the south of France. And here's the strange part. Seems the Special Branch is helping him to lie low. So why does he need to disappear in the first place, with a top lawyer and your pal Terry McGann? It makes no sense. Let's talk money and sex."

"Oh Moss, I thought you'd never ask."

"No, serious. It's nearly always down to money or sex. Think. Why would all three of them need to disappear at the same time? What do they have in common?"

"The old boys' network?"

"Sure. And going fishing and flying together. But it must be more than that. The banker is well off; Terry McGann leaves behind a wife and mistress – who dies of a drugs overdose and a broken heart; and the lawyer and his wife are getting divorced anyway – all very amicable, the Reillys simply drifted apart. People do, apparently."

"Don't keep reminding me."

Oh shit. I've forgotten how Maggie Dardis has been separated since last summer.

"Maybe it was down to money, not sex," she continues, "But if they did a runner they'd have to leave *some* kind of clues behind."

"Like what?"

"On their PCs?"

"I thought of that. Johnny Kettle's home computer went to the scrapheap years ago. When I rang his office they said their old PCs are scrubbed and recycled as standard bank procedure blah blah blah. As for the lawyer's laptop, they checked it at the time. Even managed to find out what he ordered from Amazon the night before the flight. After that, no one knows what happened to it. Not very cooperative are Kevin Reilly's old solicitor pals. As for Terry McGann, I haven't a clue what happened to his."

"Don't look at me. I was only there three months, and it was worse than a mushroom farm."

"You what?"

"We were just the coder slaves back on the coalface, where they kept us in the dark while they did their deals and presentations and photo ops with the Minister."

"Right."

"What about their log files? Like an ISP has to keep log files for so many years … "

"Sorry, Maggie. These guys aren't legally dead yet."

"So?"

"We can't access their private data."

Inspect the café's clientele again. I'm first to break the silence.

"I don't think you should be in my office at the moment. It's … "

"Sure," she says.

"And don't ring me on the landline. Just my mobile."

"Yeah yeah."

"And even then, nothing sensitive."

"You know who you should talk to? Teccie Deccie."

"Who?"

"Declan Siggins. He was our sysadmin in Terry McGanns's old firm. If anyone would know about his laptop … "

"Cool. Text me his number. I have to see a man about a drone."

Dave Smedley, Dave the Drone.

Twenty-Nine

We've arranged to meet in the Phoenix Park. Dave originally suggested the zoo. Kids love the zoo but zoos give me the jitters. It's like that sign they used to have: *Do not stand, sit, climb or lean on zoo fences. If you fall, animals could eat you and that might make them sick.*

The alternative venue I've suggested is the polo grounds. A few local lads are in a five-a-side match, with polo sticks and bikes instead of horses.

While the Irish didn't invent polo, only an Irishman could have come up with bicycle polo. Richard J. Mecredy invented it in 1891.

For a time Ireland were world champions. We thrashed England 10-5 at Crystal Palace in the first international in 1901. At the 1908 Olympics a nation held its breath and we beat Deutschland 3-1 in the final. Ireland looked unstoppable, nothing could halt the rise of our boys in green on their green bikes with their tippy-tappy possession polo. Then the first World War came along. And the second.

Yet here they are today in its spiritual home, the Phoenix Park, zipping about on their fixed-gear bikes with no brakes. The sport has all the speed and skill of horsy polo, but without having to feed the bike, muck out its stables or buy a horsebox. A sport with no fame or fortune, not even the kudos of playing for your county in the GAA. With no prima donnas and divers with their WAGs and sports cars. Just a few local lads enjoying the sheer thrill of the game, a match in which the players outnumber the supporters.

A stray ball whizzes past me as Dave's white van arrives. He slides the side door open and takes out a large packing case.

"Alrigh' mate? Best find somewhere quiet."

We traipse over to a spot near the Wellington

Monument. He opens the case.

"Let's get one thing straight, Maurice. It's a quadcopter, not a drone. And this is just a junior model. And we're not supposed to but ... Fancy a go?"

"No thanks but you go ahead."

"It's a doddle to handle. Wotch."

The thing takes off, flits, hovers like a humming bird. It's already higher than the Wellington Monument, the tallest obelisk in Europe.

"Bloody brilliant and far cheaper than a chopper." He is shouting to make himself heard as it whizzes around above us. For such a small thing it's noisy – they're not called drones for nothing – and flashy. It has a red light on one side and a green one on the other, just like an airplane.

"They've even started using 'em in the Tour de France," he says. "Not shots from the race itself but pre-recorded inserts for sticking in with the live shots. Sure you don't wanna go?"

I shake my head.

He flicks and swipes at his iPad. The aerial footage is being streamed to a little rectangle on the tablet's screen, which he swipes to enlarge. "What you fink?"

I'm hardly listening as the drone dips out of sight.

"No panic, Maurice," he says. "If it gets out of range it automatically turns back to its take-off point. Like an 'oming pigeon. You can even program its flight path with Google Maps."

It reappears and hovers above us.

"They're all the rage, mate. Soon they'll be the size of a sparra, with solar cells to keep 'em in the air for days at a time. Wait till the paparazzi get their hands on 'em. Flying robots, hanging around outside nightclubs all night, with cameras and facial recognition technology. No, serious mate. Amazon is testing them to do home deliveries. Next it'll be driverless cars from Google. Imagine."

Imagine.

The quadcopter lands a few feet away.

"Cop a loada this," he says, swiping the footage back to the start of the flight and going into full-screen mode. "High definition images."

They do drone on a bit, these boys with their toys. Yes, Dave, imagine the high-speed car chases with Google Cars, the gangsters shooting at cop cars while the getaway cars drive themselves. Or as terrorists pack them with explosives for a self-driving bomb.

I can't afford a drone, even one of these small ones, though I could always tie my iPhone to a five-euro kite from Lidl.

"Go on. Have a go, mate."

"No thanks. I'd rather not."

The footage is spectacular yet there is something unreal about it. Or hyperreal, as though it is computer-generated for a video game or a film's special effects.

"I fink you should talk to Phillo. He's one of arse."

Arse?

Oh. *Ours.*

"Phillo," he repeats. "Phil Breen. Our chief pilot."

The footage towards the end is even more mesmerizing, as the quadcopter flies over a man and woman leaning on a car several hundred yards away. Hard to make out the woman's face because she has binoculars. Which are pointing not at the drone but at us.

As for the man, he is pointing something else at us, something that could be a gun or a megaphone or God knows what. I'm sure I've seen him before. It's Detective Superintendent Coleman.

"Sorry, Dave, I really do have to go. Can you set me up for a session with your pilot pal?"

"Phil Breen? No problemo. See ya, Maurice."

He took out his earplugs, leaned into the back seat, put the recording gun down and clicked the laptop to stop recording.

"Did they see us?" she asked.

Of course they did, but he decided to say nothing.

"So we fucked up?" she continued.

"No, Mullen, don't say anything."

"Are you pissed off about something?"

"Just do the job, er, just … " Coleman could never remember her first name. Calling her by her second name sounded odd, cold. But he could hardly ask her again what her first name was; that would sound downright rude.

He was still getting used to working with women. Or rather younger women on Inspector rank. She was younger, prettier and smarter than most of the planks he was usually lumbered with. DI Mullen, whatever her first name, was a high-flier from the Murder Squad. And for reasons unknown she was on loan to Special Branch. To him.

Her binoculars followed the private detective and the Englishman. The binoculars drifted over to the former as he split off from the latter.

"Just do the job and say nothing," Coleman said. "Back at the station I mean."

Because no one needed to know. If they did know you'd only be pissed on from a great height. Because height is everything, Coleman nearly told her. And right now he and she were in a vulnerable space, on lower ground.

Tall skyscrapers were still a rarity in Ireland. Most people saw the world at street level, from five or six feet up. A mundane, grounded vision. But in business or war, height is everything. And in modern policing too. Height is power, status, aerial superiority.

The "God's Eye View". That's what they called it in the film business, in that thing he saw on BBC4 the other night. The view that messed up all your familiar perspectives. The bird's-eye view, the privileged view from high up, at boardroom or even satellite level. From, say, the top of Liberty Hall or the old bank HQ in Baggot Street.

Where else had he seen that kind of view before? From the observation tower at the top of the old industrial chimney in Smithfield Square a few years back. But the tower was closed now for safety reasons.

Or from a penthouse in George's Quay Plaza. The complex of buildings had pyramid tops that formed an even bigger pyramid. The locals called it Canary Dwarf.

Or what about the view through the floor-to-ceiling glass at the top of the Montevetro building in Googletown – or Google Docks as they called it when the dot com empire moved in? He'd been there once too.

The Galway Three would have been well used to that, to those dizzy heights, to a view from on high. Those in power and those in the know were always in the room at the top, looking down on everyone else with their CCTV, with their traffic cams, eyes in the sky and executive jets.

Once in a while the man in the street got a small hint of it. On a no-frills airline for instance, seeing his city from the air: the sandbanks and marinas and the red-and-white striped cooling stacks of Poolbeg.

They got back in the car. DI Mullen started the engine. Coleman put his headphones on and listened back to the start of the recording.

What was that Englishman, Dave Smedley, droning on about now? How the EU and US were working on a new aerospace for drones. There would be a battle for air supremacy between the heavy guns – large corporations and State agencies with huge resources, from Google to the CIA – then at the other end of the spectrum there was the light brigade: the small drone kits that you could buy online for a few hundred quid. Little quadcopters that could carry a camera for their payload. A camera, or something just as heavy.

Coleman wasn't sure which type of drone was the more dangerous: the cuddly-toy drones – Dave Smedley's drones – or the flying killer robots, the new "frontline troops" in the War on Terror, in Yemen, Afghanistan, Gaza,

Pakistan.

The Gardai would be getting ones soon. What did it feel like to control one? What was it like playing God?

Killer drones were just the latest in a long line of laser-guided smart bombs, Cruise missiles, Tomahawks, Reapers, Predators – *who thinks up these names?* – Kamikaze pilots, V-1 buzz bombs, Doodlebugs, V-2 rockets, the high-altitude bomber, the sniper. It was killing at a distance, with an unseen hand. Your target? A rebel with a missile launcher, a military leader, a vehicle, a school, a village, a wedding feast, a tribe, the name of a city on an old Cold War map that hadn't been updated yet.

Remote-controlled warfare, a rigged poker game, the odds stacked in favour of the one with the latest murder machine.

The target had no foresight, no vision. No way of seeing it coming.

What was that Smedley guy wanging on about now? Solar cells? So the next generation would be "loiter" drones. Carrying out missions for months without needing to refuel. It was like something out of science fiction, yet terribly real and just around the corner.

The sheer noise of the things would kill you though. From the drone's view it was a mute world, dumb figures down there. In that sense drones were no sound, all vision.

For the people on the ground it was the exact opposite. All sound and no vision. A low-grade, low-pitched buzzing sound, day and night like an evil lawnmower. A paranoid delusion up in the clouds, the new sound of terror, watching everything you do.

What was it like, a life under drones, under *that* sound, that perpetual reminder of imminent death … ?

Thirty

His car is as arranged, at the edge of the park near the Infirmary Road gates. I get in the back and slither out of view.

"Hey, Moss." Alan Brennan, my lawyer, is in the driver's seat. "What's with all the cloak and dagger?"

"I'm being followed and my office is bugged."

"Oh shit. Anything I can do? Get an injunction or … "

"No point. It's the cops."

"Oh sugar."

"But I think I've lost them for the moment. What you got?"

"On your dead solicitor friend?"

"He's not legally dead and he's not my … "

"But if he were legally alive he'd be locked up by now. It's all in the spreadsheets."

"You know I hate spreadsheets, Alan. It's bad enough trying to read people's faces."

"Seems he's not the only thing went missing. So did three million euros. From a dozen clients. No wonder his partners won't talk to you."

"What did he need it for?"

"The usual. A flutter."

"The gee-gees?"

"Nah. Stocks and shares and a few properties."

"And the gamble didn't pay off?"

"Got it in one. Siphoned millions from his client accounts to fund his gamble. When that didn't worked he gambled on the gamble, bought shares and contracts for difference. I'll skip the technical details. Normally the Law Society would compensate the victims. But he's not practising, he's neither dead or alive. So it's a right mess."

Alan's eyes are fixed on his car mirror. He explains how the compensation fund has paid out more than €20 million in five years. At least forty solicitors have been struck off.

"Anyone tell you you're in a crooked profession, Alan?"

"Oh, and he rewrote his will several times. Before you ask, it's not that strange. At least some of us know about the need to have a tidy will. Which reminds me … "

"Not now, Alan. When was the last one drawn up?"

"Two months before the plane crash."

"We still don't know if it was a crash. What was the gist of it?"

"He was as good as divorced and they had no kids. So he left his favourite paintings to his ex, and a few bits and bobs to his sister."

"The ex wife was basically written out of the will?"

"Jayney Mac. The man was bent, he was broke, but his will was no secret. So don't go all conspiratorial on me. He had another solicitor draw it up, his own office had a copy. It's as good as in the public domain and there's nothing irregular about it as far as I can see."

"Have you an address for the sister?"

"Thought you'd never ask." He hands me a scrap of paper: Caroline Reilly, with a mobile number and an address just off the North Circular.

"What about the wills of the other two?"

"The banker, John Kettle, a third of his estate would have gone to the wife, with the other two thirds to be held in trust for the son and daughter till they are twenty-one. Which they can't get their hands on because he's not legally dead yet. Thing is, he'd already transferred most of his money to the wife's account, so it's no longer part of his estate."

"Is that unusual?"

"Not if you knew a tsunami was about to hit the banking sector."

"His wife gave me a down payment in cash. Quite a lot of cash. She's not working, and her daughter's shop is a terminal case. The kid thinks daddy is alive and well and he's run off with his sister-in-law. Your typical crackpot family. What you got on Terry McGann?"

"Sitting on a small fortune at the time, if you could believe the business pages. But it was a paper fortune. After he disappeared his companies went into liquidation."

"What about *his* will?"

"Shares and savings, all his worldly goods and his stake in the business, everything to go to the wife."

"Hence her current penury?"

"Uh-huh. She'd get a hundred per cent of nothing."

"Look Alan, I gotta go. Ring me on my mobile if anything else turns up. But not my office number."

For the first time in his life Alan actually looks worried about me. "Good luck."

"Yeah." I head quickly through the park gates.

At the top of Infirmary Road it's easy enough to slip into the corner shop cum off-licence without being seen. Last time I bought wine here there was still a little Internet café at the rear of the shop.

What did we do before the Internet and Google, before we had a single place to store all the facts of the world? You'd learn things in dribs and drabs, in conversations and trips to the library, in card indexes and microfiche. Traipsing miles across town to find out a scrap of a fact that, two decade later, you can get with a flick of your iPhone on the top deck of the bus.

That's the theory. In practice it takes an hour of surfing and false starts in the cybercaff to discover what happened to Terry McGann's mistress.

The only report I can find of the inquest is from a Waterford online forum. This post in turn is a copy-and-paste from a local paper that no longer exists.

I'm trying to picture the scene.

A dead body on a bed. Under the bed the police will find several pairs of knotted tights and a burnt spoon. In the bedside locker is importation-quality heroin, stashed in a pink cloth bag. The bathroom's medicine cabinet has drugs paraphernalia – syringes, alcohol wipes, cotton buds, another spoon, several grams of a brown powder, large traces of a brown residue.

A forensic scientist tells the inquest the heroin had a purity of sixty-two per cent. The officer leading the investigation says the drugs "far exceeded the twenty-six per cent purity usually found at street level". They had a street value of six hundred euro.

There were no other suspicious circumstances. Nothing to suspect the death wasn't self-inflicted either. The post-mortem identifies a puncture mark on her right forearm, another on her left thigh. No older puncture marks to be found, no other injuries to suggest any "trauma inflicted by a third party". The blood has a high level of morphine, suggesting she died shortly after taking heroin. There are signs of irreversible brain damage. The pathologist is unable to give a cause of death "due to the severe state of decomposition".

The coroner's verdict: cause of death is "drugs related", a "tragic overdose", a "misadventure". No shit Sherlock.

But severe decomposition? And why only two puncture marks? What am I missing?

The lawyer's sister, Caroline Reilly, lives less than ten minutes away on the North Circular Road. I take the bus there on spec.

"I've only a couple of questions."

"Sure," she says, "come in."

Caroline Reilly is much younger than her brother would be. Say early forties, brown eyes, wide cheekbones, a waterfall of golden hair.

Sometimes you need to focus less on Goldilocks's breaking and entering and more on why Mummy and Daddy Bear don't sleep in the same bed any more. So I'd better cut to the chase.

"Everyone says their divorce was amicable. What was

your reading of it? Was your brother seeing anyone else?"

"Kevin? Of course not."

"Was his wife?"

"Olivia?" She tilts her head and touches her mouth. "No. Definitely not." Her hand is on her throat. Is she trying to cover up something? Next she'll be shuffling her feet and pointing a lot.

"It's like this," she continues. "I like Olivia. Kevin did too. But she wasn't having an affair. Neither of them was. The truth is, she was getting fed up with all his wheeling and dealing. Nobody noticed at the time but … I guess you heard about the trouble with his clients' accounts."

"This and that." How come other people's living rooms are spotless, like nobody lives in them? "You wouldn't happen to have a few of his things?"

She laughs. "To put it mildly. There's boxes of his stuff in the spare room. Technically I'm not supposed to have it because, well, what with the hassle with the will … Anyway, Olivia said I might as well have them."

We go upstairs to the spare room.

"See? It's junk mostly. I'll leave you to it."

Excellent.

Skip the clothes and obvious things. Look for his diaries. *Yesss.* Diaries going back to the year dot. His 2008 diary tells me little: niece and nephew birthdays, four meetings about his divorce, several outings with the Galway Three. And that's it.

The 2007 diary is almost as blank. There's a set of digits on the inside back page. Same for the 2008 diary, and 2006. Always the same numbers, year after year. Numbers for a bank account? Too short. The PIN number for his credit card? Hardly. For his safe? His house alarm? I photograph the back page with my iPhone.

There are four bunches of keys. For yachts, cars, God knows what. I pocket all four.

Thirty-One

Back home to Stoneybatter. Shut the curtains, check the landline. It has strange sounds, weird volume changes, static, popping. Am I imagining it?

Oh yes, imagine the incredible shrinking man, deep inside your telephone, looking for a capacitive discharge. You get that when two conductors are connected together.

As in a bug, a tap on the line.

Call directory inquiries for a number, any number, a betting shop in Athlone will do. Hang up. Wait for more strange sounds from the handset.

Possibly caused by a hook switch bypass.

Sometimes, for a fraction of a second, you also hear a high-pitched squeak.

Maybe that's feedback – your telephone receiver has been turned into an eavesdropping microphone, and a speaker.

Or the phone rings, you pick up, nobody's there.

Possibly an infinity transmitter, a harmonica bug, maybe in the caller ID device.

Or maybe it's just a wrong number. A befuddled old fax machine out there looking for friends.

No, it's not paranoia. The FM radio and TV have also developed strange habits. Strange interference.

A pro would use a drifting frequency just within the FM band, right?

Turn the stereo function off, put the radio in mono mode. Move it around, slowly, sweeping the room until the sound becomes high pitched. Which can only mean…

Another bug.

Right, that's it. Slam the front door, walk a hundred yards up the street, calm down, figure there's no point in bursting a blood vessel over spilt milk.

The street is dark. On my mobile I give Dave the Drone a call. He says his pilot pal Phillo has agreed to meet us tomorrow morning. Good.

Before going back in, do one last check for strange cars. Something darts and disappears behind a railing: a black and white cat.

We live in a strange universe. It's ruled by quantum physics yet sometimes makes sense, kind of. Life has many possible outcomes; that bit I get. And new technology means someone like a PI can indeed be in two places at the same time, a bit like Schrödinger's Cat.

And the very act of observation changes everything.

It's like the sound of that tree falling in the empty forest. Which isn't quite so empty any more because the forest is bugged.

Or like the face of a football fan as the camera turns his despair into delight.

Shine a torch on something, and the act of shining changes everything. Once you know you're being watched you start acting differently. You can't think straight, you know what it's like to be neither here nor there. You feel like Schrödinger's poor cat. Though not quite so poor if the most famous cat in physics charged appearance fees.

It was probably a northside Dublin cat too, because Schrödinger spent seventeen years here while concocting his strange stories about boxes of curious cats that were dead and alive at the same time, in a world of baffling probabilities instead of dead certainties. When does the poor thing die – when the event happens or when you open the box? Is it still alive until you cast a light on it? Is that why they say the cat is in both states until you open the box? The legendary physicist was in two states too: Schrödinger was Austrian and Irish, both at the same time, a naturalized Irish citizen. *Did Schrödinger have two passports?*

Do another recce of the street for unfamiliar vehicles. Get back in my car. The car radio is acting weird too. The interference is making a mess of a late-night phone-in, in which two people are swearing a lot and giving out yards about each other.

Look at the car aerial. The very act of looking at it changes everything. It wouldn't take much for an eavesdropper to turn a radio antenna from a receiver into a transmitter, right?

Switch off the radio, get out of the car, walk back inside and hope I don't talk in my sleep.

That night I have nightmares of waking up to an incoming text on my mobile. And seeing a picture on my phone, of me sleeping. I live alone.

I dream I'm watching Dave the Drone as he watches drone porn, video clips released on the Web by the US Department of Defense. Each long narrative leads up to a big explosion: the money shot.

Now Dave and his mates are in an oblong, windowless container. It's a large trailer, the air-conditioning kept at a constant seventeen degrees. Dave and his pals sitting in front of a bank of monitors, keyboards and joysticks. Press a button in New Mexico and watch someone die on the other side of the planet.

That's drone power for you. The power to kill remotely, at the flick of a switch, a swipe on a touchscreen. Easier than swatting flies. To exterminate a dot on a screen.

"Hey Chuck, mate! Did we just kill a kid?"

"Nah, Dave. That was a dog."

And re-running the video. A dog on two legs?

Then leaving their windowless tin can and going back to life, back to "reality", driving back into town. Dave and his drone pilots, driving into town to have a few beers and catch the big game tonight.

Thirty-Two

Ever since we first crawled out of the primordial soup, a large subsection of our species has had a natural fascination with watching things take off and land. A subspecies called planespotters.

Planespotters hanging out at the perimeter fence of Dublin Airport. Sitting in their cars with their sandwiches, binoculars and notepads. Switching on the windscreen wipers every so often to sweep off the incessant rain.

My mam and dad used to go to Dublin Airport when I was a kid. Not with me in tow of course, and it would have been Collinstown back then. They'd go there to watch the planes and have dinner. In the good old days when airports and air travel and even airport food were still *très chic.*

Die-hard planespotters would also drive to Weston aerodrome to see a couple of De Havilland Chipmunks from the 1950s doing a formation flyover this morning.

Drive to Weston. Or, in my case, take the 66a bus from the Liffey quays to Cooldrinagh Road in Leixlip. I don't trust cars any more.

From the bus stop it's a five-minute walk to the aerodrome. Dave the Drone is easy to spot in the terminal building. He starts into a potted history of the place while we track down Phil Breen, his pilot colleague.

"They filmed *The Blue Max* here."

"I know, Dave," I reply.

"And the Roger Corman film about the Red Baron. The runway would have been grass back then. Been an aerodrome since the Thirties but they only got the tarmac runway in the 1980s."

"Right."

Yes, Dave. Must have been a quiet little aerodrome back then, until a businessman bought it at the turn of the century. The man who made his fortune selling machinery leftovers from the Falklands mess.

The businessman had a dream. He upgraded the hangars for corporate jets and helicopters, extended the runway, revamped the main terminal, added a control tower and a fuel farm and several flight training schools and the Skyview restaurant. And, above all, a growing number of low-flying aircraft.

The locals protested. Some marchers even flew kites. Dangerous, but that wasn't the new owner's scariest problem.

The economy went belly up. So did his empire. Most of it ended up in receivership in 2010. The following year the National Assets Management Agency (NAMA to you and me) grabbed his remaining scraps, including the airport at Weston.

"Anyway." Oh feck. Dave is still droning on. "They sold it eventually for three and a half mill. A knockdown price, not bad for hundreds of acres and all those buildings and hangars. Oh, and the period home with dozens of stables. Hey! There he is. Oi! Phillo."

The tall man strolling towards us isn't in a pilot uniform, though neat enough in smart jeans and sweatshirt. Astronaut-handsome with Colgate smile, the kind of guy who probably gets a dry cut at the barbers once a fortnight. We shake hands.

"Catch up with you later in the restaurant," Dave shouts as he fades into the distance behind a big red fire truck.

Phil Breen looks at his watch. "Fancy a flight? I'm going up in an hour." The watch is fancy, no doubt with built-in altimeter and depth gauge for scuba diving.

"No thanks."

"No problemo. But ignore anything Dave says about aeronautics. *I* do the flying around here, he just does the drones and balloons and cameras. So what can I tell you?"

"How would you crashland at sea for a start?"

"Ditch your aircraft? I wouldn't dream of it."

"Yeah, but if you had to."

"No, I mean most pilots don't think about it because they've never had to do it. Never been trained to. So they keep it at the back of the head. Mind you, there were always arguments in training school … "

"About the best way to ditch?"

"Yeah. Always someone who'd read something somewhere, or knew somebody who knew someone who heard about somebody who vanished in a big pond on a fine sunny day after a botched ditching, you know the kind of thing."

We walk past giant hangars with dozens of helicopters and a flying boat. Phil watches a small plane coming in to land. A Cessna? Don't ask me. Not a Spitfire anyway.

"You cut your engines and glide down. Everyone knows that. But it's what happens next. Like do you land wheels up – a belly landing – or wheels down?"

"What would most people do?"

"If you were crashlanding in Hollywood you'd go for wheels up."

"Why?"

"Cos it looks better in the movies. But in real life? I've heard more arguments down the years about wheels down versus wheels up than the bloody price of Avgas."

"What would *you* do?"

"Wheels down I guess."

"Even on water?

"Oh yeah. Ever watch swans landing on water? Feet first, never belly up. Your landing gear is like a swan's feet. It's a shock absorber, protecting the aircraft spine on impact. When you're coming in at a hundred mile an hour the water is like a solid. It deflects you. So your landing gear breaks the surface tension, absorbs the force and protects you against hitting the bottom in shallow water."

"What about deep water?"

"Out to sea you mean? Gear down every time. Mind you, some pilots say gear *up* will let you skip gently in a bobbly bobble along the top."

"With gear down, aren't you more likely to flip over?"

"Doubt it. There's this stuntman guy I know from Macroom. He says most times you don't flip, even when you need to do it deliberately. Usually you dig in one wing, turn and settle upright. Or you settle straight ahead with a bit of nose under because it's heavier. Even if you do flip over it's not the end of the world – if you're strapped in and don't land too hard. The plane could be a write-off but at least you walk away in one piece."

"Or swim away. When you land on water, how long does the plane stay afloat?"

"Depends. Maybe it's still afloat the next day, or it goes down in seconds like a sub, nose first. It's all down to the design, the buoyancy from the fuel tanks, how bad the waves are. Anyway, the landing bit is the least of your troubles. It's what happens next – surviving in the ocean long enough to be rescued. How far from land were these guys?"

"We don't know."

"You're talking about the Galway Three?" I nod. "Did they have a life raft or PFDs?" He can see I'm puzzled. "Personal flotation devices. Life vests."

"Are they compulsory?"

He shakes his head. He's dealing with an amateur. "There was this Piper Aztec that ditched off the coast of Florida late at night. The two passengers didn't get out. The next day they found the plane still floating, and the bodies still pinned inside."

"What happened? No life vests?"

He shakes his head again. "The investigators said it had something to do with the way the bales of marijuana shifted."

Phillo takes me to the aerodrome's restaurant for a quick coffee, my shout. We sink into seats of claret red leather. He keeps looking at his watch. Checking what depth we're at, or maybe it's nearly time to start his pre-flight whatsits.

"Sure you don't fancy a spin?"

"No way," I say. "Look at the bloody weight of them. How do they stay in the air? And I *don't like heights.*"

"OK, so your ignorance of the laws of physics makes you think its jet engines or propellers support it in the air."

"Yeah."

"And you think an engine failure will cause it to plummet to earth … "

"But I haven't. Got. A head. For heights."

"Yeah but a fixed-wing aircraft will glide down naturally. You only use the engines to maintain altitude. It's not magic, it's basic physics. So that's what you do in a crash landing. You glide."

"Or crash."

"You're not being logical. Look at the stats. You hear about an air crash and think 'Oh God, air travel is terribly dangerous.' But they never mention the number of flights that *don't* crash. The stats don't bear it out."

No. I will not be strapped into a tin can, miles up in the air with just a bit of carpet between me and the gaping nothingness.

"In life you're either a pilot or a passenger, Mr Reid. It's up to you."

I don't get. "Can we move on?"

"Sure, but you don't know what you're missing."

I don't know and don't care. "I'd like to get back to the facts."

Phil is full of facts. He reels them off from a thick clipboard of factsheets, while keeping one eye on the runway through the restaurant's wide windows.

The Beech Model 76 Duchess. An unusual sight around here, but a nifty twin-engine four-seater all the same.

More facts: its empty weight, maximum takeoff weight, cruise speed, Garmin GNS 430 Dual Nav/Com, HSI, RMI, Dual ADF autopilot …

"Can we skip the jargon?"

"OK. That cockpit was stuffed with fancy avionics, integrated GPS, terrain database ... quite a package for a four-seater. But it don't matter how flashy your cockpit display or how fancy your gear is. None of it is any use if you lose control."

"So what do you think happened?"

"It's November, right? Cold enough. So. A faulty cabin heater? Exhaust gases in the cabin? Carbon monoxide? Sabotage? God knows."

"What was airport security like back then?"

"In 2008? Fairly basic. I can't remember Customs and Immigration having a permanent presence. They might have had an X-ray machine for the baggage, and they'd search an aircraft maybe once a week, based on profiling and intelligence."

"Once a week doesn't sound like much intelligence."

He's fidgety. More quick glances at the runway and his watch contraption.

"OK, hypothetical question," I continue. "If you were to parachute from the aircraft, could radar detect you?"

"In theory, yeah. It will detect anything it bounces off. But in practice that could be a flock of birds or any old shite. The radar operator has to see through the mess and static, and ignore anything too small to be an aircraft. That's how stealth fighters work. They *can* be tracked, but at the size of a seagull. So if you want to spot an F-22 you'd have to track every bird in the sky. Almost impossible in practice."

"Could radar spot one of Dave's drones?"

"In practice, probably not. Aircraft move fast, they give off a big radar signature. Anything else won't be tracked. It's not worth it." Another look at his watch. "But in theory? Hypothetically? Radar could detect a parachute, *if* you're looking for it. But ATC, air traffic contr ... "

"I know."

"They'd be looking for much larger items. They filter

the primary raw radar to cut down the crap on your screen, filter out any little blips not moving at a minimum horizontal velocity. Mind you, the approach control radar would be far more sensitive."

"But they were going away, not approaching. Why did the radar lose sight of their plane?"

"That's another myth. Radar isn't constantly watching air traffic. If you're a hundred miles out to sea you'd be well outside radar range."

"But when they talk about 'flying under the radar', does that mean if they were flying low enough they'd ... "

"After a while height hardly matters. Radar travels in straight lines. The earth doesn't, it curves. It's like how you can't see a ship beyond the horizon. If they were flying say five hundred feet above sea level, which isn't that low, they'd be 'under the radar' in no time."

"But there was no distress message."

"Again, fine in the movies, but in real life – in an emergency – your first priority is to deal with the situation, so radio silence wouldn't be surprising. It's what they drill into you in pilot training. 'Aviate, navigate, then communicate.' And out at sea you're communicating largely by HF. Sorry, high-frequency radio. You'd check in at fixed reporting points, give your position, air speed and altitude. But between points you'd usually maintain radio silence."

"What about the aircraft's GPS?"

"Only tells the pilot where he is. It won't tell air traffic control anything. That's like trying to use your mobile in the middle of the Gobi desert. GPS can tell you where *you* are, because you can still receive signals from a GPS satellite somewhere overhead. But there's no cell coverage to make a call, so no one else can track you."

"Ask a stupid question ... " Because stupid questions make other people look smart. "What are the height rules again, the minimum height restriction?"

"For a commercial pilot? Five foot four I think. It's all

down to cockpit ergonomics."

"No, I mean … "

"If you're too short you can't reach the overhead panel. Stubby legs won't reach the rudder."

"I meant the minimum height for flying over towns."

"Oh. Gotcha. They're very strict on that, Rules of the Air Act. I think it's five hundred feet though I may be wrong. Apart from take-off and landing I always try to stay above a thousand feet. There's a gobshite I knew got fined thousands for flying his chopper so low that he nearly hit a radio mast. It was only on the local copshop roof. The judge threw the book at him. Now I really must … "

He gets up to leave. At least he agrees to get me a copy of Terry McGann's flight documentation.

Dave the Drone is back again. He's waiting for me at the bar.

Thirty-Three

"Welcome to my shed."

Dave Smedley opens the door. It's inset into a much larger door. His company tagline forty feet above us announces: *We Take Filming To New Heights.* Dave's "shed" is a good-sized aircraft hangar.

In the centre of the room a colony of Portuguese man o' war jellyfish are bobbing gently on the wave of air we've just brought in. They turn out to be six or seven helium balloons in various sizes, tethered to weights in the floor. In one corner is a stack of helium gas cylinders, in another is a large assortment of long tubes.

I'm baffled, and Dave can see it. "Telescopic masts. They come in sections, you can put them together in minutes. That one goes up to twenty metres. Great for high shots in tight spaces where you can't get the Cherrypicker in."

I half expect him to produce a machine for picking cherries but there isn't one. A large workbench runs the length a wall, a sort of miniature runway for a fleet of quadcopters in various sizes. Under the bench are cases and crates with cameras, aerials, fancy instruments, stacks of guy ropes, safety stays.

"What's it all for?"

"You name it. Films, documentaries, TV commercials, estate agent brochures, engineering projects, golf course layouts, aerial security at concerts and festivals, and the fancy big-screen footage of the next U2."

"Can I borrow one?"

"They're not kites in a toy shop, Moss. You can't just take one out as you fancy. The Aviation Authority has regulations. You have to consider the wind and weather and you can't use balloons at night. And some of them are far too big to be handled by one man. You need a team."

"No, I meant one of the drones."

"They're not toys either. You need a permit. There's only two dozen licensed operators in the Republic."

"So there are rules for flying them?"

"Oh yeah. Maximum height a hundred and fifty metres, and you can't stray more than five hundred metres from your control station."

The next thing he says is a real headfuck: "The last bloke to ask me that was Gino Beattie. You ever met Gino Beattie?"

"No. But I've heard of him." Gino Beattie. Crime overlord, ex-paramilitary, currently resides in Mountjoy Jail.

On the bus back to town I check my phone messages. A text from Maggie: *Were r u? Call me.*

I ring back.

"Hi Moss," she says. "I've tracked him down. That guy I used to work with, yeah?"

Right. Declan Siggins, aka Teccie Deccie.

A company liquidation has much in common with a murder investigation. There's the corpse for a start.

They estimate the company's time of death, call in the forensic accountants, quiz suspects, assemble the evidence and look for the all-important "C" word: closure.

Among those picking away at the carcass, one group is always guaranteed a tidy sum: the liquidators. By the time the office furniture supplier retrieves his desks and tables the death rituals are complete. Little else remains, inside or out. Not even a ghost sign.

The "relatives" of the "victim", those looking for justice, are the former employees. The poor sods who now know the difference between a "preferential" and an "unsecured" creditor of a penniless company, and who the real victim is in all this.

In this case one of the chief victims is Declan Siggins.

Deccie has the kind of four-day stubble that a young man can get away with until his late thirties. Then it can tend to get a bit iffy. Like Deccie's.

We're in Oscars bar in Smithfield. It's half way between our respective workplaces and does decent coffee, and the window seats have a great view of the comings and goings on the square. I'm preoccupied with comings and goings at the moment.

"You fire away, Moss. Anything you need to know."

"I'm trying to trace Terry McGann's laptop."

"Probably sold with the rest of the kit. When the company went under our pay cheques bounced, the liquidators came in, they locked us out and sold the assets. A dealer auctioned off the kit to pay the preferential creditors, starting with Revenue and the VAT man. Terry Fuckface had underdeclared his VAT for years and hadn't paid our PRSI for ages. First we heard of it was when Eamonn whatsit tried to sign on."

"Where was Terry McGann's laptop the day he disappeared?"

"Probably on him. They were inseparable."

Damn. I see a white Apple MacBook Pro fluttering down into the Atlantic's murky depths.

"Aha." Declan has an idea. "But there's always his email. We had one of those Gmail-for-business packages, and I set up everyone's accounts."

"Did you keep a list of their passwords?"

"Not exactly."

"Damn."

"Well. Kind of." His voice becomes conspiratorial. "Each password was unique, with upper and lower case and numbers and all that. But with the same overall format for everyone. Made it easier for staff to remember.

"Each one started with their initials in upper case, 'TM' in Terry's case, then 'p4', as in 'password for'. Then the account type, 'gmail'. Then 'D2', our postal code. So Terry's would have been 'TMp4gmailD2'. It's like a mnemonic: 'Terry McGann password for gmail Dublin 2'. You get?"

I get. I nod. I like. The good old systematic approach of a sysadmin.

"So once they log on for the first time they're supposed to change their password, right?"

"Yeah." He grins. "Which no one ever did, of course."

"So if the company went into liquidation, who paid the Gmail business account? Wouldn't everyone have been frozen out of their email?"

"Not right away. In those days it was still free – the version of Gmail for small businesses with your own domain name and all that. So you could still get into your email."

"But surely not half a decade later?"

"That's the other thing," he says. "As soon as we knew the company was banjaxed I set up new free accounts for everyone, and imported the email from their old accounts. You see, they might need to look up old contacts and so on, after the Nazis pulled the plug as it were."

"So you copied all Terry's stuff to a new account?"

"Damn right I did. The fecker wasn't officially dead, but he wasn't officially alive either, so it's not exactly a breach of anything, right?"

"Sure. Your secret is safe with me."

"Gis a minute."

On his smartphone he logs on to the transferred copy of Terry's old email account. I can see him typing the same old password: *TMp4gmailD2*.

"What have you got?"

"A load of bullshit really."

Where's my reading glasses? It's hard to make out the subject lines on the phone's small screen: ancient staff memos, junk mail, email newsletters about eCommerce, confirmations for online orders – DVDs, CDs, history books from Amazon. And a folding bicycle.

"Can I see that order for the bike?"

It's a Challenge Folding 26-Inch Trekking Bike: not ideal for bicycle polo, but the product description says it's "discreet, lightweight, compact when folded, easy to fit in the back of a car".

"Can you do a search for 'Galway'?"

He does. Six emails from 2008. The most recent ones are about a business meeting in Galway on the day of the flight. The messages are like the bike from Amazon: short, discreet, lightweight, compact when folded. No mention of the agenda that fateful day. Just a *See u tomorrow in Galway* and a *Yeah fine, galway it is.* And the *To:* and *From:* fields and empty *Subject:* lines. To and from Terry McGann and one TJ O'Malley. And the date stamps. The meeting was only set up a day before the flight.

"Have you heard of this TJ O'Malley?" I ask.

"Oh yeah. Owned half the company. You know him?"

I nod. I've had my dealings with TJ O'Malley, a millionaire of the "self-made" variety. How come you never hear of self-made labourers, self-made nurses or self-made private eyes?

TJ O'Malley comes from a new class of land speculators, privatised refuse management operators and nursing home owners. A nasty little cartel who decide where our future generations will live and die. The same parasites who'd sell you a three-bed semi built on pyrite on the outer fringes of civilisation and tell you how much you owe for the privilege for the rest of your life, because they'll also "manage" every facet of your tenancy. Squeezing every last penny out of you, for all your essential services (water, heat, rubbish, medication, breathing) until the day you breathe your last gasp in one of their nursing homes. If you can afford it.

Deccie digs around in his bag for a disk. "After you rang I thought of this."

"What is it?"

"An old documentary he was in."

"You've been very helpful."

"Anything I can do to get that fecker. And any friend of Maggie's … "

Thirty-Four

My car is a liability. So I walk to the North Circular and take the 46A bus to Patricia McGann's house in Stillorgan.

"Oh yeah, his *den,*" she says. "Any of his work stuff that's left would be there."

"Mind if I have a look?"

"Be my guest."

It's at the back of the garden, which is a mess. What was once an idyllic Eden of fruit and veg is more akin to the "Before" shots in a garden makeover show.

The shed is one of those self-contained home office things, all mod cons. She unlocks the door, switches on a light and begins to take down boxes and box-files.

Every bookshelf tells a story. Like Gandhi says, "Almost anything you do is insignificant, but it is very important that you do it." Countless insignificant acts become significant. Or so I hope.

But even the most avid reader with a long life will have some books they'll never get around to: titles to tease them, reminders of long-lost dreams and unfulfilled passions, spur-of-the-moment buys next to stray waifs that refuse to be completely abandoned. Each insignificant, yet all adding up to something more significant. We hope.

Terry McGann's waifs include *Russian Philately, Java for Dummies, Scuba Diving for Beginners, A Brief History of Time, Cooking With a Microwave* and *Air Rifle and Air Pistol Maintenance and Repair.*

"Did he own a gun?"

"Ah no. It's just a stupid book he bought on a whim."

My iPhone takes a few photos to remind me of these bookshelf whimsies. Books on computer languages jostle with how-to-get-rich guides, entrepreneurs' biogs, maths and science books on chaos theory, two books on the topography of Lough Erne – antiques that were published in 1821 and 1836 – and an old atlas of Ireland. I'm a catholic reader, but Terry McGann takes the biscuit. More maps and atlases and books about the two World Wars. Terry McGann's specialist subject in *Mastermind* must have been "U-boats in the Battle of the Atlantic". The Atlantic? Some would call that ironic.

But the Galway Three were hardly flitting about the Atlantic in a secondhand U-boat bought on eBay.

A book about cycling with bright yellow covers catches my eye. *Domestique* something or other.

"Mind if I borrow this?"

"Go ahead. Sure I've no use for it."

I also persuade her to lend me half a dozen of his history and war books. As if the books and paintings of a dead man will let you into his troubled mind.

The cycling book's inside page has a handwritten message: *To Pete, hope you enjoy it, love Susan. 8th March 1994.*

Who were Pete and Susan? Is Pete still alive? Was it a spur-of-the-moment purchase, or a gift carefully lovingly chosen by Susan all those years ago? Was that the date of Peter's birthday? Did he kiss and hug her as he unwrapped his present, "It's exactly what I wanted"? Are Pete and Sue still together? Or gone their separate ways, as the book must have done too, ending up in the dusty corner of a secondhand bookstore or charity shop?

Or is Pete her brother, and Sue worked with the publishers? She was the one who handed out the plonk at the book launch, and after the speeches and glass-clinking she took the unsold copies home, giving one to her brother because he might be into cycling, but turns out he wasn't.

Or was Pete a friend of Terry McGann – who borrowed it and never gave it back?

We'll probably never know. It will remain a secret.

"Did your husband have any business secrets?" I continue.

"His whole business was a secret," Mrs McGann replies. "Everything they were working on was hush-hush in case the competition got wind of it. Sometimes I think his own staff didn't know what was going on. 'Everything strictly need-to-know.' That's what he was always saying. If they won a big contract they'd be made sign an NDA. You know what one of those is?"

I nod. A non-disclosure agreement.

"Then when he disappeared the secrets died with him. They couldn't go on without him. The headless chickens without the head chicken, the company with all its flaming need-to-knows."

"Do you have a job yourself?" I figure she doesn't, given her availability during business hours.

"Yes. I teach English."

"In college?"

"I give grinds."

Grinds. Extra tuition for those too lazy to read their textbooks, or whose teachers are too lazy to teach them properly. Thus avoiding the danger of failing their exams and falling out of the middle class or being forced to become – I can't say this to Mrs McGann – a poor schoolteacher who has to give English grinds.

What do they have in common, the three wives? All widows, all with husbands in the old boys' network. Three women who'd probably describe their class as "middle", a term so vague and imprecise nowadays. Middle of what? A vast middleness that stretches from the proprietor of a dying corner shop to the head of a financial services centre. Patricia McGann isn't penniless, but judging by the state of her house she's not half as wealthy as Áine Kettle's lot.

Three women. All middle-aged, fiftysomething, not quite in the nursing home yet. Three women who, with the occasional minor differences, probably have much the same outlook on life, love, class and society. But there's no conspiracy between them. Not as far as I can see.

"I'm sorry," I say, breaking the silence. "I didn't mean to get personal. Where did he go to school?"

She explains how he'd gone to the Portora Royal in Enniskillen. That would explain the photo of the proud faces on the rowing team. And the bronze and silver medals from the inter-schools rowing competitions.

Another framed black-and-white photograph is of a woman who looks familiar: possibly early thirties; boyish figure, boyish grin; hands on hips, short tousled hair; light shirt and trousers, a long silk scarf around her neck, knotted loosely almost at her midriff; a dark jacket that, like the rest of her clothes, is casual, functional yet stylish – maybe suede rather than leather. She is standing in front of the huge propeller of an old-fashioned plane. Maybe it's taken in an aviation museum. In a corner of the picture you can make out half a dozen onlookers and an old-style microphone.

"Is she a relative?"

Mrs McGann laughs. "God no. That's Amelia Earhart." Oh shit. Only one of the most famous missing persons on the planet.

"A bit of a fan he was," she continues.

"Can we get back to the final hours before he disappeared?"

"Like the night before? I wouldn't know."

"What d'you mean?"

"He was with his tart, wasn't he?"

She means Mary Buckley.

That's when I notice the framed print above the desk: the birdman cradled in his broken wings, a large downy bed that takes up half the canvas. Wings so immense that the frame cuts them off at the top left and middle right.

It's like a modern photograph, that way the artist has cropped the image, truncating what's visible within the frame. So maybe not a Renaissance painting after all.

Each wing is outstretched to twice his height. He's in the arms of a naked nymph. A second nymph is egging her on or something. A third nymph is emerging from the water like a sea sprite, wondering what the fuss is about.

They have golden lyres, garlands in their hair. All three women are naked, yet he gets the strip of cloth. How come in some old paintings, a bit like a Hollywood movie, the guy gets a discreet loincloth while the nymphs get the garlands, a nice gold harp and a full frontal?

But if he's dead the nymphs don't seem discombobulated. If anything they are curious, as if they have never seen a man before. Maybe they are about to have their wicked ways with him. "Ways" plural, because each is looking at him in an ever so slightly different way.

What does it all mean, Terry McGann and his three nymphs?

I look at the caption at the bottom of the picture: *The Lament for Icarus.* In smaller print it says the print uses sustainably sourced paper and soy-based inks. Soy-based. I can't help thinking of soy sauce. Kikkoman, the one in the conical glass jar with a red top.

Would I learn any more from seeing the original in the artist's studio? Or in its final resting place, the Tate in London? Hardly.

Ghost flights and ghost signs. Is there something the print is trying to tell us? That Terry McGann was a big ego, fond of heights, a high-flier? We know all that already.

Or is it that, like Icarus, his wings were feathers and wax? Huge wings that didn't work when he ignored his father's warnings, flew too close to the sun, the wings melted, he had engine problems? Is that it? Overambition, epic fail, a sudden cabin decompression or a fuel leak?

Or maybe it's more straightforward. Simply that Terry McGann had a proclivity for pretentious old art on the walls of his den, the Victorian equivalent of a Page Three Bird.

I thought I knew the Icarus story, the fly-too-close-to-the-sun and melting wings fable. Yet something is bugging me about those wings in the painting. There's nothing wrong with them.

That's the problem: they are still fully intact.

I go back to the cycling book. And Terry's online order for that foldable bike.

"Was your husband into cycling?"

"He hated cyclists and cycle lanes and bus lanes. He'd say 'Bloody bus lanes? Why do poor people have to get to places quicker than me?' "

"If you don't mind me asking, what was he like?"

"In bed you mean? In work? After too many pints?"

"I mean in the days and weeks leading up to the flight. Was he acting strange?"

"No stranger than usual."

"What about on the phone?"

"To me?"

"No. To other people."

"Terry had – what would you call it? – a close personal relationship with his mobile."

I've seen the symptoms often enough: leaving the room to take a call, whispering, deleting texts.

"And he never used to do that before?"

"Let's not beat about the bush. He was on to your one from Waterford. He got bored easily. He would have gotten bored with her too, eventually."

"I'm sorry. Stop me if I'm getting too personal. But was there anything else? Anything. Anything strange, any unusual bank withdrawals, things going missing?"

She shakes her head. "I dunno. Unless … "

She digs around in the boxes and finds a file of old bank statements and credit card statements.

"You want strange? He bought her a snorkel and flippers. And you were saying about cycling? He bought a bike. He liked swimming but you'd never see him on a bike. Like I said, he hated cyclists."

She scrambles among the sheets of statements.

"Where is it?" she continues. "See? He bought them online. They were supposed to be delivered here. Snorkel, flippers, foldable bike. The credit card payment went through but the stuff never arrived. I rang the website to query the payment but they said the order was definitely delivered here. He must have sent them on to that bitch in Waterford."

"Sorry I have to ask you this, but … Did you ever meet her?"

"No."

"And you knew about her at the time?"

"Oh everyone knew about her. Everyone except … Isn't that what they're always saying? Yes, I was the last to know. All of them, laughing behind my back."

"When did you find out?"

"After she committed suicide."

"When exactly?"

She sighs. "When the guards interviewed us about the crash, I guess. They were back and forth for weeks."

"But it wasn't, officially, was it? A crash I mean."

"Oh yeah. They crashed alright. Probably pissed out of their heads. Live fast, die young and all that. Or not so young in Terry's case."

"How did she die?"

"The Buckley tart? Drug overdose. The next door neighbour kept hearing a radio on in the flat at all hours of the day and night. After a couple of weeks of it he had enough, and called the guards after he saw the big pile-up of mail through the letterbox. Then there were the curtains."

"What about them?"

"The windows. They were live with bluebottles. That's what the guards said. She would have been dead for weeks."

Oh shit. Hence the newspaper references to "grim discovery" and "decomposition". It must have been two months before they found the body.

"Can we go back to your husband? Why the U-boat obsession, all those war books?"

"His granddad was in the merchant navy. His ship was sunk by a U-boat."

"Lots of people's grandfathers were attacked by U-boats, but it doesn't explain why ... "

"You don't know his grandfather. Neil McGann? Now he could tell you things. After the wedding I only met him the once or twice. You know how they say some people don't like talking about the war? Neil McGann was the complete opposite. Stories and stories."

"They were floating in the life raft when the submarine surfaced. He said they half expected a hail of gunfire but the hatch opens, and this fella in an officer's uniform with a long brown beard pokes his head out and says *'Spielkarte?'*

"They all looked at each other and the officer threw a pack of playing cards into the raft. The U-boat submerged and went on its way. Neil said the cards kept him and his shipmates sane until they ran adrift in Newfoundland. I think that's how Terry learned poker. From his grandfather. Maybe that's why Terry was into U-boats."

I pick up a small silver trophy. From a flying club. Club Person of the Year 2003.

"Tell me more about Terry's family."

"Not much to tell. Neil died years ago, and Terry's mam back in 1998. In the end all he had was his dad, Davey McGann. I don't know what happened to the aunts and uncles, Terry rarely mentioned them. Anyway, when he disappeared I think it broke his dad's heart. Terry was always flying up to see him. I mean literally. 'I'm just hopping up to Café St Angelo,' he'd say, 'off to see dad'."

"Café what?"

"The airport at Enniskillen. Terry promised to take his dad on a flight over Boa Island. It's where Davey and his brothers and sisters grew up, Terry's aunts and uncles, while the grandfather Neil was off with the U-boats. Boa Island. Here, that's a photo of it. The family had a farm on it. But Davey his dad never got to see it again."

"He's dead too?"

207

"Passed away two years ago."

I'm not sure where this is leading us. Plod on anyway. "Did your husband have a laptop?"

A big shrug. "Sure. It's not here. Maybe it was in his office."

"Would he have taken it on the flight to Galway?"

"Maybe."

"One last question: who was he meeting in Galway that day?"

"I haven't a clue."

"Does the name TJ O'Malley ring a bell?"

She shakes her head.

One last look at all those books. Thumb through one of the ones I'm borrowing. All those U-boats.

Chapter headings, lists of illustrations, maps. A black and white photo of Grand Admiral Donitz: *The focal point of the war against England and the one possibility of bringing her to her knees is in attacking sea communications in the Atlantic.*

Thirty-Five

I phone Áine Kettle to set up another quick meeting. It's dark by the time I get home.

I'm seeing the place with fresh eyes. The front door for a start. It's not bashed in but the lock doesn't feel right. It's "sticky", a sure sign it has been picked, manipulated, bypassed. I stand there staring at it.

If I were them would I go to all that trouble, or do something more subtle? Fake a utility outage: phone, power, cable TV, plumbing, gas even. The repair people would turn up in yellow jackets to fix "the problem" and leave behind a little herd of eavesdropping devices.

Or maybe if they are that smart they would have already sussed me out as the distrustful type. No one turns up to fix your problem without you ringing them. Not in Dublin 7. That's as iffy as you calling the takeaway and them arriving with your chow mein and prawn crackers half a minute later.

So they're smart. But the clock radio in my office? The so-called free pressie from Viking? That was almost too smart.

I go inside, close the curtains, turn up the TV, look for a torch. Its lightbeam darts here and there, searching for phone and internet cables, the wifi router, any wall sockets that would be ideal nests for a bug or two.

A socket near the door is a likely candidate. I unscrew it to inspect the wiring.

Nothing.

Check upstairs.

Usually eavesdroppers are like burglars. In a hurry. Seldom putting the furniture back in just the right place. Rummaging in drawers but rarely in a neat, orderly fashion.

There's only one fatal flaw: my drawers are never neat and tidy in the first place.

My watch says 7:26 pm. The old clock radio on the bedside table says 7:26 too. It would be flashing 0:00 if they'd turned the power off. But if they were smart they would have known that and reset the clock.

Back in the living room my watch now says 7:27. So does the ancient DVD/VCR player. It says the right time.

Which is the wrong time.

I always keep its timer five minutes fast, in case I need to record something and the programme starts early. It should say 7:32. Somebody has been messing with it.

From my car to my landline and my TV equipment, I am well and truly buggered.

The grill goes on for cheese on toast. I put the disk into the DVD player. The disk from Declan Siggins, Deccie's old documentary about Terry McGann.

Can eavesdropping devices pick it up? Can they watch what you're watching?

Fuck it. Find a pair of old earplugs anyway. Hit play.

Some of the sequences are familiar. Library footage, clips rehashed on the news at the time of the crash.

The documentary shows Terry explaining what it's like to be an entrepreneur in the Celtic Tiger years.

Terry on the next big tech trends.

Terry on what he thinks about *The Apprentice*.

Terry on why this newfangled Twitter thing hasn't a hope.

Terry on how the property boom is like Monopoly with real money.

Terry on how we are a nation of begrudgers who don't understand that entrepreneurs often fail a few times "but in America they see failures as par for the course when you're trying to think different".

Terry on his ambition to buy a yacht and sail the world.

The one thing Terry McGann seems to think about most of the time is himself. The centre of the universe. The centre of everything. An entrepreneur who knows everything and can do no wrong.

Eject the DVD disk. Feed it into the paper shredder, to a horrendous noise.

That night I dream of drones and patriot missiles raining down on Dublin's northside.

There are thousands of dead schoolkids.

And several hundred baby skeletons in a septic tank in the grounds of an old orphanage.

Bad dreams of an island of saints and sadists, tales of missing children and forced adoptions, strange medical experiments and malnutrition in orphanages.

Women raped, force-fed, compelled to give birth, women told they weren't suicidal enough to have an abortion but too suicidal to hold onto their babies. Children and mothers as lesser beings, the children of sin.

Thirty-Six

The next morning I'm on the bus to Weston aerodrome again. Phil Breen has managed to track down the GAR.

"The GA ... The General Aviation Report form," he says. "And the flight plan. A lot of it was flying IFR."

My face says: What???

"IFR," he continues. "I Follow Rivers. And they had PPR for Galway."

Face says: Not another flaming aeronautical acronym?

"Sorry," he says. "Prior Permission Required. If you're landing from outside the State it's a mandatory twenty-four hours' PPR. They're more relaxed for internal flights, but Terry McGann sought PPR nine days before the flight."

"So it wasn't a sudden whim?"

"Hardly."

Yet the emails with TJ O'Malley set up their Galway meeting at the last minute. And Áine Kettle and Patricia McGann gave the impression that the flight was a spur-of-the-moment thing between three mates. Maybe these are yet more instances of Terry keeping everyone else out of the loop.

"Can I keep these?"

"Sure." Phil hands me the papers.

"Is there anything about the weather that day?"

A shuffle through more printouts. "Here. Good VFR conditions. VFR: visual flight rules."

"What's its maximum range?"

"A Beech Duchess? Hold on ... " More shuffling. "Seven eighty nautical miles."

"What's that in English?"

"Sorry. Say nine hundred miles, cruising at ten thousand feet."

"And cruising speed would be ... ?"

"A hundred and fifty-four knots."

"I don't do knots."

"Say a hundred and seventy miles an hour? And they refuelled before they took off from here with Avgas – aviation gas or 'blue'."

"A full tank?"

"No. See here? That's their maximum range and maximum fuel payload, but there's no point weighing yourself down with a full tank for a short trip."

"So let me get this straight. They take off from here with X amount of fuel, fly for Y knots or nauticals, land in Galway, take off again, fly due west in a straight line, possibly on autopilot, then begin to turn north west, heading towards Greenland."

"Or crashing."

"Can you show me how to do some calculations? Suppose their plane was turning back and heading east again, on that trajectory, how far would they get? Would they make landfall? Oh, and one last thing … "

I'm beginning to sound like Columbo.

" … do you know what time it got dark that day?"

Maggie is in the aerodrome's car park on her old Honda 50. On the minus side, the scooter will need to take a roundabout route back to town. On the plus, once we hit the snarl-ups on the quays we can slip in and out of bus lanes and bicycle lanes. The only way anyone could follow us would be in a bus or taxi. Or on another bike.

Ghost signs are all around us, if you only care to look. Hints of the city's trade history and dead businesses. In Stoneybatter, *Kelly Plastics* and *Chas O'Brien & Sons* on Benburb Street, the rotting *Worldwide Discount Airfares* in Arbour Hill, the white *General Stores* lamp globes outside the Belfry pub in Manor Street, and *D Miller & Co Ltd Coppersmiths and Brassfounders* on Church Street. The *Café Ritz* sign jutting out on Abbey Street, the square clock of *Independent Newspapers Limited*, and *Cummins and Sons – Plumbing and Paints*. The neon *Why Go Bald?* sign in Dame Lane. Faint traces of a large Bovril sign on a corner building on Dorset Street. The old *Sick and Indigent Roomkeepers Society* building around the corner from Dublin Castle. The stone or metal lettering of the *British and Irish Steam Packet Company* on Sir John Rogerson's Quay. The old *Nuzum Bros* shopfront on Pearse Street, coal agents with Huguenot roots, an exotic name in the tiles and terracotta, with the ghost of some gilding on the letters.

We're nearly there.

The former Lennox Chemicals premises on South Leinster Street – bold gilded letters announcing *PURE CHEMICALS. LABORATORY APPARATUS*. The big old lettering of *Finn's Hotel* a few buildings away.

Maggie parks the Honda in a back lane near Trinity College. Inside the college grounds we find Colley on a bench in the path between a cricket pitch and rugby pitch.

Maggie boots up her laptop to find the Google Street View of the legal practice where Kevin Reilly used to work. It takes up two floors, next door to a burger joint near the Four Courts. The ground floor is an empty retail unit with a *For Lease* sign. The top floor is possibly a flat – impossible to know without seeing it in the flesh. The office and flat share their own entrance and stairway. An old building, so probably a higgledy-piggledy layout.

"C'mon, guys. I can't just break in. I'm a gumshoe, not a hobnailed boot."

"Couldn't we get a floor plan?" Maggie asks.

"From?"

"I dunno," she says. "The planning office?"

"Maybe. But we've no time."

She gives a little pout.

Colley says, "I can case the joint if you like."

"Thanks, but let's keep your distance from this one."

"I could go in as a cleaner," Maggie says. "Office cleaners are the most anonymous people on the planet."

"Suppose they use young illegals from China?"

"Never thought of that."

"I know," Colley says. "Do a fake fire drill and empty

the gaff."

I don't like it. "Too messy. It's a small office, their website shows only half a dozen staff. You wouldn't have found the filing cabinets by the time everyone is accounted for. But I like the fireman angle."

They both wait for me to reveal my cunning plan.

"Right. Maggie, I need you to print up a badge for me. Nothing too fancy, just something to make me look like I belong in that environment. You'll need to take my mugshot for it."

I pose for her phone camera then scribble down some details and fire off more instructions.

"Colley, you check out the burger joint, the general lie of the land. And Maggie? Look after these for me."

I hand her all the flight plan stuff from Phil Breen.

"Any questions?"

She thinks for a second: "Are cows just horses that made bad life choices?"

"I meant questions about casing the joint."

I don't do breaking and entering. Not normally. But social engineering? To get into a building? Do it all the time.

For example, there's "tailgating". You hang around an outside smoking area, wait for staff to take a break and simply follow them in the back door. If you don't smoke you'll need to fake it, because a cigarette is a social engineer's best friend.

No point sneaking about. Do the opposite: draw attention to yourself, exude confidence. And while I'm not the biggest flirt, a dash of humour helps. Bung in a compliment, do them a favour.

It's all down to your body language.

Take the security goons at a big concert. They're not looking for the right badge or backstage pass. It's your general posture, the difference between a fan trying to sneak in and a worker who has the run of the place.

The first-floor receptionist hardly bothers to look at my

badge. It could have said *You've A Fire In the Basement* and she'd still have waved me through.

She pages the safety officer. A Mr Mahon, a young weasel of a guy. Probably ranks his onerous duties one step up from Deputy Acting Vice Head Prefect.

I look up from my clipboard. "This won't take long, Mr Mahon. Four main rooms on this floor and the same upstairs?"

He nods. Coming from the legal profession, he should know his rights and duties. No point in boring him with the Ease of Escape Regulations or threatening him with my powers of inspection under Section 18 of the Blah Blah Blah Act, the harsh fines and/or imprisonment.

No, Mr Mahon, I know you'll comply.

Because I have a badge.

And a clipboard.

"I'm pretty sure everything is order, Mr Mahon, but we just need a quick walk-through. Alarms, exits, you know the routine."

Bombard him with questions. I'll take an electrical reading at this wall outlet. And this wiring under the desk. I'm thorough, see? Trust me. *Like* me. You must be fierce busy but you can leave us to it if you like. Don't worry, I won't make a mess on your carpet, I won't test the fire extinguishers.

I'm only here to case the joint, check the locks and doors and where the filing cabinets are, then feck off before you're none the wiser.

Inspect clipboard again. "Right. On to the main office."

A row of battered old filing cabinets. Look around, get a lie of the land. Imagine what it looks like at night-time. No point checking the door keys I nabbed from Kevin Reilly's sister. Not yet.

Next, the fire exits. The one at the rear of the building opens onto a car park, which is probably locked at night. Messy. Another goes into the burger joint next door. Perfect. Colley said they might do that. For fire and safety.

"Do your staff use this door much?"

"A bit of a sore point, Mr Wright," he says. Oh oops, he's referring to me. "We like to know where people are."

I give a knowing nod. "Absolutely." So that's how they sneak out for a quick fag. Or a burger. "You could always put a camera on the door."

"Isn't that a bit drastic?"

"Well just make sure they're not blocked," I tell him.

No, no sign of CCTV inside or out.

"Of course," he says.

What's Colley always saying? You start with the end: how you leave.

No point in breaking in if you can't get out again. And your escape route won't necessarily be the same as your entry point.

Thirty-Seven

It's probably the most common lock: a pin tumbler. A Yale.

Kevin Reilly's old key for the Chubb lock has worked fine but the Yale won't budge. They must have changed it over the years, or at least once since he did his vanishing act.

Spies and PIs on TV pick locks all the time. But I don't. Not normally. For starters, the gardai don't like it. It's burglary, criminal trespass.

I don't do fistfights and firearms either. The things a TV private eye gets up to on a typical case (assault, intimidation, unlawful discharge of a firearm, all the usuals) would put you away for three to six, in the kind of facility where good-looking TV actor types are in big demand.

And another thing: you're doing it in the dark, against the clock, and it's my first time, and everything is happening in slow motion.

So stay calm. Steady. Insert the bent tension wrench into the bottom of the keyway. Apply torque. Wiggle the lock's plug left and right, keeping the lock slightly turned with the tension wrench. Insert the pick, feel around for the "weirdest" pin. Apply light pressure to lift it. Have an almost unbearable urge to scratch the back of your neck.

Good, the "weirdest" pin is set. Next, apply more torque on the tension wrench. Slowly, calmly. If Colley were here now he'd make a bad joke. *Torque is cheap.* But he's outside and I'm alone. Let's keep it that way.

Rotate slightly more. Continue setting each pin, in order of weirdest to least weird, turning the plug as you go. Once the final pin is set, the plug is free to rotate – just as if you'd inserted the proper key. That's the theory anyway.

In the movies it takes seconds. Or they skip all that and use a credit card. As if.

Pin tumbler locks aren't exactly my speciality, and the

lock is turning out to be a right awkward bollix.

Switch to Colley's smallest screwdriver, then a sturdy paper clip (straightened out but with a bended loop at ninety degrees, just long enough to fit into the key-way), then the Allen Wrench. It's two sizes too big for the key-way but Colley had the good sense to file it down. Don't ask how Colley knows these things.

It takes a good ten minutes to get the pins just right. Yet when you hit the sheer line you know it.

You feel it.

A kind of deja vu as the plug turns, the whole thing turns at once and you think: it's your first time for real, you're doing it in the dark, and all that reading and practice with my *Dummies Guide To Lock Picking* have paid off after all.

And you're in.

The room isn't completely dark. City-centre buildings rarely are. There's usually a dusting of streetlight and moonshine, even through blinds or curtains.

Put the small backpack on a desk, close the blinds. You can just about make out the outlines of furniture, filing cabinets, a coat stand. Various machines are glowing or blinking on standby: an extension cable, a sleeping desktop PC, a snoring TV, a thermostat, a blinking alarm.

This particular alarm isn't blinking. It has just been disarmed. The secret combination came from the back of a dead lawyer's diary.

A further glow from my mobile as I text Colley: *I'm in.*

Don't ask why Colley happens to own a fancy Digital Night Vision Scope, with a 50mm lens that works not only in the half-glow of the street lighting but also in total darkness if necessary, thanks to IR illumination.

A text comes back from him: *Clear.*

A thin but powerful ray of a flashlight scours the room. Not a hand torch – for jobs like this I prefer the headlamp. Nothing fancy, just a Duracell thing I bought on a whim for a tenner years ago, for jobs around the house. It doesn't splash light everywhere, and it's hands-free.

The filing cabinet I want isn't locked. The files are alphabetical. The ones I need are easy to find. Take them to the relative seclusion of the toilet, to snap away with my iPhone. Page after page of them.

Lawyers are serious paper addicts. They even print out client emails. Emails, letters, forms, the whole shebang.

I'm on the final file when another text message arrives: *Get the FUCK OUT.*

Suddenly another light crashes into the room: a blue one this time, flashing.

Then another.

No need to look out the windows. The street must be crawling with cop cars. Well, not exactly crawling. Leaping and jumping more like. How the hell did they know I was here?

Shove files back into filing cabinets.

Rush down to the fire exit.

Burst a little too loudly through the door.

Stroll to the table, nobody in the burger joint bats an eyelid. No one apart from Maggie Dardis.

My mobile buzzes. Another incoming text. I ignore it. Switch it off and curse myself.

Nobody knows how many mobile phones are bugged in Ireland. The official line is that it's only done in extreme cases, crime and terrorism. In reality it has become so normalised that tapping is done on a day-to-day basis on tens of thousands of calls. Phone taps without warrants, without visibility or transparency.

Telecom operators have begun to admit that direct-access wires or "pipes" are connected directly to their networks, so the powers that be can listen in. To record not just conversations but times, dates, who was on the other phone, and lots of other metadata. Like the location of the device. The fecking location.

My mobile phone is bugged, buggered, banjaxed.

Maggie slides her frothy coffee towards me.

"Hi."

"Hi."

"Trouble?" she asks.

"You could say."

I put the backpack down and point to her milk moustache, which she rubs off. "We need to meet somewhere tomorrow where we won't be watched.

She thinks for a moment. "How about IMMA?"

"Yeah, but not indoors. Too many cameras."

"The gardens then."

"Fine."

So that's sorted. The gardens at the back of the Irish Museum of Modern Art in Kilmainham.

Through the window the cop cars are still flashing and moaning away, to the hiss and crackle of walkie-talkies.

"I need you to buy two pay-as-you-go phones," I tell her. "Nothing fancy, not a top-of-the-range 4G gizmo with Google Glass. Something cheap and nasty, something you can actually use to make phone calls. And pay for it in cash."

"Starving freelance?"

She needn't remind me. I slip her some of Mrs Kettle's fifty-euro notes as discreetly as I can.

"I also need an airline ticket. In my name, on this date." I scribble down the details. "And that's my passport number. On that date, anywhere out of the country, on the cheapest flight you can find, one-way. Here, use my credit card."

"Not cash again?"

"No, credit card is fine, but just for the air ticket."

"I thought you didn't like flying."

Yes. I've aviophobia, aerophobia. Fear of flying, fear of crashing, a fear of heights. Blame the media. Doris Day had a fear of flying. So did Stanley Kubrick. Whoopi Goldberg has to travel by bus or train to other US states.

"Yeah, Maggie. I'm Whoopi Goldberg. If there's any change left over get me some sedatives."

My foot pushes the backpack towards her.

"A couple of other things," I continue. "My iPhone is in that bag. It's a liability. I need you to go somewhere, miles from anywhere, switch it on, download the pics from it as fast as you can, switch it off again, get rid of it and scarper. Got all that?"

"Yeah."

"Put the pics on a memory stick and dump the phone as far away as possible. Get it stolen, give it to a beggar, drop it in the Liffey."

"Is that it?"

"Have you a spare laptop I can borrow?"

"Sure. Anything else, mister detecty man?"

"Could you swing by my house and grab some spare clothes?"

"Oh yeah. And do the laundry while I'm at it and feed the cat."

"You know I don't have a cat."

"Anything else?"

"Do it quietly – the place is bugged. And tomorrow, at IMMA, bring along the flight plan stuff I gave you earlier."

"Anything else?"

"I need a ruler and a compass. Try the desk in the living room. A compass to draw circles, like you used to do at school."

"Is that it?"

"Be careful."

She takes the money and backpack and leaves.

Thirty-Eight

No sign of life at Colley's. It's an artisan two up two-down in the heart of Stoneybatter. Not the best time of night to bother him, but needs must.

That Special Branch detective's words from France spin in my head as I ring the doorbell. *We can track you through your email, your mobile, your laptop, your passport …*

The house is still dark. Ring again.

Try ringing one last time. Colley is already opening the door.

"That was a right disaster. Tea, Reidy?"

Tea. The biggest cliché when something's wrong is to put the kettle on. He follows me in, closes the curtains, switches on a light.

"Sorry, we've no coffee," he says. "D'you take milk?"

"No."

He starts making the tea. The room is open-plan, high ceilings, period fireplace. The shelves are coming down with vinyl and CDs. Colley has this theory that middle age is the point at which the amount of music in one's record collection begins to outrun the time left to enjoy it.

I grab an LP, a slice of early Motown, and put it on the turntable. Crank up the volume, beckon him to join me at the kitchen table, lean in conspiratorially.

"Hope your neighbours don't mind."

"You're grand, Reidy. They're on their holliers."

"Do airlines give their passengers' passport numbers to the security people?"

"I dunno."

"What about ferries?"

"How the feck would I know?"

"I need a passport."

"A false one? What kind of eejit d'you think I am?"

"I just thought, what with your connections … "

"Well you thought wrong."

"I need to disappear.

"Sure. Fine. Disappearing is all the feckin' rage at the moment."

"I need to get back to France without anyone knowing. I'm not asking you for a passport – just spell out the options, you being a man of the world and all."

Because how would I know? I'm just a plodding PI, not a state-sponsored secret agent with a nicely printed licence to kill. I don't have a safe deposit box in Zürich containing guns, cash and two dozen passports.

Colley scratches his chin, a day's grey stubble. "What about identity theft? The *Day of the Jackal* thing."

"What? Trawl through graveyards looking for a baby who would've been your age?"

"Yeah, Reidy. Copy down the name and date, get a copy birth cert from the Registrar, send it in with your photo and passport application form and… "

"That was half a century ago. Surely they've closed off the loopholes by now – *and* it would take too long."

"Then get one of those emergency travel documents you can use at a foreign airport."

"No way. That would just draw attention."

"Right." He thinks a bit more. "OK. Bribe an official for a blank passport and fill in your details. Or nick one from someone who looks like you and make a few alterations."

"It takes more than a biro and a pot of glue to change a modern passport, Colley." He looks annoyed. "Sorry. I like the bribe-an-official idea though."

Because Ireland has had its fair share of cash-for-passport scandals. One passport officer at the Irish embassy in London provided false passports for cash and sex (twenty four thousand dollars per passport, and I don't know how much sex). Fake Irish passports also keep turning up on dead bodies of jihadists on the Iraqi-Syrian border. Or what about the dodgy Irish passports that pop up in intelligence fiascos, such as the Iran-Contra affair –

Ollie North, aka "John Clancy", using a false Irish passport to visit Iran? Or the Israeli hit team in Dubai four years ago, they were on Irish passports too. The only upshot was that an Israeli embassy official was sent packing.

"So that's all I have to do? Bribe someone in the passport office or an Irish embassy?"

"Yeah, Reidy. Or an Israeli one."

Half an hour later we're discussing how to find a forger. I'm picturing dark alleyways and grubby backstreet lockups.

"Ah no, Reidy. Not face-to-face. Everything's done online nowadays."

So we flick through a few sites on the dark side of the Net. Seems you can buy most things on the Silk Road. Drugs, guns, bodies (dead or alive). The going rate for a fake Irish passport is $350. With lots of loving detail about the technical processes involved: thermal printing, ultraviolet overlays, embossing, holofoils, you name it. Sites whose preferred online payment method is anything but credit cards or Paypal. *We prefer Bitcoins, cash, cheques or postal orders, with the payee field left blank.*

"I don't like it, Colley. How can you trust anyone who's in the business of faking stuff – whether it's fake passports, fake luxury goods or fake orgasms?"

"True enough."

"Mind if I kip on your couch?"

Heuston Station is waking up, the sun hasn't begun to burn off the early morning mist, and Arnaud is grumpy. He hasn't taken too kindly to being rung at six in the morning from the last working phonebox on the northside.

"Then what about Julie?" I ask, plonking two paper coffee cups down on the counter in one of the station's coffee bars.

"No," he says, "don't bring her into it."

"But if anyone would know about fake papers and passports, Julie would."

"No."

"And she still owes me one."

Julie is a kind of ex-client of mine who has been in Ireland for a couple of years. A long story. She's also Arnaud's dish pig: a pot washer, sud buster, pearl diver. And an illegal.

"I've had to lay her off, remember?" he says. "She's lost in the wilds of Connemara at the moment, so you can't ask her where to get a passport."

"*And* a driver's licence. I'll need them in this name." I push a folded piece of paper towards him.

"Not asking for much, are you?"

The bell of the Luas and the smells of burnt hops and damp leaves drift into the station. Autumn is creeping in again.

"It must be far easier to fake a driver's licence than a fifty euro note," I continue. "And if I were a forger I'd get a lot more for a driving licence than fifty euros. So if you could ever ask Julie … "

"I think I have a name. Jenny Jameson. She's in the film business. That's how I … "

"I don't need a bloody movie star, Arnaud, I need a fake passport."

"Yeah. But she's not an actress. She's a … "

Arnaud leaves first, while I spend ten minutes in the photo booth for my passport photos.

It's a five-minute walk from the station to the leafy lane that leads up to the art museum.

Maggie's Honda is by the rear of the main building, and she's standing at the steps down to the formal gardens. We walk down to their far end, which you can hardly make out in the dewy fog.

"You dumped my phone?"

226

She nods. "On the Luas. The Red Line."

"Perfect."

She flops on a bench and puts down a large carry-bag.

I open it for a quick look. "You got everything?"

"Uh huh."

Spare clothes, airline boarding pass to Glasgow-Prestwick, sedatives, the flight plans that Phil the pilot gave me earlier, a cheap mobile phone, ruler and compass, and Maggie's spare laptop.

"Nothing incriminating on it?"

"A clean machine. No sexually transmitted diseases."

I take my passport photos out of my pocket. "Give these to Arnaud. Tell him they're for Jenny." And I hand her back the boarding pass. "But I won't be needing this."

"I thought you bloody well wanted to fly somewhere."

"Yeah. That's what I want them to think."

There's one last person to see before doing a Houdini: Áine Kettle. I'm back at her place in Clonskeagh, trying to find a backup of her original memory of what happened.

"Sorry, can we hold it there a sec? What were the first words your sister said on the phone?"

"It's like I told you."

"Please. Her exact words."

Because that's the trouble. The human brain doesn't start off as an empty attic where you decide which furniture to store in it, and some people bung in a bit of old tat from IKEA while others pack it to the rafters with junk because downstairs has gone for the minimalist look.

The walls, floors and ceilings keep changing for a start.

The ways we store our memories aren't neat and precise. It's not like an attic or a hard drive or a photographic archive. We turn past events into stories. These become open to suggestion and elaboration. They keep changing. So when you drag something up from your memory you're recalling not the incident per se but the last time you thought about it, the last story.

Even a flashbulb memory isn't like a photograph, a moment fixed in time. It's a story that is retold, refashioned, remodelled – less a single snapshot, more a movie that's constantly being reshot and edited, even splicing in extra sequences that were shot at a different time or that never happened.

Within months most of the memory will drain away; the remaining fragments become a partial story, with more and more gaps and forgotten sections. Nobody likes stories with big holes in them, so you begin to fill in the gaps, to infer, to add twists and turns that keep changing, without you even realising, until these gap fillers become so integrated into your memory that they're as good as true. Meanwhile one or two small but absolutely crucial facts have dropped through the bloody cracks, Mrs Kettle.

"What do you want me to say?" she says.

"Her exact words, that's all," I repeat.

Through the front-room window the long drive and streets look empty. If anyone were following me he'd stand out a mile.

"But I've told you."

"You said 'My sister said she saw *him.*' "

"Exactly."

"But did she ever say who *he* was?

"Of course she did."

"No. Her exact words. What did she call him? 'Johnny'? 'John'? 'Mr Kettle'? Did she say 'I've just seen that lazy lump of a husband of yours'?"

"I can't remember."

"Because she didn't, did she? She only said *he* was there. *He, him,* that's all. A man from five years ago who was older, balder, and possibly taller and skinnier too."

That's my problem. The most untrustworthy thing in this whole case isn't DS Coleman, or the French cops, or the waitresses in Mentidera. Or even Áine Kettle's husband the banker, or her sister with her "condition" about faces. It's Áine Kettle's memory bank.

Thirty-Nine

Your passport is a most peculiar document.

Technically it's never yours. It doesn't belong to the bearer.

It evolved from medieval times, from the letters of introduction from a traveller's home State to the State being visited, asking it to accord the traveller respect and not infringe his or her rights. A magic document allowing you to cross borders and swan past Immigration without let or hindrance.

All a load of tosh really. What may have started as a handy letter giving travellers special privileges has become a compulsory licence. It's not so much about the bearer's freedoms as about State control of moving bodies. Without those papers you're going nowhere.

My fake papers will take a week. That's what Jenny Jameson has told Arnaud. So I need to keep my head down for seven days, starting at the central bus station.

Its official name is Busáras. In Irish, a building (*áras*) for buses.

By rights this bus house shouldn't exist. Busáras was built when our fledgling State was even more broke than today, but at least at a time when the country still had ambitions and dreamers. What they dreamt began to emerge on the city's skyline: a building that was both Irish and international, ancient and futuristic, local and outward looking, from its design ideas to its globally sourced tiles.

The bitter twist was that this thoroughly modern (some would say postmodern) structure was going up at the same time as the State was organising a cultural clampdown on writers, film-makers and other big dreamers. The list of forbidden books reads like a who's who of Irish twentieth-century literature. Even today, hundreds of crime-fiction magazines are still banned.

Dubliners have a love–hate relationship with Busáras.

Most probably don't know half its secrets. I was on its top floor once, during a case four years ago. Its mosaic oculus wouldn't look out of place in a mosque or Moroccan palace. In the basement I seem to remember there was a tiny theatre without wings, the Eblana, though I can't recall ever being in it. Instead of doing first runs of plays by John B. Keane, Brian Friel and Tom Murphy it now does left luggage lockers.

Today the main drama is on the ground floor, in the atrium. It's a watering hole that is constructed around the needs of the buses: their need to move, eat and drink.

Each morning the buses flock together around their feeding trough, like spokes around the hub of a wheel, as they devour their passengers, drink their diesel and head off to the countryside.

I'm the kind of traveller who hates cutting it fine. Normally I'd arrive at the departure gate hours before the final call. But there's no point in hanging around at a large feeding trough under all those cameras. So I kill half an hour with a slow coffee in the Robert Reade pub across the road.

I've bought plenty of reading material along with me, including half a dozen of Terry McGann's history books and *Domestique Labour,* his book about cycling.

The peloton is the main pack of riders, a large, densely packed grouping that flows as smoothly and naturally as a flock of birds. Like birds in formation, each "unit" of the peloton obeys simple mathematical rules — each makes slight adjustments in response to the units around, beside, and particularly in front of you. These simple rules produce complex patterns, like a huge cloud of starlings as they weave their mesmerising dance in the skies.

Unlike airports, bus stations can afford to cut it fine. Some drivers will only begin to let the passengers on less than five minutes before departure time. That's when I walk quickly from the pub to the atrium, with five minutes to go. I can hear engines ticking over, the PA announcing departure gate numbers, a robotic voice warning *No pedestrian access. No pedestrian access.*

I lug my bag onto the bus, hand the driver cash for a ticket. Above him, a video screen shows two stragglers struggling to put their cases into the luggage compartment at the side of the bus. I doubt if the footage of uneventful journeys is kept for much time.

We set off. Small towns pass by: Virginia, Butlersbridge, Belturbet, Derrylin. We're heading north towards the lakes of Enniskillen, the mountains heaped up in slow motion, the valleys carved out over millions of years. If the glacier that carved out this particular side of Fermanagh and Donegal was in no hurry, it wasn't particularly kind either. It was ruthless. Its deep scars left a beautiful countryside, though you can't eat scenery.

After Enniskillen there are hilly fields and sheep and forests and windfarms with windmills doing slow gymnastic cartwheels. The bus hurtles through a corridor of trees, a thick wall of greenery with the occasional glimpse of Lough Erne's silver waters and wooded islands. The shore road to Ballyshannon is twisting and rattling. I'm about to give up trying to read.

It is better to be closer to the front of the peloton, to avoid crashes and the "elastic band effect". This is where a change in speed becomes amplified as it ripples to the back of the pack. The guy behind a rider who is changing his speed must adjust slightly faster in order to avoid collisions. Sometimes, though, you reach a tipping point, a point where the fragile equilibrium breaks down …

Almost four hours from Dublin we pull up at a bus station by the steep banks of the River Erne.

Ballyshannon has been battered and beaten after several rounds of the recession, and the umpire forgot to stop the fight. The town clock has fallen in a recent storm, and many shops on the main street are abandoned.

The little bus station's glass wall has some taxi numbers. I ring one with my new mobile phone. The cab arrives quickly enough and takes me the ten kilometres or so down the road to Rossnowlagh. "It's *Ros Neamhlach* in Irish," the driver explains, "the heavenly headland." Our small-talk is about placenames and holidays, the changeable weather, the farce with the new water charges, the unemployment and emigration. I tell him I'm here for the fishing.

Rossnowlagh strand is a wide expanse of flat sandy beach. Two women and a gaggle of toddlers paddle in the shallows. Several hundred yards out are two dots, possibly a pair of surfers.

At the Sandhouse Hotel the young receptionist says paying by cash is no problem (my excuse is that my credit card has expired). She says the best bedrooms are the "Deluxe Sea View", looking out onto the strand.

Would Tony Blair have had a Deluxe Sea View during his idyllic childhood summers here? I try to imagine the little Blairite sitting back in his armchair by the picture window, planning his meteoric rise to world domination.

I don't want a room overlooking a mile-long beach and an astonishing seascape. It costs more, it's high season and most of these rooms are gone.

I take a "Mountain View" instead. It faces inland, overlooking the tennis court and main road: the only way in. If anyone comes looking for me, I doubt they'll be arriving by sea.

It's hard to imagine this afternoon, yet the Sandhouse used to be a thatched cottage bar with only three rooms. In the late 1940s the new owners transformed it into a hotel for English tourists. That trade dried up overnight when the Troubles came; the Blairs, too, stopped coming in 1969.

So they switched focus to the Yanks (as we all called Americans back then), investing heavily to turn the place into a four-star hotel. Then came the economic crash of 2008. They went into voluntary liquidation – an unusual step for a hotel at the time – and carried on trading.

Nobody would buy the place, so three years ago it was sold at auction to its manager for €650,000. That's cheaper than the cost of a three-bed house in the posh parts of Dublin at the height of the boom.

The height of the boom. When everything in the world began to unravel.

My borrowed laptop is on the bed. It's opened at a folder with a series of pictures. Photos of files from the law firm's office.

It takes next to no time to piece it all together, this old boys' network built on mutual backscratching. Kevin Reilly's legal practice did much of the paperwork for Terry McGann's main company: memoranda and articles of association, annual returns, change of directors, setting up subsidiaries, office leases, a B5N this, a B6 that, NDAs, IP, contracts with staff and with other companies.

The solicitor also looked after Terry McGann's personal stuff, such as the conveyancing of a series of family homes over the years, from Harold's Cross to their final one in Stillorgan.

In turn, several of McGann's holding companies banked with Johnny Kettle's bank. Nothing unusual in that either; Ireland had a narrow choice in banks back then.

Next, the list of Kevin Reilly's clients. Mostly criminal work in latter years, a rogue's gallery including one Gino Beattie. There is no escaping that name.

Next, all three wills: Kevin Reilly's, Terry McGann's, Johnny Kettle's. The bequests are all exactly as the widows and Reilly's sister and my solicitor Alan have described.

Last but not least, the papers related to Reilly's yacht. The *Nora Barnacle* is owned by a trust set up two months before his disappearance. So despite the lawyer's mounting debts from his property deals, at least his yacht was safe. Maybe that's why nobody was chasing after it, nobody asking questions when the *Nora Barnacle* upped and vanished.

It's still bright so I take a stroll along the beach. Down at the gently crumbling waves is a long stick, a bit of driftwood. I use it to doodle five words in the sand:

Who?

Where?

When

How?

Why?

Cross the first three out, one after the other. The stick stops at *How?*

It's staring me in the face yet I still can't see it.

An advancing wave washes the words away, though you can still make out their traces.

Yachts. What did Arnaud say again? Yes, why all the palaver with the plane? Why stage a ghost flight? Why not simply skip off in Kevin Reilly's boat?

What would a reasonable man on the 46A bus conclude?

That he's on the wrong bus.

Or that he took two buses.

Back at the hotel I spread the maps out on the bedroom floor, with copies of Terry McGann's old flight plans on the bed and dressing table. The names of airports and aerodromes in Ireland and the UK are circled. So too are ones in France, Belgium, Spain, Portugal. Terry McGann got around alright.

Boot up the laptop, find its calculator. Take out the ruler and compass. Draw lines and circles on the map, just as Phil the pilot has shown me. Do the interconnected sums on the calculator: total fuel, payload, mileage, distance.

Even with my rotten maths I'm able to figure out that it would have been possible – just – for the aircraft to turn back towards land and make it as far as Donegal town or its hinterlands. But where could it land?

Donegal Airport – Carrickfinn to the locals – is a

stretch of land at Kincasslagh on the northwest coast. From the air – from the satellite images – it's narrow, flat, quite dramatic. But it's too far north and out of range.

I'm getting tired. It's getting late. What about Donegal Bay, further south?

What about it? Donegal Bay can wait until the morning. It's time for some light bedtime reading.

Cycling has a hierarchy, a class structure if you like. At the top is the queen bee, your team leader, the guy you want to win the overall race. At the bottom is the humble domestique. He is the tactical footsoldier who must be willing to sacrifice everything so that "our guy" and the team pick up the points.

The domestique's mundane roles include water carrier, tow truck, minder and wind break. The merde *work.*

To understand cycling, to truly understand the shapes of the pelotons and echelons and the overall shape of the race, you need to grasp the physics – particularly the aerodynamics.

Much of your effort is to push aside the air in front of you, until you learn that riding in someone else's slipstream is far easier than taking the lead.

That is your main job much of the time: to create a slipstream in front of your team leader, and shield him from the crosswinds.

"Drafting" like this can save your guy a third of his energy in a long event. So you ride into the wind, sheltering your guy, giving him a much easier ride while he's tucked behind your wheel.

That is your role: to protect and safely deliver him to the final stretch before the finishing line. Above all, you shield him from the wind.

It's all about following the path of least resistance …

Forty

The next morning the same taxi driver takes me to Donegal town, to a white cottage-like building by the pier. It's the ticket office for the Donegal Bay Waterbus.

As buses go, this one is big: a blue-and-white ship, which is moored a hundred yards down the quay. A sign says it seats 160. What it doesn't say is that most of the 160 are pensioners and tourists. It takes a while for all of them to board, by which time the ship has become a Babel of tongues and accents, from Brooklyn to Beijing via the Black Forest and Birmingham.

The bay is a smooth mirror. As we pass a seal colony I skip the zoological, geographical and natural history commentary and hit the bar. It serves beer, spirits, tea, coffee, biscuits, crisps and a slew of ice cream. I order a Merlot and quiz the woman behind the counter.

"Ah no," she says, "sea sickness is never a problem. It's almost always calm on Donegal Bay."

"Would you get many airplanes around here?"

"Hmm. One or two. Helicopters mostly."

The cruise takes eighty minutes. On the journey back, the cabaret and loud singalong are impossible to avoid. You could never tactfully ditch a Beechcraft Duchess in Donegal Bay. It's not quiet enough.

Back at the hotel, boot up the laptop, spread out the maps on the bedroom floor. More mucking about with ruler, compass and calculator.

If not Donegal Bay or Donegal town, what about the airfield at Letterkenny, the Swilly Aeroclub? Too far east. Anything around Derry would be even further again.

Or how about Finner Camp to the south of here, outside Bundoran? Hardly. You'd have the army crawling over you in no time.

Or Sligo Airport, even further down the coast? Way

too busy. You'd be bound to be seen.

If you can't go north and can't go south, that only leaves east. Somewhere east, across the border.

The maps tell me little but the history books say a lot. That particular area of Northern Ireland is peppered with old RAF airfields from the second World War and from the Troubles. And one place stands out: St Angelo. It's a former RAF base outside Enniskillen, and still a working aerodrome.

Of course: St Angelo. What did Terry McGann's wife say he was always telling her?

I'm just hopping up to Café St Angelo, off to see dad.

Terry McGann would have known it well.

Then there's that news story from 2008, from my trawl of stories about the Galway Three. It's the one about mysterious flying objects in County Fermanagh.

UFO spotters said members of the public had contacted the police about the sightings. Although army personnel conducted a search of the area they found nothing. The Armagh Observatory said it wasn't a meteorite either.

Check Terry McGann's old flight plans. Yeah, he had flown to St Angelo often enough. If they had headed due east they could have reached the little airfield. Just about.

But they hadn't, had they?

No one had seen them. Unless, perhaps, you count a couple of UFO spotters. And who'd believe them?

So if the plane didn't land at an airport, what does that leave us with? Donegal Bay can be ruled out, and there aren't enough flat fields around Donegal town. As for landing on a main road or motorway, that's just for the movies.

I'm distracted by the noise in the hotel's car park below my bedroom window.

It's a car pulling up.

Just a family. Three or four kids pour out of the back seat.

I am walking along the strand. At its southern end is a shortcut to the narrow cliff road up to the headland.

The road rises steeply, quickly. It soon gives a near-panoramic view of the beach and the bay, with a hint of the Bluestack Mountains further north.

A muddy old blue car drives down the cliff road towards me. As it passes, the hand on the steering wheel gives a little flicker of a wave. If he were walking past me instead of driving he'd probably give a casual country nod. I nod in return and salute my own imaginary cap.

Near the summit is the Smuggler's Creek Inn. Its bar and restaurant have comfortable old furniture, dark wooden floors, exposed brick, an open fire for chilly evenings. Like the Sandhouse, the Smuggler's Creek oozes character, decades of it. Like the Sandhouse, it was reborn during the recession. The new owners bought it five years ago.

"Yeah, you do be seeing them flying over from time to time," an old man with a coffee at the bar says. "But at a good height, what with the cliffs and all."

Down near the strand a white dot begins moving up the cliff road: Dave the Drone's white van.

Soon the two of us will be driving back to Ballyshannon. To the oldest town in Ireland, the town of Allingham the poet and Gallagher the Rory. *The music of the waterfall, the mirror of the tide ...*

How hard can it be to fly and land a light aircraft on a big stretch of water, if the stretch is as long and as complicated as Lough Erne? Only one way to find out.

If you can't afford to prang an aircraft, there's always the next best thing: one of Dave's drones.

We're about to use one of his quadcopters to make a home movie that begins in Ballyshannon. Everything has gone smoothly so far. If this were a real movie the director would probably be called Alfred Cock, what with there being no hitch.

The blackened old stone bridge crossing the river is too exposed and open for a take-off, even of a little drone. Ballyshannon's new concrete bridge of the bypass is almost as bad. So we drive down the Mall, past a large old warehouse or factory that has seen better days. We reach a recently restored handball alley, a playground and a small park. It's only a couple of feet above sea level. Perfect.

Dave takes the quadcopter – a seriously big model this time – out of the van. We wait for a woman with a Labrador to go out of sight, then Dave does his stuff.

The drone takes off. He puts it in a holding pattern at around fifty feet up while we get back in the van. I'm driving while Dave does the droning, as it were.

He swipes the iPad's screen. The drone rises and flies due east, following the water. Over the bridges and sluice gates of Cathleen's Falls. Over the generating station. Over Assaroe Lake, an artificial reservoir for the hydro-electric scheme. We are heading upstream and east towards Belleek and Lough Erne, to its Lower or North Lough. The van's satnav map shows the lake stretching for twenty-six miles to the Upper or South Lough, with Enniskillen in between, straddling a wide river.

If it's windy there can be waves on the lough of open-sea dimensions. Dave is more worried about the drone getting out of range or hitting a tree. We're not even over the border at Belleek he loses his nerve. We pull in, he lands the drone and puts it back in the van.

At one time, one of Terry McGann's history books says, *in summer the Erne was in Fermanagh, in winter Fermanagh was in the Erne.*

The Erne suffered winter flooding until the 1880s, when a drainage scheme lowered the loughs by six feet. Metal plaques around the lakes show these new levels, which were enshrined in a statute. Nowadays the water level is maintained at around a hundred and fifty feet.

Deep enough, in other words.

Now fast-forward to January 1941, and a top-secret

meeting between Sir John Maffey, Britain's representative in Dublin, and Ireland's Taoiseach, Eamon de Valera.

Sir John says the Brits have a problem. Or rather two problems.

Problem number one: every mile of cover that the air patrols from Northern Ireland can provide for Atlantic convoys is paramount. But the mid-Atlantic has an unprotected section. This is the so-called "Black Gap", where U-boats can roam free from detection.

Problem number two: it's a war, Ireland is neutral. So the patrols have to fly north over Lough Foyle before heading around Donegal's northern coast and back down to the Atlantic battleground.

And the solution? The Donegal Corridor.

At the secret meeting Dev agrees – unofficially of course – to relax Ireland's neutrality, to give the patrols a direct route out to the Atlantic. *The path of least resistance.*

The flying boats will take off from their base on Lough Erne, fly across to Belleek – still in Fermanagh, UK territory – skip over the border to Ballyshannon in County Donegal and on to the Atlantic to meet the convoys bound for Derry. Thanks to this narrow, four-mile-long strip of "neutral" airspace, the air patrols increase their range by a hundred miles to cover much of the Black Gap.

Thus this stretch of lake that we are driving beside is dragged into the front line of the war. It becomes a turning point in the Battle of the Atlantic.

So that's the Donegal Corridor, and Terry McGann knew all about it. Was possibly obsessed about it.

Kids from Belfast, evacuated to the South after the first blitz on the city – kids no longer kids now but old men and women – can still remember the night flights over the big hotel at the bottom of Bundoran's main street. Despite the blackout the hotel kept a bright light shining. To guide the aircrews back to Lough Erne.

The airmen were briefed: *If you crash in the South you must say you were on an air-sea rescue mission. You were responding to an*

SOS from an unidentified aircraft, possibly German.

Meanwhile an armed trawler was secretly stationed up the coast at Killybegs, for air-sea rescue and to supply planes that had run out of fuel.

Terry's books would have told him all of this. They listed all the crashes and forced landings, and told of how the Irish Army would hand the bodies over at the border, the coffins draped in the Union flag, a guard of honour, the priest giving a final blessing, a bugler sounding the Last Post.

Locals can still remember pulling bodies from the wrecks at Abbeylands and Tullan Strand on either side of the River Erne. Bodies identified from dog tags, love letters, burnt ID cards.

The ghosts of Allied airmen still haunt these hills.

We drive through Belleek's main street to switch to the Lough's northern shore. At a discreet distance outside town the drone takes off again.

I've one eye on the road, the other on Dave's iPad, as the quadcopter flies parallel to the shore. I'm not quite sure where this is all taking us, but the footage is amazing. The screen shows little white dots in the slate-grey water below: boats, marinas, pontoons, slipways, jetties. It's busy this morning, as it often is since they opened the Shannon-Erne Waterway twenty years ago.

During the war this would have been isolated, rugged, swampy terrain. Not many roads, no electricity, no water or telephones. Perfect seclusion for the training camps before the invasion of Normandy.

The nearby hills made it unsafe to land in darkness or bad weather. And the flying boats didn't have satnav or all the other modern crutches we have.

Not all crashes were fatal. One evening in December 1942 a huge Flying Fortress, *The Devil Himself,* circled noisily over north Sligo and landed safely on Mullaghmore beach. The crew were feted at a local hotel and Finner army camp for seventeen days while awaiting a replacement engine.

Dave is thinking of crashes too. The drone is low on power, it's too far out, there's too much of a gap between the road and the lake. He's too worried.

I pull in at a picnic spot. The quadcopter flutters safely back to land.

He puts it back in the van and gets back in the driving seat. I rewind and watch the footage as we continue along the northern shore road.

Forty-One

Towards the Enniskillen end, the North Lough is dotted with coves, inlets, and hundreds of small islands. Islands often completely covered in trees, as if woods have sprouted fully formed from the waters.

By the end of the war many of these islands were still inhabited; I don't know if any are still now. It was a tough life. In winter the islanders would set out in their flat-bottomed boats or "cots", to break a path through the ice to the neighbours on the next island. Then on to the next island, and the next.

Our main road reaches Boa Island, the largest, least isolated of the islands. "Island" may give the impression that you see water all around you, though Boa Island is more like a narrow strip of fields and hedges about five miles long, close to the shoreland and with no sight of water for long stretches of the road. Short bridges at either end connect the road to the mainland. Mainland to island to mainland again. At times it's hard to tell where the one begins and the other ends.

Boa takes its name from Badhbh, the Celtic goddess of war. Kind of appropriate, given Boa was also a satellite of the flying boat base at Castle Archdale during the war.

Boa Island.

Where have we heard that name before?

Of course. Terry McGann's grandfather, Neil the merchant seaman, came from here. Terry's father Davey grew up here too. You can almost see Terry's dad with the brothers and sisters. Davey McGann, just another fresh-faced kid on the farm, feeding and playing with the aircrews of the flying boats, the exotic young airmen from another world.

A couple of miles up the road is Killadeas. I haven't a clue how to pronounce it. The placename is underlined in Terry's history books – it gets a serious amount of biro and highlighter.

On the ground, you'd think not many wartime reminders would remain, not much to look at today. Not unless you knew where to look.

A deep crater marked by a memorial cross; a piece of a Catalina's wing that is now the roof of a sheep pen; large rings that once held the flying boats down in winter gales; a sunken barge by a refuelling jetty; the remains of a slipway for the Catalinas, now owned by a local yacht club.

At one time they planned to turn Killadeas into a Butlins. Maybe someone was struck by the similarities between military camps and holiday camps. In the end it came to nothing. Corrugated iron scrap from the buildings was sold to businesses in Belfast. Some of it ended up in the Casement Park stadium in Andytown, of all places.

Boa Island and Killadeas were satellites of the RAF's flying boat base at Castle Archdale, another book chapter with plenty of Terry's underlinings. The base was built by the US Navy in early 1942 and handed over to the RAF later that year. At one stage its Nissen huts had three thousand personnel.

Its wartime reminders include the operations block, the pump house, refuelling jetties, slipways, maintenance docks, and fragments of a punt that would bring the depth charges out to the flying boats at their moorings on the lough. Somewhere nearby are the remains of a directional finding station near Duross Point, as well as three navigation lights in the lake and the welded steel pontoons that were used as floating landing stages.

What you can't see – unless you have sonar – what you won't see fifty metres down on the bed of the lake are the skeletons of the crashed and scuttled flying boats.

Little else remains apart from a few memories. Memories of local people in their seventies and eighties, memories sugared by candy, cookies and chewing gum from the US personnel. Memories and the two granite plaques we drove past in Belleek and on the bridge at

Ballyshannon. The two memorials to the Donegal Corridor.

St Angelo is three miles from Enniskillen. The airport's narrow strip of car park is sandwiched between the main road and a fairycake yellow-and-white terminal. Apart from our van there are only three cars. The runway is almost within touching distance on the other side of a perimeter fence.

In 1943 this was home to squadrons of flying boats and fighter planes on anti-submarine patrols. On an early autumn day like today it's hard to imagine wave after wave of Spitfires and Hurricanes taking off from here to intercept enemy reconnaissance aircraft off the west coast, or rushing to defend Belfast.

After the war St Angelo had multiple makeovers. During the Troubles it became a centre of helicopter operations and a barracks for the British Army and UDR. Personnel were housed in a vast array of temporary portacabins. The IRA made several mortar attacks and attempts to shoot down the army helicopters.

By 1996 that particular war was as good as over. St Angelo became a private airfield. Although the army portacabins were demolished, most of the wartime buildings survived: the blast shelters around the airfield, where the aircraft could be scattered to make them more difficult targets; the massive blockhouse; the defensive pillboxes that faced inwards, towards the runways – ready for an attack from within, by German paratroopers.

But the paratroopers never came. St Angelo was the best-preserved wartime RAF station in Northern Ireland.

Ten years ago they announced plans to list St Angelo as an historic monument. The owners pre-empted the decision: the perimeter defences and most of the wartime architecture were demolished overnight. Buildings that had managed to survive the Luftwaffe and IRA.

From everything in Terry McGann's history books, this was where the Galway Three were headed. Had to be. Somewhere towards St Angelo, somewhere between Boa Island and the village of Kesh. To McGann country, to the land and waters that Terry would have known like the back of his hand.

His war books have a surprising amount of technical detail too.

The Catalina pilots called Lough Erne the most beautiful runway in the world. Yet landing in summer sunshine from clear air to calm water was a puzzling danger. Navigation, hundreds of miles offshore, was another dangerous puzzle, particularly in the dark, freezing, blinding fury of winter Atlantic gales and driving snowstorms.

Even in modern times, though, to ditch a small plane? On waters as complicated as Lough Erne? In winter, shortly after dusk?

You'd need to have guts.

Or be stark flaming mad.

You could wreck the plane. Tip it over. Drown.

But Terry McGann was calculated. And he calculated. Must have spent days working it out, done all the fuel and distance sums, as I too have tried to do.

And picked his spot.

Just close enough to the shore to get out of the water quickly and avoid shock. Yet still far out enough and deep enough to make two tons of metal disappear. Two tons and a body or two.

Dave locks the van. We stroll up a couple of steps to Café St Angelo. I fancy the special of the big dirty Ulster fry, tea and toast and dessert for a tenner.

Forty-Two

Back in Dublin I'm about to meet a slug from the fourth estate. A slug called Harry Street.

You've heard of police informers? Informants? The ones who give information to the cops? Harry is the opposite: the cops give him the spicy information.

And of all the joints in Stoneybatter he had to pick this one. Harry said he was stuck for time. "I'm on a case," he said on the phone earlier.

This is the place where they play a strange game. A game in which a small elite charge a small fortune and dress up in wigs and dresses and play on a court, with the ref sitting on the bench. It's a game called The Law.

Most of the wigs may have gone but it's still a courthouse: the new criminal courts on the corner of Parkgate Street and Infirmary Road.

From the outside the building is an optical illusion, a large four-storey cylinder of glass and steel, looking in at what appear to be stacks of cardboard boxes. These are an acoustic barrier and an energy-efficient double skin.

Once through the large front doors and airport-style X-ray machines you arrive at a huge main hall with shiny marble floor. The circular central atrium is surrounded by ten storeys of courts, offices, cells and jury rooms. On one side is a seven-storey window, on another a transparent shaft with four large glass lifts. Seen from below, the walkways and ceiling lights form a series of white concentric circles, not too unlike the underside of a spaceship in *Close Encounters.*

There's no sign of Harry in the second-floor restaurant among the garda uniforms, barrister gowns, legal assistants and one or two of the accused. Then his ugly fat mug appears. He's waving at the window from the outside smoking area. As I open the door he gives a furtive look in at the diners. He gestures for me to follow him further out onto the balcony.

"I need a favour, Harry."

He takes a drag of his fag. "OK, Moss, but make it quick. I've only time for a quick breather."

"It's just one or two things, the kind of stuff you hacks know about."

He flicks the cigarette end into a flower pot. "Fire away."

"Do dealers really cut cocaine and heroin with strychnine or arsenic, or is that a myth? I mean, poisoning your customers isn't exactly great for repeat sales is it?"

"They do it for two main reasons, Moss. Reason one: cutting it with something psychoactive makes the gear stronger. So it's more in demand. That's why they stretch cocaine with local anaesthetics. Lidocaine, benzocaine, procaine … "

"And Michael Caine. I'm not a flamin' pharmacist, Harry. Stick to the strychnine."

"Small amounts won't kill you. But it will get you high. Your liver breaks it down quickly – you could take the same as two lethal doses over twenty-four hours but there's no toxic effects, so they say. And the thing is, strychnine looks and tastes like unadulterated heroin. When you snort it, it's hard to tell from the real thing."

He lights up another fag before continuing.

"Only a complete sap would use something sweet to cut their shit – lactose, dextrose – cos the punters will spot it in no time. But strychnine is bitter. So everybody does it, for – what do they call it in *Dragons' Den?* Yeah. Added value and brand identity. But there's one minor problem: dealers buy from other dealers."

"So?"

"So the shit changes many hands along the chain, with everyone looking for their cut, if you know what I mean. After a while it's impossible to tell what the previous guys cut it with. Like it's not as if the stuff you buy on the Liffey Boardwalk comes with a nice fancy list of active ingredients printed on the side."

"No, I don't suppose it does." I'm picturing a label. *Horse tranquiliser 2%, baking soda 6%, caffeine 5%, scouring power 8%. Warning: may include the kitchen sink.*

"You said there were two reasons," I say.

He takes a big puff. "Yeah. Reason two is the conspiracy theory. Arab dealers go all political and flood Tel Aviv with bad shit. That kind of theory."

"And do they?"

"I dunno. Nice story all the same. Or there's the 'death cut' theory. A dealer kills a few addicts who've ripped him off once too often."

"Or he wants to kill off witnesses. One last question."

"Fire away."

"You ever hear of a DS Coleman?"

"Sean Coleman, Kerry fucker, Special Branch?"

"Yeah."

"Maybe."

"So what would the Special Branch be doing in France?"

"On holiday?"

"Serious, Harry."

"No, really. Generally they only do local stuff, back home in Ireland. Cash-in-transits, counter-espionage, counter-terrorism, Emergency Response Unit."

"Never abroad?"

"Oh I'd never say never. You'd sometimes see a Branch guy or two making sure our esteemed President and the Queen of England don't trip over and bang their heads together when they do the peck on the cheek thing in Buck House but ... "

"What about France?"

"With no queens or Michael Ds? Witness protection I guess. Can't think of anything else it might be."

He flicks the butt over the balcony and heads back inside.

"Thanks, Harry. I owe you one. Oh – do you still have

any contacts in the PSNI?"

"Cops in the north? Buckets of them."

"Then I might have a story for you."

"Thanks. Mind you, you owe me a favour. Fancy a coffee?"

"No, Harry, you're grand."

With its cameras and its panopticon views, its marble corridors of a thousand whispered conversations, with its Harry Streets and favours owed, the courthouse is beginning to give me the heebie-jeebies.

In the Criminal Courts of Justice the dark suits and white shirts come and go. Out on the street, in the real world, nothing is quite so black and white.

Forty-Three

The next day fate steps in, as it often does. A body turns up. In Lough Erne.

They weren't looking for a crash. Not initially, not per se. It was just one of those coincidences.

A local pensioner has gone missing. The police in Northern Ireland get a tip-off from a journalist friend in the South, one Harry Street. On foot of this they shift the focus of their search. By the time they stumble upon this body, this other body, the missing pensioner has been found alive and well, down the road in Blaney.

The rumour machine spins into action. This other body, the dead one, is male, from years back. A boating accident perhaps? A suicide? Paramilitaries, a gangland hit? The body dumped in deep water, weighed down with fat chains?

But there are no chains. And despite the rumours none of this is what actually happened.

I'm back at the Lough watching the search and rescue. An hour ago the Enniskillen RNLI launched another lifeboat and two more rescue craft. Little point in rescuing corpses that are at least five years old by now. But they're just doing their job, and giving the news crews something to do.

After that it isn't exactly fast. Or furious. Not even dramatic. Underwater search and recovery is slow, patient, complex and … Sorry, but a bit boring when you're trying to follow the wetsuits hour after hour on cheap binoculars.

Each team has three divers: the main one; his assistant who stays on the surface to signal and communicate; and the overall bossman who directs operations and does the walkie-talkie stuff. One team has sonar but the one I'm watching this morning doesn't.

They begin with an "arc search" or "pendulum search", with the main diver at the end of a blue nylon rope. It's painstaking, plodding, methodical work.

He prods around in the search area of the arc, after which the assistant diver moves the rope and the centre point to the next search area. It reminds me of rulers and compasses.

The radius of the arc depends on what you're looking for. For, say, a bicycle, the second diver might release a foot and a half of slack between each arc rotation. For something smaller, a gun say, the arcs would need to be much tighter.

After three hours they've little to show: plastic bottles, two shopping trollies, a traffic cone, a waterlogged laptop.

So they switch to a snagline pattern. The main diver and assistant diver swim in parallel lines from the shore. They are searching in a fixed width from each other, like the width of a fridge or a car. That's the width, seeing as the first corpse was wearing what looks like the remains of a safety belt, and the supervisor has decided that they are looking for a motor vehicle. Not quite a Beech Duchess but there or thereabouts.

Sometimes when a car – or, indeed, a plane – crashes into water, the bodies inside stay submerged. Particularly if they're wearing seatbelts, or with the doors closed and windows intact. But even seatbelts don't last for ever.

That must be how the first body turned up eventually.

The lead diver is called Mad Dog. A team member on the shore tells me it's to do with Mad Dog's technique for keeping the bogey man at bay. Mad Dog sings away while he gropes in the pitch-black water for dead bodies and the twisted metal of a wrecked car. Mad Dog sings so loudly underwater that even I can hear him from time to time. Maybe that's why he makes so many bubbles.

The pathologist has given them strict instructions. If you chance upon an object, Mad Dog sends up a signal marker. Then the two divers bag the evidence underwater, not for the sake of onlookers but to maintain the integrity of the evidence. The item comes up on balloons and is secured by the assistant diver, and the bossman records the GPS coordinates.

Like I said, it's methodical. Slow but very methodical.

Shortly after lunchtime they find the aircraft.

And body number two.

The radio newsreader skips the gory details. She says both bodies are male, well preserved, and probably died prior to hitting the water. The newsroom wouldn't know how that last detail was deduced in the preliminary report: there was still air in their lungs, after all this time.

She says it's too early for a DNA match. In real life DNA reports take days, not seconds of TV time. Besides, you can't look for a match when you don't have a name to match it against.

It also takes time – though a lot less time – for the toxicology tests to come back. Both men had consumed a substantial quantity of cocaine. Cocaine, the clichéd "drug of choice" during the boom. Cocaine laced with something that would popularly be described as rat poison.

I rang Arnaud in Dublin as soon as body number two turned up.

"Two bodies, and you can make a predictable prediction. Their DNA will be two of the Galway Three."

"Get real, Moss. Nobody's gonna be checking the dental records or the … "

"I know. You know and I know who they are, but no one else does, and someone high up wants it to stay that way. I want you to ring Harry Street."

I give him the details.

"Right. Oh Moss. Before you go – your passport's ready."

Adieu to Belashanny and the Erne's winding banks. On the bus back to Dublin I try to figure it out. It's like those fictional detectives say: "When all else is impossible, that which remains must be so."

I can't help thinking of an analogy someone once made between Joyce's *Ulysses* and the Velvet Underground. Something Brian Eno once said about the Velvets' first album, the one with the "banana" cover that's about as famous as the record. An image that's so typically Warhol: slippery, contradictory, as unknowable as modern life itself. Mind you, I think I prefer the jeans cover Warhol did for *Sticky Fingers*.

Anyway, Eno is supposed to have said that they only sold a few thousand copies of the banana album, yet everyone who bought a copy formed a band.

Complete bolloxology of course. James Joyce did influence generations of writers. The Velvets did indeed inspire many other bands to form. But by 1970 the banana album had already broken the six-figure mark, and Eno never said anything of the sort.

It's a nice line, it's made up. Just like Leopold Bloom, Ziggy Stardust and the Galway Three myth. Made up by Terry McGann to weave a perfect story and throw everyone off the scent.

So how did the aircraft land? An educated guess?

Gear down. Softly, gently, slushing and slithering smoothly across the waters of the lough – surprisingly smoothly.

Then what?

The water would hit you like a slap.

What next? Pull off your shoes. That's the first thing they tell you to do, if you fall in water: kick off your shoes. So I guess that's what he would have done, before grabbing the snorkel and flippers. Oh, and the bike. It's folded up, reasonably light, but awkward. And it won't float of course. You can't swim with it like that.

So he leans back, grabs the bike and ties it to a lifejacket, reminding himself that you have to get out first before inflating your lifejacket. By which time he's also probably thinking: *What mad eejit would put a folding bike on a light aircraft and hope to swim ashore with it to make your getaway?*

Absolutely mad alright.

Outside the plane now, the heavy bike is dragging him down, deep into the lough. A single thought is gripping his mind:

So, after all this, this is how you die? Dragged down by a stupid foldable bike – when you hate bloody bicycles?

So what does he do? Think.

Cool it. You've thought about little else for weeks. No point in panicking at the last minute in the final furlong.

So you spit out a mouthful of freezing lake water, take a deep breath and dive. Down, down to grab the bike, surface again, spluttering, pull the toggles to inflate the two life jackets – yours and the bike's.

Swim, struggle and swim several hundred yards. Your left arm hits the bottom of the lake – you've reached dry land. Which is still wet. Haul the bike out of the water, by which time the plane is already sinking. The flashing red tail light is the last thing you see, slipping under the waves. The ghosts of two Irish businessmen.

Terry McGann is dead too. The old life is gone. Now you can start to be someone else.

What kind of madness drives a man to do all that? To kill his two best friends, to crashland in the dark on a lake, to swim ashore then cycle to the nearest hotel, then bus it from Enniskillen to Dublin, and another bus or train to Waterford to murder his mistress, using yet more rat poison?

The height of madness.

A madness whose depths you can't even begin to calculate.

Forty-Four

You can't control your IQ.

You can't control your DNA.

You can't control your neighbour's dog.

But sometimes you can make your passport toe the line.

"What do you think?" she says after unwrapping it.

I don't know what to think. She is wearing white cotton gloves, as if she's holding something contagious.

After letting me in she has perched herself on a tall stool at a large workbench. Jenny Jameson's workshop is a large loft space of whitewashed brick, stained floorboards and dark joists, with some rafters so low that you need to duck your head. Every available patch of wallspace and workbench are covered with photos, clippings, sketches, blow-ups, PCs, scanners, printers, cameras, paintbrushes, ink bottles, blades, glue, tins of spray paint, mounting sprays, rolls of wallpaper – all the kind of clobber you'd expect in Jenny Jameson's line of work.

She's not exactly what I expected a passport forger to look like: tall, thin, pretty, with ringlets of light brown hair, and wearing a clean white apron over T-shirt and jeans. I guess she looks exactly like someone who does what she does for a living: making models for the movies.

Props, fake newspapers, documents, old treasure maps, boxes of vintage cigarettes. And passports.

I rustle through its crisp pages. Two have visa stamps. It all looks genuine enough, but how would I know?

"Yeah," she says, "I know what you're thinking. It might look OK to the naked eye but it won't fool a scanner, ultraviolet light and all that."

"That's fine." In fact I couldn't have asked for more.

"It should pass for ID in a bank, or in a small regional airport maybe. They might have scanners but sometimes they just take a quick look and wave you through."

Exactly. This thing isn't sophisticated enough for a major international transport hub. For that you'd need the works: holographic script, fine guilloche lines and other background security printing features, fluorescent inks and fluorescent fibres in random places at varying depths and different on each page, UV features, anti-copy patterns, a holographic "identigram" photo of your mugshot, micro text, machine readable zones, collation marks, tamper-proof laminate with embedded wavy lines, the correct binding and … At least it doesn't have an embedded RFID chip. I don't fancy having documents that have been buggered around with inbuilt chips. For all you know they could be tracking devices.

Her white gloves deal out four more ID cards in quick succession. "That one was easy. And that one too. And the driving licence. But this one, the international press card? I was pushed for time so I took some liberties."

"It's grand. The least of my worries. What's the damage?"

"I can't take anything."

"No, really. How much do I owe you?"

"You're fine." She takes off her gloves like my dentist does after a good springclean. The handover is complete.

"But it must've taken you ages. The least I can do … "

"No. It's better this way, if anything goes wrong I mean. It's like this: Arnaud said he had a good friend in a spot of bother, and I'll not ask how you got into this because I really don't need to know."

"What about you?" I wave a hand at the tools of her trade. "I mean how did you get into … "

"The film racket? This stuff?" She giggles. "Long story. If you want to really hurt your parents, and you don't have the nerve to be gay – before you ask, I'm not – but the least you can do is go into the arts. Or an art department. No, serious. The film work keeps my head above water, but the arts aren't about making a living. It's about making life more bearable. You've just created something. With real art, you have power over things."

What an incredibly strange young woman.

At first I considered flying. I really did. Tried to go through what I would do, how to act, how I should look. The body language.

How to dress for airports. I should write a book about that. How to dress for security, for the worst-case scenarios and the negative "trust no one, anyone could be a terrorist" vibes. How to dress and how to act. How to consider every step.

For example, say you arrive at a French airport and someone has been following you. If they're smart they won't tail you from the plane. I wouldn't, not in their shoes. No, I'd be ahead of me, if you know what I mean. So no looking over your shoulder every five seconds, drawing attention to yourself. There's only one direction you can go: forward, to passport control and Arrivals. So if I were them that's where I'd be: ahead of me. Them with the body language of a tired would-be holidaymaker.

That's just Arrivals. Departures are worse. Where else in life are you forced to queue up, put all your metal in a tray, walk towards some serious-looking strangers, then – as the doorway bleeps and flashes – all the usual rules and social norms about privacy and touching go out the window? All that frisking and patting down while someone else tears your luggage apart.

The first rule of flight club is to wear comfortable shoes, for all that standing around. With not an ounce of metal in them because I'm a serial bleeper. I don't have a dozen metal pins in my bones yet I'm always getting bleeped as soon as I step through the archway of death.

I hate airports, the way they've become a cross between a town square and international shopping centre, with food to be consumed on the go, joylessly, until everybody has been squeezed out the other end of the pipe.

Second rule of flight club: expect to feel lost, because

those airports are always in a state of flux. Out go the cursory security checkpoints – remember them? – to be replaced by elaborate screening regimens. Out go the old rows of check-in desks, in come the self-service kiosks and smartphone boarding apps, or people in face masks checking your temperature for a deadly plague.

Everything is geared to the constantly changing needs of the pipe and border control, the efficient processing of passengers and consumers.

In some airports you can go ice skating or host the kids' birthday party. Amsterdam Schiphol even has a casino, a museum, a wedding chapel and a morgue. They are building our everyday lives and deaths around the rules of global transport and consumption.

All I want to do is arrive, get through security, hop on the plane and fly away in the minimum time. Not wasting time in a giant shopping mall under the glare of all those cameras. And not having to gamble that this time they won't bother to shine my toytown passport under a UV light.

That's why I'm not flying. I'm on foot. I'm taking a train. And a ferry. And about to take a second, much longer train journey. Down the hexagon of France.

Forty-Five

It's a complex transaction. I think she's trying to tell me they only take credit cards or cheques – the French are still big into cheques.

So I'll have to pay in my real name, with a real credit card. The trouble is, I need two named drivers on the documentation, just in case. When the woman on the hire car desk asks to see both "our" driving licences – my real one and my fake one – it takes some explaining to get out of this one.

"Oh *oui Madame*. The reason he looks so similar is that we're almost twins. He's my step brother. He'll be back here in a minute. Shall we just get on with it?"

That's what I'd like to say but I don't know the French for "step brother". So my other alias, Monsieur Barry Murphy de Dublin, ends up being *mon frère de mon papa's deuxième mariage*.

Sling the bag in the boot. Make damn sure there's enough breathalysers and *gilets jaunes*. Drive.

My first stop is Le Moulin, the restaurant in Mentidera. No sign of anyone following, but I park the car a good distance away from the place, and ramble past another faded Forvil sign.

Sometimes I'm worse than a journalist. Thinking too much, asking too many questions.

Like that sign, *Forvil: brilliantine parfumée*. Who decided it should go there? Why in this particular village, on that wall above the old water pump? Did the wall's owner get paid for the use of the side of his house? Was it a one-off sum or annual fee? Who painted it – a local signwriter or house painter, contracted for a one-off job, and sent a set of instructions and three tins of primer in the post from Paris? Or was it a specialised team, employed directly by the manufacturer or the advertising agency?

The French probably have a word for it, for this particular occupation, for these descendants of the cave painters. A band of artisans wandering from village to village, tailoring each display to the local situation, adjusting the typeface and logo to fit the size and surface peculiarities of a given wall.

Walls have ears. Walls were once able to speak too, but recently lost the ability, after loud billboards and screens muted their voice. The walls used to speak in clear voices with short, unambiguous messages. No puns or difficult word associations or complex image editing. Just one basic, no-frills, easy-to-remember fact of life, stripped down until shorter than a tweet and perfectly adapted to twentieth-century driving:

Beer = Mons
Cognac = Martell
Hair = Forvil

I too have stripped down my list of questions for Gabrielle and Angélique, the two waitresses in Le Moulin. A list with just two items.

Was this the man?
What kind of boat?

Forty-Six

Terry McGann may or may not have been on a canal barge that day in Mentidera. But it's his yacht that Angélique remembers.

The waitress can't recall whether it had a little set of steps to climb down, or a rope ladder or gang plank. She couldn't tell me its make or type or name. But it was definitely a yacht and definitely him. Slightly different from the photograph, but him alright, at the port of Sète.

So Sète is where I've ended up.

You need a good cover story to hang around boats asking questions. Mine is that I'm a galley cook. I've a good idea what the life is like because I did it once, very briefly, years ago. Once was more than enough. But enough to spin a line to prospective employers that …

Oh yes, Monsieur, it's all about making great food on limited rations and minimal fuel and water, with space at a premium, feck all counter space, and no ceramic utensils unless you want smashed plates. Oh no, Monsieur, I prefer those stainless steel cat dishes. Don't scoff. I really do. The ones with the rubberized bottoms. They don't slip and they stack well.

All the tricks. To save on precious drinking water you use clean seawater to cook fish and to do the initial dish washing. You avoid pungent cheeses that make people seasick, and you wrap tomatoes – deliberately bought underripe – in newspaper. You can cook on a gimballed marine stove top and oven combination that swings from side to side but stays horizontal as the boat tilts. You know how to use a galley strap in stormy seas, and store you knives with extreme caution (flying blades bad). You know the value of lids, clamps, microwaves, pressure cookers and bag-in-box wine.

Convinced yet? I can tell you about the joys of cooking with UHT milk, powdered milk, vacuum packs of pre-ground coffee, home-grown bean sprouts and granola bars for emergencies. And how you never use the oven when it's thirty degrees outside, and if you burn dinner twenty miles out to sea you can't call the takeaway. You can't rely on catching shoals of tuna or *loup de mer* all day long either.

So I've had the life of a galley cook. I only stuck it three weeks before being thrown overboard, metaphorically speaking.

The main thing, just about the only thing this unemployed galley cook has learned so far from his inquiries among the yachts and the boat owners of Sète, is that this stretch of the Med is a melting pot of culinary influences. France meets North Africa meets Italy and Spain.

The restaurants and bars around the port and docks have their own local variants of *bouillabaisse* – the fish soup you see everywhere in the Languedoc and Provence – and their versions of stuffed mussels and *rouille de seiche* (cuttlefish stew). They have *langouste à la sètoise* (similar to the more famous *homard à l'américaine),* another fish stew called *bourride de baudroie* (based on *lotte* or monkfish), a serious amount of couscous dishes, a *macaronade* (pasta in tomato sauce with beef, pork and sausagemeat) and above all *la tielle sètoise:* their octopus pie, a sort of spicy ragout encased in dough with a brilliant sunny crust – the Languedoc equivalent of a Cornish pastie.

As part of my cover story I've even been forced to try one. While the *tielle's* golden pastry looks charming, its feisty flavours remind me of tinned sardines in tomato sauce.

I've heard my cover story so many times that I'm beginning to believe it myself. I'm about to give up for the day, going through my tale one last time with the Italian couple on a large motorboat, when I come to the bit about how "a friend says this man … " – produce photo – " … is looking for a galley cook. I'm not sure if the man is English or Irish."

I've next to no Italian, this Italian couple's French is

worse than mine. They don't recognise the man in the photo, though they say the Americans next door might.

I knock on the hull of a large yacht. An elderly woman emerges from a stairway.

"Young man, what you looking for?" It's an American accent.

"Work. I'm a galley cook."

"Well I do the cookin' round here, sonny."

I give her the story.

Call me Marnie, she says. Marnie Epstein from Boston. Or Concord Massachusetts to be precise – as if I should know her neck of the woods. She and husband Zack spend their summers chugging up and down the Mediterranean.

I tell her I wasn't given the man's name, just his photograph.

"You say he's English?"

"Yeah. Or possibly Irish."

"If he's who I think he is, he's a good deal older than that, but – *Hey Zack! Zack?* That's Peter Boyd. *Zack?*"

An ancient mariner emerges from the cabin. Introductions are made.

"Zack, tell him about Pete Boyd's yacht."

Zack runs his fingers through a long grey goatee beard. "The Jeanneau Sun Odyssey you mean."

"That's its name?" I ask.

"No. The make. Damn fine boat."

Sugar. I should have brought some photos of Kevin Reilly's yacht to show around.

"Do you know where I might find it? I think it's called the *Nora Barnacle* or something.

"Don't think so," Marnie says. "Isn't it *The Trojan* or *Troilus* or … "

I feel a sick joke coming on. "Not *The Troika?*"

Zack slaps the hull of the boat. "That's the one!"

"Where did you see it last?"

Marnie looks over at her husband again. "Honey?" She

gives the slot machine handles of his brain a good tug.

"Em ... ? Oh sure," he says eventually. "Further up the coast. The Camargue."

After a lifetime as a galley slave I'm going up in the world. My next stop is the local boat salesrooms. I'm on the lookout for a brand new Jeanneau Sun Odyssey.

"Oui Monsieur. What kind of model?"

Oh shit. There's different kinds?

"Oh, something like a friend of mine has. You probably know him, a friend from Ireland, Peter Boyd. Oh gosh. What's his tub called again? Oh of course. *The Troika."*

"Ah! Your friend is Monsieur Boyd, with the Sun Odyssey 45DS? A superb choice, with the raised deckhouse, the wrap-around windows, the curve lines, the big porthole, many porthole. It is *une nouvelle conception de l'espace,* the design by Garroni, and the furling main sail. I show you *les brochures."*

"How big is it?"

He consults one of the brochures: "The three cabin, the two *toilette,* the ... "

"Perfect. What's the galley like?"

"The *cuisine?* It comes with the oven and grill, the *frigo,* the freezer, the four-burner 'ob ... "

"Excellent. Because the galley and its hob are the very heart of the ... Pardon me for asking: what's a furling main sail?"

"Oh Monsieur." His voice has gone down several scales in disappointment.

"No, sorry. *Desolé.* I mean it's not for me. It's for my son Tarquin. Twenty-first birthdays and all that. For him and his girlfriend to muck about on the Med."

"Then the furling main sail is an excellent choice. It is easy to sail I mean, if you are two-'anded. It is exceptionally stable at sea, the Jeanneau Sun Odyssey, the 45DS. An excellent choice for your son if I say so,

Monsieur … "

"You can call me Charlie. How big … how long is it? And none of your metres and centimetres."

"Oh. But of course, Monsieur. It is – how you say? – a forty-five footer.

"Right. I'll think about it. Can I take some of them brochures?"

The Camargue. Golden beaches, broad saltwater lagoons, flat wetlands, reedy expanses teeming with pink flamingoes. Farmers who look like cowboys, with lassoes to chase wild white horses.

Monsieur de Beauvoir is the only skipper to be found with a boat for hire. It has a small cabin at the front, and a back deck with enough room for three anglers, four at a pinch. He also has a leather stetson and grey whiskers.

I tell him I'm on the lookout for a friend's forty-five footer, a Jeanneau Sun Odyssey called *The Troika*.

Monsieur de Beauvoir thinks he saw it around here two days ago. Should he get it on the radio?

No, I tell him, I'd like to play a surprise on my friend.

He can take me out first thing tomorrow morning.

The smell of the sea. It was so different here to Dublin port, he thought. Or Sandymount Strand or the Liffey, or Dingle even.

From a safe distance Coleman watched the private detective haggling with the old sea dog at the dockside. He left them to it. They weren't going anywhere tonight.

Forty-Seven

Coleman put down his binoculars and felt hungry. Next door to the bar near the end of the marina was a fish restaurant. More a shack than a restaurant, though it had promising smells, the menu looked cheap and the dishes changed depending on the catch that day.

Too early for supper though, so he had time to have a stroll and stare at the waters.

What did he expect to see? A little sign, any sign, of life at the water's edge. The kind of life you'd find in any rock pool or shallows. Fry and fingerlings, a few minnows darting about, shrimp-like things galloping among the anemones and sea glass – the small glass fragments that have been tumbled and smoothed by decades of sand and waves. Algae, barnacles, mermaid's purse, crabs scurrying over seaweed.

Sometimes that's what he felt like. A crab walking sideways.

When he was growing up crabs were comical things. The stuff of cartoon strips. Cartoon crabs that could nip your cartoon toes, or latch onto the real-life string that you dangled off the pier, and just as suddenly let go again. That's what he'd like to see: the tiniest of crabs, going about its chores in its sideways universe.

He tried to focus on the water below the surface but his eyes were too far gone. When you were a kid you could see everything. Playing soccer in Jimmy's Field until dusk, the grown-ups calling you, *Sean! Sean! It's bedtime, Sean,* the adults forgetting that kids had Superman vision and could still make out the ball and the other players for a good hour yet.

When you were a kid you could still see into the rockpool's waters. See but not yet fully understand that beneath the calm surface was a deadly fight. Feeding, fighting, breeding, killing for every scrap of food.

When you were no longer a kid you could understand far more but could see far less.

He hadn't brought his glasses. The surrounding world was a soft blur. Maybe try the binoculars. Or then again, no, not binoculars.

What must he look like, staring down at the water, unable to zoom past the sparkling reflections and into the depths? No, he couldn't see into that little world. He might understand it but he couldn't see it any more. He'd been in the big bad world too long.

In the shiny waters he could no longer make out the mermaids' tears, the tiny things that despite their size – no, *because of their very size* – were signs of far worse crimes, of the terrible things that we do to the life around us, from the strands and rockpools of childhood to these blue-green waters around the Camargue.

The Med was getting so bad they should rename it the Plastic Sea. Forget the obvious flotsam and jetsam and fishing gear, the ubiquitous plastic shopping bags fluttering among the hedges or trees on the shoreline. That was the obvious stuff, the stuff you could see.

What about the seabed? A giant rubbish tip of bottles, discarded nets, clinker even – the residue of burned coal from steam ships. Centuries-old clinker trails along the same main shipping routes of today.

When marine explorers did deep-sea dives – supposedly the first time humans had seen these sites – our rubbish had arrived there before them. It must be like landing on Mars and finding its canals already stuffed with shopping trolleys and traffic cones.

The plastic soup could be seen by satellites out in space. It covered huge stretches of ocean, a vast floating rubbish dump that would last for centuries. The North Pacific "gyre" of plastic trash was the size of France, a vast vortex slowly swirling round like a giant clock, choked with dead fish, marine mammals and birds.

Plastic crap thrown away in the late 1950s was still

bobbing away in it. Some plastics in the gyre wouldn't break down in the lifetime of his own children, or the grandkids of the unthinking bastards who threw them away in the first place.

Coleman couldn't see it, though last night he dreamed about it. The mermaids' tears as they started off as the tiny plastic pellets that leaked from the injection moulding factories, that spilled into drains and gutters and water system, and ended up flowing down to the sea. The mermaids' tears, with the sunlight slowly breaking them down in their millions and billions, into more microscopic fragments, into all the shite you can't see.

All that toxic crap in the food chain, in the fish, the seabirds and marine mammals. They found syringes inside the stomachs of seabirds. Syringes, cigarette lighters, toothbrushes, biros. The poor things mistook them for food.

But it was the plastic pellets from the factories, the pellets that turned into microplastics, thinner than a human hair, they were his biggest nightmare.

A torrent of mermaids' tears, turning the Med into a gigantic dustbin of death. Plastic molecules being swallowed in huge quantities by the wildlife that mistook the stuff for nourishment, with six kilos of poisonous plastic for every kilo of natural plankton.

And they say fish is good for you?

He decided to give the little fish restaurant a miss.

Forty-Eight

Finally, suddenly, it comes into view. Lying at anchor, four or five hundred yards to the – which one's starboard and which one port again?

After nearly six hours scouring coves and sandy stretches we have finally found the yacht. Too far away to make its name out yet, but Monsieur de Beauvoir is sure it's the one. *Regardez, Monsieur:* just like the brochure.

He cuts the engine. We take out fishing rods and binoculars, sit back and wait.

The girl is on deck. Olive skin, dark brown hair in a short bob, as per the descriptions. She's wearing maybe shorts or short dark jeans and little else. Sunbathing.

From the cabin a man appears. Tall, slim, not so tanned. Hair could be grey. May have a little grey beard too. Hard to tell at this distance.

Out of the silence comes a humming sound behind us, growing louder and louder until it becomes a growl, a roar, a big bird that swoops and hovers above us. A police helicopter. A megaphone appears out of its side window. A man is telling us in copshop French to return to shore. Seems we're under *arrête* again.

Back at the marina five or six cops surround us, pointing five or six guns at us, as Monsieur de Beauvoir ties up the boat, as if it were the most natural thing to do.

The helicopter settles down on the beach two hundred yards away. One man gets out: Detective Superintendent Sean Coleman, Special Branch.

"Oh look who it isn't," he says, still catching his breath as he shoos the French police away. "Moss Reid PI. Or is it Barry Murphy this week?"

"What are you doing here?"

"I could ask you the same. You could say I'm looking after the crap you don't normally see. The stuff you can't see or don't want to see. Mind if we take a walk?"

"Have I much choice?"

We stroll along the marina. He's silent, thinking what to say next.

"You know the Attorney General … "

"Not personally." I can't even recall the AG's name.

"And Peter Boyd?"

"You mean Terry McGann?" I reply.

"Yeah. Boyd, McGann, whatever. He has a special relationship with the AG. It's a criminal offence to even contact him or publish his whereabouts."

"Even in France?"

"Especially in France." Coleman stops walking. "Can't we be civilised about all this? When you fight monsters you need to take care you don't become one too. Come on."

He guides me to an outside table at a bar near the end of the marina. The tiny room inside is decorated with nets and pictures of oysters.

"Red or white?" he asks, the perfect host. "The rosé is quite good around here … "

"Red is fine, so long as it's chilled."

"Yeah." He's taking off his tie. "I like the way they do that around here."

He orders a litre half of the house red. The waiter returns with a carafe. It's chilled.

Coleman pours two generous glasses. "Right. Now tell me everything you know."

After I finish my edited highlights, he gets up for a moment. He paces around silently, slowly, respectfully, as one might do at IMMA or the Tate.

"Well you're half-way there," he says, sitting down again. He's all smiles and offering to fill in the blanks. At least some of the gaps.

"You know the Witness Protection Programme?"

I nod.

"Any idea how many people are in it?"

I shake my head.

"Me neither," he continues. "I don't think anyone has a clue any more. It's a mess. Some witnesses wind up dead. Others start making lavish demands. The people we protect aren't exactly innocent bystanders, you see. They're usually criminals and subversives. And touts of course. Informers and double-crossers, one way or another. Not exactly the kind to keep vouched expenses."

He has a glug of wine before continuing.

"So the State relocates them, we pay the mortgage, find them a job, keep 'em out of trouble, sometimes might even get them in the witness box. Terry McGann isn't the worst. Oh yeah, the State loves Terry. His demands aren't extravagant, he's a man of independent means. But it wasn't always so. How's the wine?"

"Fine."

He tops up our glasses. "Six years ago he was a right mess. But then his lawyer friend … "

"Kevin Reilly?"

He nods. "One of Reilly's clients is Gino Beattie. You do know Gino Beattie?"

"Heard of him."

"Gino has Reilly on a retainer, to look after his business's legal requirements. Reilly gets wind of Terry's money problems and puts the two of them together, Terry and Gino. Terry has a plane. Gino needs a plane. Terry gets the gig, bringing in high-volume shipments to Ireland. It's still not enough. He's still a financial mess. So he decides to go freelance, figuring there's no point skimming half a kilo off the top here and there … "

"Or cutting it with rat poison."

"Yeah. Because they'd soon find out. But he can't afford to set up his own deals. That's where Reilly comes in again. Kevin Reilly and – what's the banker guy?"

"Johnny Kettle."

"Yeah. Kevin and Johnny bankroll the operation, He likes the odd flutter does Kevin Reilly. There's only one snag: how to sell the stuff. Terry's only contacts are Gino's lot. So he has to set up his own deals. Now Terry is way out of his depth. He's drowning, because he's dealing with our lot."

"It's a sting?"

He nods. "Terry's company is going down the tubes, the Garda Drugs Unit is closing in. Terry has feck all to give us except Gino and his gang, only Gino is a pro. He always leaves it to his couriers and footsoldiers to handle the drugs."

"So what happened?"

"It was a good sting. Sometimes stings get nasty, but if you do it right you control everything. Lure the buyer into a meet-and-greet, initial negotiations somewhere ordinary, a McDonalds at the edge of town rather than a city-centre hotel. Give them an unmissable introductory offer, shit-hot merchandise at an excellent price. They report back to Gino, and Gino is hooked. We set up another meeting to conclude the deal. Usually the undercover guys come with a real kilo of stuff but the rest is fake, all shaped like bricks."

"Yeah yeah, like in the movies."

He ignores that. "We bust the buyers, seize their cash and cars, and that's where the maths can get a tad vague. Most of the money ends up in evidence bags. Some of it gets recycled – as rewards for informants, or to buy special kit, overtime payments. Some of the real kilo of stuff gets recycled too. All unofficially of course. So that's a lot of white powder and cash sloshing around in the hands of respectable officers.

Cops, cash and cocaine? Sounds wild dodgy to me.

"Don't get me wrong," he continues. "It's all above board, kind of."

"So you busted Gino Beattie's lot."

"Wait for it. It's a huge consignment. None of it fake, because this is the real deal. Terry McGann pretends that he's acting as a go-between. He has flown it in, it must have taken up half the plane. He refuses to wear a wire. We say fine. He drives the stash to one of the gang's apartments in Rosslare. We're in luck – this is supposed to be a new supplier but Terry is delivering the stuff in person. Gino figures there's no harm in checking it out himself, because only Terry and he know when it's due to come in. So Gino and his two senior lieutenants get caught red-handed, we get a result and it's four months before Gino can figure out how much of the stash has gone walkabout and where it might have ended up."

"Terry held onto it?"

"Yeah, left most of it down the road at his mistress's place. Now Terry has three choices. Stick around and get pumped full of lead. Sit around under twenty-four-hour armed guard, with the best we can offer him a poky little four-cell unit at Arbour Hill. Or spend the rest of his life on the run."

"In the Witness Protection Programme?"

"Strictly speaking Terry was never a witness. Not in the court sense. In return for all his information and for keeping schtum, he gets immunity and a nice new identity abroad. That's the deal and we tell him it's almost but not quite over yet. These scum don't have a long shelf life, but it's only a matter of time before Gino's gang implodes. Or so we thought at the time.

"So Gino is put away, his bagman dies in prison after a drugs package explodes inside his arsehole – it's called body packing, we can skip the details – and half his gang are locked up with a long string of convictions. On the outside there's gun feuds every night, young savages with a pathological hatred of each other, you know the kind of thing and most of them end up dead."

He pours two more glasses.

"I'll take your word for it," I say.

"Three do a runner to Spain and end up under six feet of concrete. New gangs take their place. Small fry are quickly replaced by even smaller fry. Gino is locked away but the latest feuding factions aren't his enemies. They're his new customers."

"What do you mean?"

"He runs the whole operation from his cell in Mountjoy."

"Where's Terry in all this?"

"That's the snag. Terry McGann has cut a deal with the DPP, signed and sealed, not quite a comfort letter but as good as. He has immunity from prosecution. Then he stars in *When Witness Protection Goes Wrong*. How were we to know he'd disappear with a yacht full of white powder? Usually they're trying to smuggle the stuff into Ireland, not out of it."

"And it's absolute immunity?"

"Yep."

"Even from the plane crash?"

"That was one of Terry's maddest ideas. He needed a big convincer, otherwise Gino's mob would be on his tail for ever. But it wasn't as if it was costing us anything. It was his own plane."

Total immunity. When the Cold War started they even gave SS officers and rocket scientists a new life. Clean slate and all that, for the bigger picture, the next enemy.

"Let me get this straight," I say. | He smuggles drugs, fakes a plane crash, kills his mates, poisons his mistress, bumps off his sister-in-law in Mentidera or Aigues-Mortes or wherever, and … "

He shrugs. As if to say it's not his call. "So?"

"He's getting away with murder. What makes Terry McGann so special?"

"Like I said. The State loves him."

He makes an air-scribble sign to the waiter for the bill.

"So a couple of dodgy businessmen are dead," he says, "after they dabbled in a bit of drug smuggling. What's one or two more deaths, in the grand scheme of things? What would you prefer? All that eye-for-an-eye stuff? It only makes the world go blind."

The waiter comes with our bill.

Coleman stares at it, like it's a secret code. He takes out a pair of reading glasses.

"See that helicopter?" He's referring to the one he was just on. "They do specialised patrols out at sea. You know how many people have died trying to cross that sea in the past fortnight? Look out there, Mr Reid. All sunny and peaceful, tourists and fishing boats. But ask those guys in the helicopter to show you the reports of the mass drownings, the multiple stabbings, what it's like to find hundreds dead from asphyxiation in the hold of a tiny fishing boat. And God knows how many are trafficked for body parts. I'm talking about the boat people, Mr Reid. The ones who come from Tunisia, Libya, Syria, or further again – Eritrea, Ethiopia, you name it. They can't all become Premiership footballers.

"The French call it *faire l'avenir*. Maybe that's their only crime, to dream about a future. Maybe they heard stories about the men who made the journey to Italy and came back with fancy cars and enough money to build a house in the village for the kids.

"So week after week they bundle up their dreams and hand over their life savings, to be mugged and shoved into overcrowded dinghies and unseaworthy ships, packed into half a square metre of space with no food, no water or life jackets."

He stares out at the sea and sky as they dissolve into each other on the horizon. A world blue at its edges, with the blue light that got lost on its way from the sun.

"So then, if their luck holds, they are finally in sight of Fortress Europe," he continues. "Don't get me wrong. We all have our orders, no one gatecrashes your country without a proper invite. That's the rule. But there's another rule: *Don't get involved.* I mean, take your Monsieur de Beauvoir. Say he's out there," he waves at the sea, "and he comes across several hundred boat people crammed into a sinking boat. What does he do? He steers well clear of it.

Rescuers could face charges – for helping illegal human trafficking. The big commercial ships don't want to be dragged in either."

I'm not sure I need any more of this cop-with-a-conscience stuff, but like I said: what choice do I have?

"Sorry, Mr Reid. Am I boring you? You know what they call it? The 'left to die' policy. Last month they left five hundred Eritreans who'd set off from Libya. It was a tiny boat. The motor failed, the weather turned bad. Got the picture so far?

"But they're not far from the Italian shore so the passengers set fire to a sheet to attract attention. The fire spreads, the boat capsizes, most of them drown. They are so tightly packed they don't stand a chance. You want to hear the sick bit, the final twist? The Eritrean diplomats arrive in Sicily to claim the bodies. Line after line of coffins, of all these people who were trying to flee their country's repressive government and these same bloody officials.

"That's on a bad month. In a better month it's 'just' three hundred deaths a fortnight. So that's – what? – six thousand a year? That's what's out there." He holds a hand out to the Mediterranean. "A sick fucking cemetery. Now think about the families they leave behind, the ones back home who don't know whether they were lost at sea or ended up in a living hellhole in Fortress Europe."

"But you changed the subject," I say, finally getting a word in. "What about Johnny Kettle and Kevin Reilly's loved ones? And Niamh McElhinney? And Terry's mistress, Mary Buckley? They were murdered."

He shrugs, takes a final look at the bill and puts a few coins on the plate.

"Those women," I continue. "They were all … "

"What? Innocent? Sure. So call Interpol. You'll find everyone's too busy with the next invasion. The boat people, Islamic armies, the next plague from Africa, whatever. Too busy or don't care. No one gives a fuck about your Terry McGann any more, Mr Reid."

Seconds pass. He breaks the silence again to give out about dying planets, ice caps and mermaids' tears.

"Sorry," I interrupt him again, "how did you find me this time? My credit card?"

A flick of his eyelids. "Yeah, at the hire car. You still have your passport? I mean your real one?"

I nod.

"Then would you ever feck off back to Ireland." Not a question, more a polite order.

"I can go?"

Another flick of the eyelids says yes.

"And you'll leave me alone?"

"Sure. If you leave our friend alone. That's the rule: don't get involved. Deal?"

He grabs the drinks receipt and continues, "Expenses. Vouched, see? You've cost us a small fortune you know."

He gets up to leave. "Deal?"

"Deal," I tell him.

Forty-Nine

As I walk back to the hire car he calls me back again.

"About Gino Beattie. You said you didn't know him."

"I don't. Never met the guy."

"Well he knows you."

What???

"Didn't your big pal Dave tell you?" he asks. "Gino became very interested in you after Dave the Drone told him about your French adventures with Mrs Kettle."

"Gino and Dave Smedley know each other?"

"Oh yeah. Ever wonder how they smuggle drugs into prison these days, when the most likely inmates are always getting strip searched and stuck behind a thick perspex screen at visiting time? Ever wonder how Dave pays for all his fancy flying gear?"

"Gino Beattie?"

"Got it in one. The first we heard of it was when one of Dave's drones crashed into the netting over the exercise yard. The netting was there after the neighbours complained about the toe-rags on their roofs who were chucking drugs packages into the prison compound. Anyway, the prisoners made off with the drugs but the screws managed to recover Dave's drone. It had a serial number, and an IP address. Like I said, we know everything."

He turns to go again but has another last word. "Oh, and you can stop blaming us for bugging your house and office. That was Gino's lot."

I am looking at the walls of Gino Beattie's cell. They are a mirror image of the wall of my office. All that stuff about the Galway Three, the clippings and pics of Terry McGann and Johnny Kettle. The main difference is that Gino Beattie's prison wall probably also has a photo of me.

By the time I've digested this I realise that Coleman has

already gone. He hasn't told me everything. But now I can see how far I've gotten arse over elbow.

The cops were following Dave, Dave was following Mrs Kettle; she brought him to me, and he brought me all over the place. All to find Terry for Gino.

On the shoreline I write "Killer" in the sand and wait for the waves to wash the letters away.

Then I notice him.

He's in a white shirt and denim jeans, barefoot, with some kind of shoes in one hand. He has a goatee beard with flecks of grey. The main thing I notice is his eyes. Maybe he did try plastic surgery, yet he still looks far older than the photographs. And one thing you can't fake is the eyes. Dark, empty, lifeless eyes.

It may sound far-fetched, but forensic pathologists are now using people's eyes to determine the age of a corpse – though Terry McGann is currently far from a corpse of course, in more ways than one. He's now far away from dozens of corpses.

When those scientists look into your eyes it's a bit like carbon dating. Or taking ice core samples in the Arctic to learn about air pollution in Ancient Rome. Or measuring the widths between the rings of long dead redwoods to discover a little ice age.

During our lives we become exposed to naturally occurring radiation, plus the stuff released into the atmosphere during nuclear weapons testing. Over decades these levels fall to trace proportions, yet still measurable within the microscopic crystallins of the eye. If only I could stick Terry McGann on a pathologist's slab and slice him open I'd be able to say with certainty that he has absorbed some of this radiation and carbon in the food chain thing and it has become fused into the very darkness of his eyes.

As I can't do that right now, I ignore his eyes and stick to his accent. When he opens his mouth it's a northern one, possibly Fermanagh.

"I'm Peter Boyd," he says. Pure Enniskillen alright

"I know. Seems I'm not allowed to talk to you."

"Oh? Why?"

"Because you're – how shall I put it? – *immune.*"

Cold, dark eyes. The kind of eyes that – plastic surgery or no – grew up through the nuclear testing times. Cold War eyes, with minute particles of radioactive carbon that was released into the atmosphere at the same time as the first floods of mermaids' tears reached the ocean.

I still know next to nothing about him. What are those eyes thinking? Fast-forwarding through scenes of his life?

Up close he smells of drink. We stand face to face in silence. Waiting for what? A sniper's bullet? For one of Gino's hitmen to run across the sand or stroll up to us with a sawn-off?

"I am the resurrection and the life," he says. The outburst is bizarre, unexpected. I must be dreaming this. I look down at the word "Killer" in the sand. It has been washed away. Or mostly away, because the past never truly dies, does it?

He continues: "He that believeth in me, though he were dead, yet shall he live. And whosoever liveth and believeth in me shall never die."

But this is no dream, so I hit back with just about the only thing I've got.

"You think you're immune, Mr Boyd or McGann or whatever you call yourself this week. But you're not Jesus. You're not God. Not even Icarus. You forgot one minor detail."

I turn away, walk back to the car and shout: "Look at your maps. Lough Erne, it's in another State. In UK territorial waters."

281

Fifty

Mrs Kettle has made her final downpayment, in cash.

So case closed, another satisfied customer.

After a discreet meeting this morning with her private detective – that's what she still calls me – wheels are set in motion.

Áine Kettle is about to tell all to my reporter "friend", Harry Street. Harry in turn will get her an appointment in Enniskillen, with some of his contacts in the Northern Ireland police. Various things will then shuttle back and forth – coroners' reports, phone calls to France, faxes (because they do still use faxes) and an extradition warrant for murder.

Sorry. I mean murders, plural.

If Terry McGann has any sense he will plead insanity.

At least Gino Beattie should be off my back. Then, born a street rat, Gino will one day die a street rat and only his fleas will mourn him. Rest in pieces.

For once in my life a hopeless case has turned a handsome profit. So I'm blowing some of it on a slap-up meal in town with Arnaud, Colley and Maggie Dardis. They deserve it.

It's a double celebration because most of Arnaud's crew are back together again. Several catering gigs are in the pipeline, everybody is happy, and water tax protesters have hit a government minister with a water balloon.

During dessert, Colley asks if I'm finally done with that book.

Which book?

The cycling one.

Oh, *Domestique Labour*? He wants a lend of it.

That's the trouble with this town; when people say, "I've just finished that book," you never know whether they are talking about reading one or writing one.

About the author

Irish writer Mel Healy is based in Dublin. *Ghost Flight* is the third novel in his 'Moss Reid' series about the private eye whose main patch is Stoneybatter in Dublin. Find out more about Mel, read draft chapters and short stories, download other goodies and get in touch with the author at
http://melhealy.wordpress.com

You can also talk to Mel on Twitter **@mossreid**

Oh, and Mel doesn't do Facebook.

Plot Spoilers

Check Mel's blog at melhealy.wordpress.com for occasional plot spoilers about this book. To access the spoilers (preferably after you've finished these pages of course), you will need to use the password **yk746**.

Also by Mel Healy

Another Case in Cowtown

Dublin, Ireland, summer 2013.

It's the middle of a heatwave, and things are hotting up for Moss Reid.

The Stoneybatter sleuth has way too much on his plate this month: an adoption trace, a missing person, a couple of cheating spouses, a series of thefts at a top Dublin restaurant, and someone has nicked his laptop.

So what's he doing sitting in an interrogation room, in an itchy boilersuit, being grilled (and boiled and finely diced) by the Murder Squad?

Another Case in Cowtown is the first novel in the series about Moss Reid, Stoneybatter's gastronomic private eye. For most of his clients it's a question of the "not knowing", from not knowing who your parents (and you) really are, to not knowing why a loved one has disappeared or where they ended up. As for Moss himself, it's often about the not knowing whether you'll get paid and eat this week.

But don't panic: it's not all doom, gloom and starvation. There are various digressions on the funny side of life (and the occasional death). And half a dozen recipes along the way.

Another Case in Cowtown
ISBN-13: 978-1493679225
ISBN-10: 14993679228
ASIN: B00GJMOGPI
Pages: 218
Available in paperback and Kindle from Amazon

Also by Mel Healy

Black Marigolds

Dublin, Ireland, December 2013

Whistle-blowers, missing persons, top-up scandals, corrupt councillors and a dead body or two… Sometimes you couldn't make it up.

It's nearly Christmas, the city's streets are full of pub crawlers and Christmas Jumpers, there's a housing crisis, and Moss Reid is trying to find a homeless person.

Meanwhile a right-wing TD is being blackmailed. He has been snared in a honeytrap. And if you're dealing with a honeytrap you might as well start with the honey: a honey as young and sweet as you can get …

In the second book in the 'Moss Reid' series, Stoneybatter's foodie PI is back with more sad cases, skip traces, tempting recipes and a problem with the brussels sprouts.

Black Marigolds
ISBN-13: 978-1499328738
ISBN-10: 1499328737
ASIN: B00L5J9BQY
Pages: 210
Available in paperback and Kindle from Amazon

Printed in Great Britain
by Amazon